NORTHLAKE PUBLIC LIBRARY DISTRICT

P9-BYO-135

the King's Rose

ALISA M. LIBBY

DUTTON BOOKS

D U T T O N   B O O K S

A member of Penguin Group (USA) Inc.

PUBLISHED BY THE PENGUIN GROUP

Penguin Group (USA) Inc., 375 Hudson Street, New York, New York 10014, U.S.A. |
Penguin Group (Canada), 90 Eglinton Avenue East, Suite 700, Toronto, Ontario M4P 2Y3,
Canada (a division of Pearson Penguin Canada Inc.) | Penguin Books Ltd, 80 Strand, London WC2R 0RL, England | Penguin Ireland, 25 St Stephen's Green, Dublin 2, Ireland (a
division of Penguin Books Ltd) | Penguin Group (Australia), 250 Camberwell Road, Camberwell, Victoria 3124, Australia (a division of Pearson Australia Group Pty Ltd) | Penguin
Books India Pvt Ltd, 11 Community Centre, Panchsheel Park, New Delhi - 110 017, India |
Penguin Group (NZ), 67 Apollo Drive, Rosedale, North Shore 0632, New Zealand (a division of Pearson New Zealand Ltd.) | Penguin Books (South Africa) (Pty) Ltd, 24 Sturdee
Avenue, Rosebank, Johannesburg 2196, South Africa | Penguin Books Ltd, Registered
Offices: 80 Strand, London WC2R 0RL, England

This book is a work of fiction. Names, characters, places, and incidents are either the
product of the author's imagination or are used fictitiously, and any resemblance to actual
persons, living or dead, business establishments, events, or locales is entirely coincidental.

Copyright © 2009 by Alisa M. Libby

All rights reserved. No part of this publication may be reproduced or transmitted in any
form or by any means, electronic or mechanical, including photocopying, recording, or any
information storage and retrieval system now known or to be invented, without permission
in writing from the publisher, except by a reviewer who wishes to quote brief passages in
connection with a review written for inclusion in a magazine, newspaper, or broadcast.

The publisher does not have any control over and does not assume
any responsibility for author or third-party websites or their content.

CIP Data is available.

Published in the United States by Dutton Books,
a member of Penguin Group (USA) Inc.
345 Hudson Street, New York, New York 10014
www.penguin.com/youngreaders

DESIGNED BY HEATHER WOOD

Printed in USA | First Edition
ISBN 978-0-525-47970-3
1 3 5 7 9 10 8 6 4 2

NORTHLAKE PUBLIC LIBRARY DIST.
231 N. WOLF ROAD
NORTHLAKE, IL 60164

*This book is
dedicated to my mother,
Bernice Vicki Moskowitz,
who likes a bit of romance
with her history.*

THE KING'S ROSE

I The Thames is a messenger of fortune, rippling smoothly beneath the prow of this barge. The curtains flutter in the cool spring breeze; silver moonlight filters through their thin silk.

When I was a child and knew nothing about court life, I watched my cousin Anne Boleyn set across this very water, not long after her secret marriage to King Henry. The king's first wife had been banished from court in order for Anne to take her place upon the throne. The gold curtains of Anne's royal barge were flung open to reveal her, gowned in sparkling white satin and draped in jewels. King Henry awaited her on the steps of the Tower of London, where they would spend the night together before her glorious coronation as queen. Anne's long black hair glistened like satin in the sunlight, and the panels of her jeweled gown shifted to reveal the round belly beneath—already pregnant with a prince, an heir. Or so we all thought.

Years later Queen Anne had a much different voyage to the Tower, this one void of fanfare—or reverence. But it is best not to think of Anne, and the sorcery she used to entrap the king. She creeps into my daydreams when I least desire to find her there.

"It will not be for long," Lady Rochford reassures me. She pulls a curtain aside and smiles, enchanted by the moonlight sparkling upon the dark water. We are not going to the Tower, of course. In the distance I see the torches lit before the red brick façade of Lambeth—my former home, from my former life. I lived here before I went to court and became "that Howard girl who caught the king's eye." I imagine my grandmother, the dowager Duchess of Norfolk, pacing the front hall and peering out the mullioned windows to spy my approach.

"I know, Jane. The king thought it best that I stay at Lambeth, for a time," I tell Lady Rochford, just as my uncle, the Duke of Norfolk, informed me earlier today. The king is not displeased with me. It is simply for the best, I was told as the servants hastily packed my trunks. I was given no further information. *The king's will be done,* as my father used to say with his strange mixture of bitterness and awe.

What would Father think if he saw me, now? The moonlight winks darkly upon the tear-shaped sapphire suspended from a gold chain around my neck. It's not the type of necklace a lady-in-waiting in the queen's household would wear, not even a lady of considerable means. And definitely not Catherine Howard, the daughter of disfavored Edmund Howard, who died penniless years ago in spite of his powerful family name. The sapphire was a gift to me, from the king. And it was only the beginning.

"I saw the queen before we departed. Her trunks were being packed, as well," I inform Lady Rochford, though she already knows. "Where was she going?"

"Don't worry about her, Catherine," she answers, her voice quiet, dreamy. "Don't waste your time worrying about her."

But I can't help but worry about the queen—King Henry's fourth bride, shipped to England from Cleves, Germany, at the start of this year. Anne of Cleves was intended to rejuvenate the king after his long mourning for his third wife, Jane Seymour. But this seems unlikely; the German princess was not as pretty as her portrait, and King Henry's disappointment was clear.

I came to court last autumn to serve the new queen, and awaited her winter arrival with the rest of her ladies-in-waiting. But by early spring the gift of the sapphire made the focus of the king's affection clear for all to see. At fifteen years old, I am on the brink of gaining great wealth and great privilege for my family. Or so I have been told. I had best act properly, I am often reminded, or else squander all of our chances. The king is forty-nine and not as well as he once was. Time is precious, fleeting.

The Thames is a messenger of fortune, be it good or ill.

II   I am swiftly ushered to my apartments upon arrival at Lambeth—elegantly appointed chambers near the duchess's own, nothing like when I lived here as one of her many charges, sleeping side by side in a row of beds in the maidens' chamber. A long wooden box lies upon the bed. The duchess's servants crowd around me, smiling expectantly. Their eyes flicker like candles.

"Where is the duchess?"

"She will be with you soon, Catherine. Look." The servant moves forward, touching the box with eager fingers. "This arrived earlier today, along with the message that you would be joining us. Don't you want to look?"

My fingertip traces the image carved into the center of the box—a Tudor rose. I've received gifts in such boxes before, but never one as large as this. With a glance at Jane, I lift the lid, the motion followed by a wave of sighs. A cream silk gown is nestled in the box before me; the ladies crowd in for a closer look.

"There is a letter," I proclaim, plucking the parchment

from the box and bending my head over the slanted script, wary of the prying eyes surrounding me.

I hope this gown will suit your pleasure, as surely you suit mine. I look forward to seeing you wear it and can think of no more lovely young lady to which to present this gift, from your

Henricus Rex

"Oh, how exquisite. I've never seen anything like it," Jane declares.

"You haven't?" I inquire, but Jane does not answer. Jane's late husband, Lord Rochford, was George Boleyn—Anne's brother. Jane was lady-in-waiting to Anne when she was queen. Did she really never see Queen Anne in a gown such as this?

It is the type of gown I've always dreamed of wearing. As a child I had only my sister Isabel's shabby outgrown dresses to wear. Even at Lambeth I was envious of the so-phisticated ladies in the maidens' chamber, only to later be awestruck by the elegant attire of my fellow ladies at court. But this far surpasses anything they flaunted before my covetous gaze. The silk is deliciously soft to the touch, the bodice embroidered with gold thread and hundreds of delicate pearls.

"Wait until the king sees you, my dear"—Jane gushes, admiring the ample silk skirt—"from a girl to a princess in just one day."

"Wait until all of those snobs in the queen's household see you," one maid exclaims, "arrayed like royalty." The ladies giggle, sharing my revelry.

"Wait until all of court sees me." I hold the gown to my chest and stand before the mirror, admiring the twinkling bodice in the candlelight. "Even the gift of a sapphire can't quite compare to this." I smile, remembering when my fellow ladies-in-waiting saw the first concrete evidence of the king's affection: the deep blue-purple refractions of the stone glittered in their eyes.

"Imagine the look on the faces of those handsome grooms," one of the younger girls waxes dreamily. "All of the courtiers, the lords and ladies. Imagine the look on the face of your cousin Thomas Culpeper."

I flinch at the sound of his name. Jane's eyes turn sharp, piercing through me—we've talked about this already. I swallow, compose myself, and attempt a slight smile. I blink rapidly, smoothing my palms over the full skirt. Suddenly my fingers feel numb, the softness of the silk no longer registering upon my skin.

The door to my chamber opens, and a tall figure emerges from the shadows. A single glance from the duchess silences the servants' chatter.

"I must speak with Catherine alone," the duchess says smoothly. The servants move away from me, receding into shadows and filing silently out of the room. Jane squeezes my arm swiftly before departing.

The duchess walks into the ring of light created by the cheerful fire and the lit candles on my dressing table. Even in this golden light she appears hard, silvery, her sterling hair swept back from her white face. She levels her steel-gray gaze at me and smiles.

"The gown is beautiful, Catherine," she says, lifting it from my arms and spreading it out carefully upon the bed;

she caresses it lovingly. "We will have it fitted while you are here."

"Is the king to visit me here?" I ask, feigning composure. For all the times I've met him in the palace gardens, played my lute for him, or danced before him in the great hall, I've never been alone with King Henry.

"Do you know why he sent you here?"

"The Duke of Norfolk assured me I had not displeased the king," I state, instantly defensive. "I've charmed him. I've done all that you told me to do."

"Calm yourself, Catherine." She moves to a corner of the room and lifts a glass decanter of wine from a small table, filling two goblets. I feel uneasy watching the duchess pour wine for me. Her face is serene, but there is a certain energy sparking around her; I can see it in spite of how carefully she moves. "Your uncle Norfolk is correct, you have not displeased the king. Quite the contrary. Please." She hands me a full goblet and gestures to a chair before the mirror. She sits across from me upon the bed, her rich black satin gown a stark contrast to the cream silk lying beside her. "It was the king's order that you were sent here."

"Norfolk told me. But why did the king remove me from court?"

"He thought it prudent that you be sent away before the queen is relocated. She will be sent to Richmond, to escape the threat of the plague and take in the country air." The duchess sips primly from her own goblet, then sets it upon the table.

"There is a threat of plague? In London?"

"Of course not, fool." But she smiles, amused instead of

frustrated. "Don't you think the king would be the first to take to the country if there were? No, no, he will stay at court and brave the false threat of contagion. It will not be long now before their marriage is deemed null and void on the basis of a preexisting betrothal contract for Anne of Cleves with the Marquis of Lorraine, and nonconsummation of her marriage to King Henry."

"He will divorce the queen," I murmur, rolling the meaning of these words over in my mind. "Already?"

"Oh, you cannot play the fool with me, Catherine. You did not truly think that our king would stay married to that Flanders Mare?"

"Will I return to court when the divorce is final?"

"In a matter of speaking." The duchess's eyes fairly glow in the dimness. "After the wedding."

"The wedding?"

She stares at me for a moment. Extending her arm, she places her cold hand upon mine.

"The time has come, Catherine. King Henry intends to make you his bride."

She smiles at me. I blink back at her.

"King Henry intends?"

"To make you his bride," she repeats. Her eyes are focused upon mine. "I expect you will be wed before the summer is done."

My heart rises in my throat, as though I have just swallowed a living thing. I knew this was their goal, eventually, but the sudden reality of it shudders through me. Cousin Anne waited years for King Henry's separation from his first wife . . . oh, but I can't think about Anne, now.

"So soon?" My voice cracks slightly. I clear my throat. "I did not know . . . it is all . . . I didn't know it would happen so soon. That he would be rid of the queen—" I clear my throat again, trembling hands clasped tightly around the goblet. "Anne of Cleves is a princess. I am not even—"

"He has chosen a common girl before—don't forget your cousin Anne, and Jane Seymour. Neither one with royal blood. But you are not common, Catherine. You are a Howard, and our family is among the most powerful at court."

My mind swims; the golden light in the room seems liquid, blurred.

"The king has made his choice, Catherine, and he chooses you. Norfolk said King Henry has described you as a jewel of womanhood. He loves your freshness, your innocence."

There is something literal about the way she says that word: *innocence.*

"The king knows that he has little time to waste," the duchess adds, and looks at me darkly. "Do you know what is required of you, as the king's wife?"

"A child," I state, "a son." I drain my wine in great gulps and set the goblet upon the dressing table.

"An heir, Catherine—your son will be a legitimate heir to the throne." She squeezes my hand so tightly that I wince. "But that is *after* the wedding. Right now you are to be the king's virgin."

I look up at these words; the duchess's eyes sparkle eerily, like twin sapphires.

"He does not want a seductress, or a temptress, or a flirt. He wants to marry a virgin—like his eternally beloved, departed queen Jane Seymour. You must be like Jane for him."

You know that isn't true, I think, meeting the duchess's gaze. Before I can say a word, she raises a hand to stop me.

"There are things now that are dangerous to even think, let alone say aloud," she says, her voice quiet but piercing. "Any admission could be misconstrued as a precontract, and could spoil all we've done. It never happened, Catherine, any of it. Your past is gone. You are a virgin, now."

Hearing these words spoken to me within Lambeth's walls is almost too much to bear. My past echoes here, the very stones of this building crowded with memories of the girl I used to be.

"That's what you've told him?"

"Yes. The king is told what he wants to hear."

"The king was told that Anne of Cleves was a beauty— just see where that lie will lead her, not to mention Cromwell."

"The king is already taken with you, Catherine. And the king wants a virgin. The Duke of Norfolk and I have made you exactly what the king wants you to be. Do you understand?"

"I understand," I murmur, my eyes lowered.

"Besides, he would not have wanted you, otherwise." Her voice is low and cold, slithering around me like a snake. "The thought of a girl already spoiled by another man disgusts him." A slight smile plays at the sharp corners of her mouth. "But we have fixed all of that. You will be queen, Catherine, because of your family. Remember that, for you could not have done this on your own."

"I will remember." I knew this was their plan, of course. But now the crown itself is at hand: too large, too grand a thing for me to comprehend. If I have a son, he will be second in line for the throne of England, behind Prince Edward, son of the dead Queen Jane. I will be crowned queen, and my son could one day reign as king.

"We have created you, Catherine." The duchess's voice trembles with excitement. "The king desires an innocent young maid who will love him." She smiles, her steel eyes wide and impossibly bright. "So that is what you must be."

"Of course," I tell her, lowering my head. I am accustomed to taking direction, but this masquerade seems frighteningly intimate, manipulative—obscene.

"That's right," the duchess says, admiring my pose. "Just like that: very bashful, nervous, and a little bit afraid."

It is not entirely an act.

III

I first met the king, my future husband, at a private entertainment at the residence of Bishop Gardiner, early this spring. Since my arrival at court the previous autumn I had seen the king only from a great distance, during the pomp and splendor of his royal wedding to Princess Anne of Cleves at the dawn of the year.

I had lived in the duchess's residences since the age of ten, taken in from my father's overcrowded household upon my mother's death. The duchess and my uncle the Duke of Norfolk arranged my position at court while the new queen's household was being prepared. I was sent to court with new gowns and no lack of instruction from the duchess on how to behave in the king's presence, though at the time I thought it barely necessary—I was but a junior lady-in-waiting, veritably lost in a sea of sleek hoods and satin gowns. We all anxiously awaited the arrival of the new Queen of England:

that serene face gazing from the portrait that had captivated our king.

But soon after their nuptials, the king's displeasure with his German bride was evident. While the marriage to the unattractive "Flanders Mare" seemed a disaster to King Henry—and to his adviser, Cromwell, who had urged the match—it also presented a golden opportunity. Nothing cheers this particular king more than the sight of a pretty young female, and every family at court was eager to distract him from his dismay with their own daughters and nieces, and thereby win attention and royal favor. The duchess took an even keener interest in my looks, my singing voice, and my dancing skills. I was given a new gown to wear to Bishop Gardiner's royal entertainment—silk as blue as a robin's egg, with a hood trimmed in pearls.

"This is your chance to charm him, Catherine," the duchess informed me. "This is your chance to shine brighter than all the other ladies. You represent all of us Howards tonight." I was not alone, of course: my cousin Mary Norris was also present and gaily attired for the very same purpose. Still, I took the duchess's desires to heart. I had never been trusted with such a charge before. I wanted nothing more than to make her proud.

The king sat in a place of honor at the head of the hall, and I took my place before him, among the other ladies assembled. In spite of my nervousness, the call of the wooden reed sang through me, the tabor drum beating the rhythm of my own heart. I danced, glorying in the music, in every step and twirl. Those late-night parties in the maidens' chamber at Lambeth did me some good after all, though no doubt the duchess would slap me for thinking it. Twirling in my blue gown, I could feel the king's eyes upon me, though I could never have imagined exactly what this would mean.

"Mistress Catherine," he said, beckoning me to approach him as the music faded to silence. I stepped forward, past jutting shoulders and bright hoods, and bent in a graceful reverence at the king's feet.

I had seen King Henry before, mounted upon his great black hunter or seated beneath the cloth of state during the wedding feast. Even from that distance he was all that a king should be: tall, imposing, elaborately dressed in gold and jewels and velvet and furs. But standing alone some few feet away from him, his eyes upon me, he was altogether massive and glittering; overwhelmingly majestic.

"Stand, child," he said, with a wave of his jeweled hand. "Let me look at you."

I stood, my head humbly lowered, my heart pounding like a rapid tabor. I looked up and met his eyes, warily: startlingly blue eyes, set deeply in his full face. His nose straight and pointed, his neatly trimmed beard the same reddish gold of his hair. He has a round chin, obscuring a strong jawline, but his mouth is pink and youthful.

I had seen that look in a man's eyes before, but never in the eyes of a king. He was quiet for a long moment, looking at my face as if searching it, or memorizing it for some mysterious purpose. His blue eyes glittered brightly as the jewels upon his hand. I felt my knees shake below me and feared they would give way. And then he smiled at me: slightly, cautiously. It was the first time I had seen him smile since my arrival at court.

"Mistress Catherine, you are springtime in the flesh."
King Henry laughed, a raucous, glorious laugh, and all the
court assembled laughed along with him. I smiled as sweetly
and demurely as I could manage.

I can assure you it is an intoxicating feeling for one so
long ignored, to be singled out in a room full of people and
looked at so closely by a king.

THE CREAM SILK GOWN slips over my skin with a whisper; the full skirt rippling like the smooth surface of the
Thames.

"Oh, how lovely," Lady Rochford breathes, carefully slipping the sleeves over my arms.

In the days since my arrival here, I've stayed to my
apartments, per the duchess's instructions. Today was a
beautiful day and I longed for a walk in the gardens, but
the duchess's fears—and my own—gave me pause. I fear
being seen by the other ladies of Lambeth, who knew me
before my departure for court: Joan, Lisbeth, Dorothy,
Katherine, Malyn. They were my friends when I was a
different girl—a foolish girl. To see them would be a reminder of who I was. And how would I explain to them
who I am, now?

*You are a virgin. You will be his departed Queen Jane, reincar-
nate.*

"You will return to court as Queen Catherine," Lady
Rochford states, pushing a pair of jeweled slippers before
me. "Lady Ashley and Lady Christina will be beside themselves fawning over you."

"Lady Ashley and Lady Christina may fawn all they

like." I slip my feet into the slippers, then step onto a low stool, grasping Jane's arm for support. "I'll not forget how they treated me when I first arrived at court, like I was not fit to be seated in their shadows."

"And now they will bask in yours," the duchess's seamstress mumbles over a mouthful of pins, kneeling before me and pinning up the hem of my gown.

In the corner of the chamber I spy the duchess, scrutinizing the trim on a blue hood. All of my gowns have been taken out and spread upon the bed and chairs of my apartment for the duchess's inspection. She stalks efficiently about the room, listing off instructions to her seamstresses and maids. To become the king's bride, I must dress accordingly. All wardrobe is strategy, the gown itself a character in my performance.

The pink silk—like a freshly bloomed rose—I wore to another entertainment for the king, my lute in hand, per the duchess's instruction. The king requested me to sing for him before all assembled and pronounced me a "sweet bird" of song. I wore the red satin on the night when he stopped the music in the midst of our dance to request that I stand at the front of the group of ladies.

"No need to hide the red rose amongst the tall weeds," he said, and all of court laughed. Even the queen seated beside him laughed, though her lips were pinched in a thin line.

Those few words from the king were enough to set me apart from the other ladies.

"We all have our place in this world." Lady Ashley had sneered at me. "A Howard girl cannot help but throw herself into the king's bed as soon as she sees the chance."

Her words made me flinch—were the machinations of my

family so evident to all? The ultimate goal wasn't so obvious until I saw it through the eyes of another: no doubt they intended for me to be King Henry's next plaything, and perhaps sire another Howard bastard with royal blood. I hadn't given any thought to the reality of coupling with the king. I was but fourteen at the time, the king forty-eight—an unfathomable age—not to mention overweight and intimidating. But I realized, perhaps too late, that my misgivings were quite beside the point. Lady Ashley was right. The frequent collision of my path with King Henry's—in the halls, in the royal gardens—was not merely the will of God, but the will of the eager Howard clan, grasping for power once again.

I soon learned that the Howards had even grander plans for me, and so did King Henry.

WHEN THE PINNING is done, Jane helps me step from the stool and steers me over to the mirror. At the sight of my reflection I feel suddenly light-headed: I am shining like a perfect pearl. The gold lace sparkles, the cream silk lush and immaculate. The bones of the bodice fit perfectly against my waist, seductively snug. The wide, square neckline displays my full breasts, the glistening gold embroidery of the décolletage pressed against my skin. The sunlight streaming in a nearby window makes the pearls glisten, my hair shine copper. I am like a dream of me.

"The sapphire." The duchess strides over toward my dressing table. "You will wear that gown and the sapphire when you see the king."

"The pearls were a gift from the king as well," Jane remarks, "and they match perfectly."

"But the sapphire was his *first* gift," the duchess says, efficiently unclasping the pearls from my neck, "and therefore the most important."

The stone is startlingly dark against my fair skin.

"It was a gift for my birthday, this spring," I tell them, touching the stone with a cautious fingertip. "I told him it was my favorite time of year, the season of my birth."

The duchess nods. "Then he gave you this sapphire, and that changed everything."

Once this necklace was clasped around my neck, the king's interest in me was made clear to everyone at court. The ladies invited me to join their card games, and I walked in front of the group when the queen was not present. I was greeted graciously, solicitously, by courtiers who had not deigned to learn my name mere months before. My favorite songs played in every room I entered; suddenly all music was played expressly for my enjoyment.

But there was more that changed, as far as the court, and my future, was concerned: I became the king's chosen, with no other claim upon my heart. At least, no claim that anyone could detect. It had all happened so quickly, like a sudden, thrilling storm in late spring, tearing the petals from new roses, leaving the world irrevocably altered in its wake.

The sapphire upon my chest feels cold, like ice against my skin.

"The king will approve," the duchess sniffs, satisfied. "You will visit me in my chamber tonight, Catherine. We have much to discuss before you next meet with His Majesty.

"Lady Rochford, Catherine will take her supper in my chambers. You are dismissed for the night."

Jane's eyes flash up at the duchess, but only briefly.

"Of course, Duchess," she says, and exits the chamber without another word.

IV   "Queen Katherine was a good queen, but the miscarriages and stillbirths that befell them—no wonder the king considered himself cursed," the duchess remarks, her rich voice turned a bit raspy from talking. We've eaten our supper and are spending the evening secluded in her parlor, the windows opened to allow a cool breeze. "And I will admit I was surprised when young Henry married his brother Arthur's widow."

This parlor is so elegantly appointed. I've never been invited to sit here before. Never been invited to share a meal alone with the duchess, nor had her talk so openly with me.

The duchess has been the closest relative in my life for years now; I'm delighted to finally be pulled so close into her company. I've long wanted to ask about her career at court, and tonight I've been given my first chance to do so. She was lady-in-waiting to King Henry's first queen, Katherine of Aragon, and had the honor of putting king and queen to bed on their wedding night, some thirty years ago.

"They had not been long married, and Arthur had been ill, hadn't he?"

"Yes, but still long enough to have consummated the marriage, making the Spanish princess an ill-suited choice for Henry when he was crowned king."

"But her only fault was no male heir. Does it not seem unfair?"

"There is no such thing as fair and unfair, Catherine. You had best learn that, now. It is the desire of the king with which you must concern yourself. Queen Katherine could not give him what he desired. He found another candidate he thought likely to do so, and he did whatever he needed to do to put her on the throne."

"Anne Boleyn." I sigh, meeting the duchess's gaze. "You took me to London for her coronation procession and I dreamed of it for years afterward. I was captivated by her."

She smiles at this observation. "As was King Henry, for a time."

I had watched as the duchess carried Queen Anne's train down the aisle of Westminster Abbey at her coronation. Later that same year, the duchess carried Anne's first and only child, the Princess Elizabeth, down the aisle of the Chapel of the Observant Friars to the baptismal font.

"Look at all he did to be with her—banishing his wife, severing the church in England from the pope in Rome. He remade the church, with himself at the head of it, just to be able to marry her." I feel my old envy boiling inside me at the mere thought of Anne's power. They said she used strong enchantments to bend the king's will to her pleasure. But fascinating, too, were the stories that her bewitchment had faded from the king's eyes and that he had begun to see the devil in it.

"She was—special, that Anne," the duchess muses, gazing into the fire. Her eyes are pale, steely gray, unblinking. "You cannot teach or learn ambition like that, Catherine. It is something that you are born with; it is a part of your soul. Or perhaps it takes a part of your soul. I think it depends on whom you ask."

The duchess tips back her head and drains her glass of wine.

"They say she tricked him with witchcraft," I remark, as nonchalantly as possible. "Did you ever see her sixth finger? They say it was a sign of the devil and she hid it with her long sleeves."

The duchess looks at me, her eyes glassy, a bit unfocused. But her face is expressionless. "Witchcraft or no, what would it matter, either way?" She shrugs. "There was more to it than that."

"What do you mean?"

"Anne was deft at charming the king, I will give her that. But she proved herself unworthy of the position once she was there. She was grasping, greedy, hot-tempered."

I can't help but revel in this, hearing the duchess denigrate my glamorous cousin, her own granddaughter. Twenty years into the king's marriage to Queen Katherine, the duchess testified that Katherine had not been a virgin upon their wedding night, thus aiding the king's petition to divorce the queen and be free to marry Anne.

"After all that King Henry had done to have her—even suffering excommunication by the pope himself—she didn't know enough to treat him kindly, to demurely look the other way when the king sought to take another lady to his bed."

"But why would he desire another, once he had Anne?"

"Ah, she wondered the same thing. But it's the way of the king, Catherine. Everyone knows it." Her eyes focus on mine, one eyebrow sharply cocked. "But Anne, in her arrogance, could not bear it. She hadn't the grace of Queen Katherine, who knew enough to allow the king to take his pleasure, here and there."

I sigh at this, my chest tight. Whatever dark sorcery Anne performed failed her in the end. Luckily, I managed to catch the king's eye without the use of witchcraft.

"But you supported Anne, didn't you?"

"When a Howard finds a path to the throne, you do not take it lightly. You show your unfailing support, whoever that Howard may be."

Her eyes settle upon me for a moment in silence, reflecting the flickering candles. I turn away. She reaches over to a nearby silver platter and selects a sweetmeat. Placing it in her mouth, she smiles.

"Anne came so far, and then it was all over." Saying her name aloud gives me a strange chill. The room has gone darker, the sky outside the window a deep, fathomless black. Now I wish I could stop thinking about the witch, I wish I had never asked. "The king's will be done."

"There are often other wills involved," the duchess remarks over her sweetmeat. When I look at her, perplexed, she only smiles.

"You won't find Lady Rochford in your chamber tonight," she states, pouring more wine into her goblet and swirling it gently. "She has returned to court, for a short visit."

"Jane returned to court, tonight? Why?"

"Tomorrow, she will testify to the nonconsummation of the king's marriage to Anne of Cleves, to support his claim for an annulment."

"Lady Rochford has testified against queens before."

When Cousin Anne was put on trial for treason, it was Jane's testimony that condemned her to death. She repeated Anne's own words—evidence of a vile temper—stating aloud that the king was impotent, and incapable of siring an heir. With her testimony, Jane also condemned her own husband, George Boleyn—Anne's brother. Their crimes were incest and adultery: treason against the king and an abomination to God. I shiver at the thought of the vile witch that once occupied the queen's throne. It must have been a terrible thing for Jane to have witnessed. Despite my curiosity, I've never asked Jane about Anne. I avoid even mentioning her name.

"Another step toward divorce is another step toward your betrothal, Catherine. Besides, all of the queen's chamber knows of her naïveté in regard to her marital duties. She unwittingly admitted as much to her senior maids, Lady Rochford included."

"Her mother in Cleves taught her impeccable embroidery, but little practical knowledge about marriage," I remark.

"Indeed." She smiles, then narrows her eyes at me. "That is one area in which I need not worry about you."

My neck and cheeks turn warm. The duchess laughs wryly.

"Just think of Queen Jane, Catherine," she reminds me, her voice stern. "She is your model—it's only a shame that she was a Seymour, and not a Howard. Still, I admired their strategy: she was precisely what the king needed, having tired of Anne's vicious temper. Jane was sweet, pious, virginal, and thoroughly English—without the Spanish pedigree or Anne's affectations of the French court. She was mild by nature and knew better than to challenge her husband. She had a proper wifely disposition."

"A wifely disposition?"

"Yes, Catherine. A wife is honest, humble, and quiet. A wife is obedient to God, to her husband, and to her king. Look at how things will be easier for you—with husband and king the same person." She smiles at this, selecting another sweetmeat and chewing laboriously.

"But what about Jane—she was the greatest success of all of them, with the birth of Prince Edward. But then she died just days later."

"Well . . ." The Duchess shrugs, picking a bit of sweetmeat from her teeth. "You can't help what happened to Jane."

Perhaps it is the legacy of the witch, wreaking havoc with her successor from beyond the grave. And now I'll be up on that throne, where she once sat. I only hope that if her spirit is angry, she will be kinder to me. We are cousins, after all.

DISTURBING THOUGHTS follow me to my bedchamber. The hall is dark and quiet and I run my hand distractedly across the cold wall. It reminds me of running through these halls as a young girl, eager for a secret meeting under cover of darkness, rushing silently down cold stone hallways, breathless, my slippers in hand.

In these shadows, a memory catches me: the way the light flickers upon the stone walls, it seems to reflect another night, so many years ago. I was skulking in this very hall when I saw the duchess in the doorway of her chamber, bidding good-bye to a cloaked figure. The duchess's face wasn't visible, but I remember how her garnet brooch sparkled in the dimness. I stand here now, staring at her closed door, as if watching the scene again.

It was just before Anne Boleyn's trial, I remember. I couldn't help wondering then, as I do now, if it had something to do with Anne. *Of course it did;* the duchess has a hand in everything related to the Howards. But I did not see the face of the cloaked figure: only a profile, in shadow, a pale white hand pulling the cloak closed. A woman's hand. In the days that followed, I waited to hear what would happen to my cousin—the cousin I had admired and envied and feared above all else. Somehow I assumed the magic she used to become queen would save her; she would be safely exiled, or join a nunnery, and we would never hear from her again. But then the French swordsman came to sever her slender neck in two, and there was no reprieve.

I wonder if Anne's violent end surprised the duchess. But somehow I can't imagine the duchess being surprised by anything. I hurry to my own chambers, eager to light a bright, cheerful fire to keep these shadows at bay.

V When Jane returns, I dare not ask about her testimony. I prefer to focus on the gifts the king has sent—a blue velvet riding habit, jeweled slippers, and pearl trim for my hoods—than to dwell upon the fate of his current wife. My days are spent being fitted for new gowns and embellishing a new hood with gold lace. I distract myself with this, and with dreamy speculation on my impending royal wedding and coronation. It is a favorite game I play with the ladies here in my company—we could spend hours detailing the potential permutations of my hair and gown, the food to be eaten, the music to be played.

"Mistress Catherine." A servant's voice permeates our chatter. "The duchess requests your presence in the parlor."

For further education, no doubt. The novelty of the duchess's company has diminished somewhat, after hours spent in her parlor receiving exhaustive instruction on my future role as queen: the administration of my household and estates, listening to petitions to present to the king, and all the finer points of court etiquette which she feels certain I am still lacking.

It's a strange irony in comparison to the life I once lived in these very halls. Making my way down this quiet hallway, I imagine colliding with Joan or Dorothy, flushed and pink from a vigorous ride, or a walk along the sunny garden paths. There was little structure to my days then, aside from morning Mass and meals taken together in the great hall. The evenings were spent on embroidery, or practicing the lute or new dances. It was an ordinary life for a girl of my birth, but very different from the propriety I had to learn at court, and even more so the life ahead of me as queen. But I can't imagine being queen is as mundane as the duchess would make it out to be.

I open the door to the duchess's chamber and I'm taken aback by the bright smile she flashes at me upon my arrival. She has features not accustomed to such smiling; it seems to break her face in two.

"Good morning, Catherine," she exclaims, and moves forward, enfolding me in a stiff embrace. I look up to see the

Duke of Norfolk standing before the sunlit window, a black obelisk against a screen of gold. I bow solemnly before both of them. It is so unlike me, but I can feel that I am being carefully inspected. Their eyes feel heavy upon me.

"Am I to see the king today?" I ask.

"You will see him tomorrow, for today the divorce is complete." The duchess's voice is low, tremulous. "The queen has been offered the title of the king's beloved sister—a title which she accepts gladly, with all of the benefits it entails."

"And she will stay here, in England?" I inquire with pretend composure.

"She's been given a number of her own residences, and is now a woman of means in this country. I doubt that she will even consider returning home." The duke steps forward, studying me with his stern gaze. A tall man with thin lips and a hooked nose, he has gained the favorable post of lord treasurer at court. He's also fought for the king, bringing down an uprising of rebels in the northern region, on the king's command. In this he was, from what I have heard, merciless. A man to be feared by his enemies.

"There is more, Catherine, and I've come here to tell you."

The duchess takes my hands in hers. Her hands are cold and shaking slightly.

"Your betrothal is ready to be made official," she tells me.

I can only blink in response.

"You will be betrothed to the King of England, Catherine," the duke pronounces. "No other betrothal is valid, or was ever valid. Indeed, no other betrothal even existed."

I catch a sharp look in the duke's eye, and quickly look away.

"It is important that you know what is expected of you, as queen," Norfolk continues, "and as his wife—for that is your job, first and foremost."

"Indeed. His wife," I echo, to let them know I understand. I am fifteen years old, and the king nearly fifty. But this is not out of the ordinary—a girl of fifteen is ripe for a husband, and older men of means often take young brides. This is one reason I was sent to court, to parade myself before the eligible bachelors and attain a profitable betrothal.

And I have. I will be Queen of England.

"It need not be difficult for you," the duke states, stepping closer. "Simply do and say little. Be cheerful; do not vex him with requests or complaints—aside from those we require from you. Your only job is to make the king happy and to become pregnant as soon as possible. You will be the perfect serene, docile maiden."

I notice a certain emphasis on the word *maiden*, but perhaps it is my imagination. Reflected in the glassy shine of my uncle's eyes, an image of Queen Jane: the most triumphant of all of Henry's queens, before her untimely death.

"You will also listen to us," Norfolk intones, "and do as you are bidden."

"Have I not done everything you've said, so far?" I've heard this warning many times before. I learned from the duchess that Norfolk did not like Anne Boleyn for her headstrong ways. But I will be better than Anne, he will see. They will all see.

"You have done well. He wanted you from the moment he saw you," the duke tells me. How much more has the duke been told? I think back to that day: I dance before the king, my silk gown swirling around me in a blue cloud. I watch it pass before me like a strange play, a tableau of the king falling in love with Catherine Howard. It all seems unreal to me, more pageantry than real life.

"This was meant to be, destiny," the duke pronounces. "A Howard upon the throne."

And that Howard happens to be me. *When a Howard finds a path to the throne, you do not take it lightly. You show your unfailing support, whoever that Howard may be.*

"Catherine, are your courses regular?" the duchess asks suddenly, her eyes narrow. I blink at her, slow to decipher what she is saying.

"They are, usually." I try, feebly, to explain the common delay of my courses, feeling a deep blush travel up my neck and cheeks, Uncle Norfolk's beady black eyes trained on mine. The duchess purses her lips and sighs in displeasure.

"Well, there is little we can do about it, now," she remarks. "He has chosen you, it has already been decided. We must simply hope for the best." She turns to Norfolk and tells him about a concoction of herbs she will prepare for me, intended to invigorate fertility. I wonder if they have forgotten I am still in the room.

"You will rest today, Catherine," the duchess says abruptly, rubbing my hands with her still-cold fingers. "Tomorrow the king will arrive here, and make his formal proposal for marriage."

"Wear the cream silk, Catherine. The king mentioned wanting to see you in it," the duke tells me. They continue to speak about when the king will arrive, and who will arrive with him, and how everything should be prepared for the occasion. I sit dumbly beside them, feeling oddly inconsequential to their plans.

When the duke leaves, the duchess turns to me and her expression softens.

"He is king, Catherine, and he has chosen you." She grasps my upper arms and holds me firmly. "You must remember all that I have told you. It is imperative that you follow all of my instructions."

All that the duchess has told me? How to look at the king, how to speak, how to walk, bow, smile, laugh—

"Your life starts anew from this moment, Catherine. Do you understand me?" She is staring steadily into my eyes. "Your past is gone. Not only is it gone, but it never happened at all." She squeezes my arms until I wince in pain. "You must burn your life, all of your life, before this moment. Burn your life and start a new one—a life for the King of England."

I open my mouth to say something, but the words catch in my throat. There is no use giving voice to those old dreams, now.

"The king's will be done," I tell her, my voice colorless to my own ears. The duchess does not seem to notice.

"That is right," she says, smiling. "Remember it, Catherine. Never doubt it. It is the will of God."

God chose Henry Tudor to be king, the grandest and most beloved king that England has ever seen. And Henry Tudor has chosen me.

I think the will of God had little to do with it.

VI

After a flurry of silk and thread and ribbon, the cream gown has been properly tailored for the betrothal. Preparations have swallowed the day; it is already twilight, and I am wearied by the barrage of instructions I've received in preparation for tomorrow.

Jane helps me from the silk gown, then drapes it carefully over my oak chest. I pull a linen nightdress over my head and plop heavily onto the bed. The silk gown lies beside me, unfolded like the petals of a rose. In my nightdress I feel smaller, diminished. I am merely the model upon which the gown was held, the gown's mode of travel. I can only hope to play my part well and live up to the gown's expectations of the girl I must become.

Turning to the dressing table for my silver comb, I notice that Jane has something else in her hand—a small box of pale wood with a rusted latch. My heart leaps into my throat at the sight of it. I open my mouth to protest, but she merely sets the box upon the dressing table with a decisive click.

"There is something I found that I must speak to you about," she says, turning to me with comb in hand.

"It isn't anything—nothing of importance."

"Good," she says smoothly, pulling the comb efficiently through my hair. "Then you will not mind if I burn it for you."

"It was my mother's jewel box," I inform her, tugging my hair out of her hand.

"Its contents, then." She blinks blandly. "You can keep the box itself."

"I did not realize it would be necessary."

"It is more than necessary, and you should know that well enough."

"Perhaps if you weren't rooting around in my belongings—"

"And who is to say a nosy maid at court won't be rooting around in your belongings? What if Lady Ashley had discovered it, or any of the others? You cannot fool yourself into believing they would protect your secrets, Catherine. A queen has no secrets."

"Then I am to deny everything, even to myself? Deny my heart—my love?"

"Oh, don't bore me with your tale of love. You sound like an ungrateful child."

"Maybe I am a child," I tell her. I feel tears burning behind my eyelids.

"I won't hear another word of it, not of the box, nor of your love. The king wants a maiden enamored with him, not a fickle-hearted girl betrothed to another."

I look away from the box, thinking of the duchess's words: *Burn your life.* Then this is it, the final fire, the purifying flame.

"Fine," I tell her, wiping the tears from my eyes. "But I'll do it myself."

"I only wish I could trust you to do so," Jane states solemnly. She lifts the box from the dressing table and offers it to me. "I am happy to do the honors, if you would like," she tells me.

I snatch the box angrily from her hand. I see there is nothing else for it—she will stand here and wait until the deed is done. I pull a folded paper—a page of music—out from beneath the various trinkets. Before I can think long on it, I thrust it unceremoniously into the flames.

"That wasn't so difficult, was it?" she asks, moving efficiently to the hearth and stoking the flames. The paper crackles before our eyes. "Better to do it now, before you return to court. And how appropriate"—she turns to me with a wry smile—"to burn your past here, at Lambeth."

I turn away from her, clutching the box tightly. True enough, this must be done, but I cannot do this with her watching; my own emotions embarrass me.

"Just look at how far you have risen, Catherine," she says gently, stroking my hair; her voice is tinged with awe. "The past is over. This is your life now."

"I did not choose this life," I mutter quietly, fearing a harsh rebuke.

"No, but you were chosen. And that is all that matters."

I know that Jane is right. No one denies the affections of a king, even if it means denying your own. I must not think about the past. I will be the king's wife, I will be queen. This will have to be my happiness, now. And this can be enough, can't it?

"No more tears, Catherine. Do you hear me? No more crying for you. The past is gone, there is no use crying about it, now."

Jane unclasps the gold chain from my throat. It slips free, and I catch the sapphire in the palm of my hand. It glints there darkly, like a wide-open eye.

KING HENRY'S PROPOSAL will take place at midday today. I am attired in the cream silk gown, awaiting the signal that the barge approaches the water gate. We're waiting in the duchess's stuffy parlor in order to conceal me from

NORTHLAKE PUBLIC LIBRARY DIST.
231 N. WOLF ROAD
NORTHLAKE, IL 60164

curious onlookers: the ladies of Lambeth, sequestered in their chambers above. I can only guess what stories they have heard from the servants, what details they rehash while resting on cushions or carding wool for thread. I try my best not to think about them.

At the signal, I'm hastily ushered outside. The royal barge arrives at the water gate, arrayed in brightly colored banners and ribbons. A series of barges follow, which carry the grooms of the king's chamber, a few of his closest advisers, and a band of musicians who serenade the king as he approaches the water gate. I stand in the sunlight, watching the royal party glide across the glittering Thames.

The sun is bright and hot, reflecting brilliantly off my cream gown.

"Stop squinting, Catherine," the duchess tells me. "Remember to smile."

The king steps from his barge and approaches me; I feel my breath catch in my throat. King Henry is tall and broad, the width of his massive shoulders accentuated by voluminous sleeves, decorated with fine slashes to reveal the glittering cloth of gold beneath the red satin. He wears a purple satin doublet embroidered with gold thread, and on a long gold chain around his royal neck hangs a diamond the size of a walnut; it swings against his full belly as he mounts the steps toward me.

"My dear Catherine," he says, and puts out his hand. I curtsy, speechless, and place my hand in his. He towers over me, monstrous—no, no, I can't think of it like that. He simply dwarfs me, in size and power and wealth and importance. He dwarfs everyone, a legend setting his feet upon common soil. The jewels on his fingers and his collar are sparkling, drenched in light. My eyes begin to tear. To those appraising the scene, I appear overcome with emotion.

He considers me for a moment, and squeezes my hand firmly in his gigantic grip. He does not kneel down, and of this I am relieved. He seems the type of romantic man to want to do such a thing. But who would feel comfortable watching a king beg, even if it is only pretend?

"Catherine Howard," he pronounces, "my red rose, Catherine, whom I know to be the dearest, loveliest creature upon this earth. Will you agree to marry me? To be my wife, my queen—to be all of England's queen?"

"Yes, Your Majesty. You do me the greatest honor," I tell him. But I do not know that anyone hears my answer. They do not need to. I bow gracefully before the king and he kisses the back of my bare, jewel-free hand. I lift my eyes to his, smiling, becoming accustomed to the new center of my focus, my life.

A flash out of the corner of my eye: a fair face with dark, glistening eyes and dark hair. Thomas is standing among the other grooms, watching. I force myself to look away.

HENRY AND I and all our glorious retinue are taken by barge to Oatlands Palace in Surrey.

"It will be a beautiful, private wedding," the king assures me, "beyond the eyes of the full court. And we will have a gown specially made for my glittering bride."

He reaches out to rest his hand upon my own. I am smiling, wistful, seated on the royal barge, the green velvet cushions laden with flowers.

"I only hope that it will please you." The king smiles.

"Of course it will please me," I tell him. It sounds so convincing I nearly believe it myself. Over the king's great shoulder I see Lambeth receding into the distance as we glide away from the water gate. As the sunlight slants, I see a series of pale faces pressed against the glass of an upper window—the window of the maidens' chamber. At this distance their faces are blank, expressionless, like ghosts', but I can feel their eyes on me.

"Do not turn pale, my dear." The king laughs. "You are leaving one home but will be provided with many others, far grander than Lambeth. Now the royal residences are your home."

"Of course, my lord." I blink, turning my gaze back to Henry. But even as the barge drifts out into the vast Thames, I feel watched, from beyond, by my past.

"I'M GLAD WE will be married soon," King Henry tells me. The sun has set upon this day and made for a cool evening; a fire scented with cinnamon and applewood crackles in the hearth. King Henry and I are seated in the main chamber of my apartments. The ladies—my ladies—sit in the adjacent room with several grooms of the king's chamber, whispering over their card games and embroidery.

"I look forward to it as well, my lord."

I am seated beside him on an embroidered dais, very conscious of our physical closeness. I glance up and spy Lady Rochford, scrutinizing my every movement, my facial expression, the reaction of the king to whatever I say. The king doesn't seem to notice. Perhaps he is so accustomed to being watched that it simply fails to register in his mind. The life of a king is a life lived in public.

I think I see a hand pass before the doorway; the edge of a velvet cape, an elbow encased in satin. Thomas is standing there. I avert my eyes carefully, gazing at the sapphire glittering darkly upon my finger.

"It rather dwarfs your hand, doesn't it?" The king laughs, tapping the stone with his own jeweled finger. "Your little fingers will be weighed down by jewels, very soon."

"You know well how to delight a young maid, Your Majesty." The king is staring at me, appraising the soft white flesh exposed above the collar of my gown.

"I yearn for you, Catherine," he whispers hoarsely. I look down at my small hand in his great one, not knowing how to react. My eyes flutter, my vision blurs.

"You must know this," he persists. "I've yearned for you since the moment I first saw you."

"I—I didn't realize."

"I've flustered you! Don't be bashful, my dear." His laugh is a low rumble, unmistakably masculine, suggestive. He rests his fingers delicately upon my shoulder; they radiate heat against my skin.

"I am glad that I please you, Your Majesty." I blink, meeting his gaze in a brief flash. "I hope that I will please you."

"Do not worry about that." He strokes my neck and chin lightly. I stare instead at the fire, the bright orange flames flickering in a frantic dance.

"Our pleasure will wait until the wedding ceremony is complete, Catherine. Do not worry, there will be pleasure for both of us, you will see." He laughs again and I smile shyly in response, my cheeks burning pink. He tilts my chin up with the tip of his finger and gazes into my eyes.

"I would not threaten your purity, your maidenhood, until we are properly wed."

I have never heard such a noble thing as purity discussed in so lascivious a tone.

"I thank you for this, Your Majesty," I whisper. I press my newly jeweled hand upon his and shift again upon the dais, my arm brushing against the sleeve of the king's doublet. My face (a measured expression, a beautifully constructed mask) reveals equal parts nervousness and eager anticipation. I must hide all weakness from my king—except, of course, my weakness for him.

The king laughs at his own passion. He rests his hand upon my leg, stroking the nap of my gown. His hand is massive; the sight of it upon my knee makes my throat constrict.

"You are a warm-blooded creature under there, are you not, Catherine Howard?"

"Of course I am, my lord." I smile and squeeze his hand warmly.

The Duke of Norfolk has done well to convince the king of my purity, chastity, devout Catholicism (without being too prim or pious), and delightful attitude. Now I need merely live up to the mythos created about my personality. The king must never know that his wife is half person, half fiction. I wonder if this is how the king must feel—needing to be so many different things, for so many different people. Lucky for me, I suppose I need only please him: as a maiden, as a lover, and as a wife.

I have only three days to prepare myself.

VII

For the wedding ceremony I will wear the royal jewels—last worn by Queen Jane—and a gown of cloth of gold. Lady Rochford and the duchess assist in the final fitting of the gown; its metallic luster is warm and provocative. I feel as if I've been dipped in a pool of gold. The double strand of rubies and pearls is cold against my neck, and each time I shift it with my fingertips I feel a certain thrill rippling over my flesh. I stare at myself in the mirror, glittering like a jewel in the candlelight.

"What a beautiful bride." Jane pats my cinched waist in approval. "The gold was a wonderful choice, for your skin and your hair."

"What a beautiful queen," the duchess remarks resolutely. "You will wear this gown when you arrive at court, and are presented as queen."

"And perhaps for her coronation?"

"No, a new gown will be made for the coronation—white and silver, perhaps, or purple and silver. Something grander, more regal, with a longer train." The duchess turns back to me, studying my reflection in the glass. I lift my hand to touch the jewels at my neck again, but she smacks it away.

"Don't fidget, Catherine. You must be poised, serene."

I stand still. She stares at me.

"You burn through the room, think of that. You are like a trail of fire in this gown, burning through the room. You must hold yourself properly, holding your head high like a lighted torch." Her eyes pierce mine. "Walk for me."

I turn and walk around the chamber, practicing how to hold my head, how to move gracefully, the gown sparkling around me. But my mind is full of the other words the duchess shared with me, in private: *Burn your past, burn your life* . . . And here I am, walking the length of the royal apartments—my apartments—dressed like a flame.

"Lift your chin, Catherine. Now try a small smile—nothing too garish."

Now that I am to be put on display as the king's new bride, there are so many things about myself, my past, and my fears that I must conceal. All weakness must be hidden far beneath the surface, and the surface must be tailored to fit the demands of the moment. I will be tailored, time and again, like a gown of satin or velvet or silk.

"That's enough," the duchess pronounces. "You must bathe tonight, Catherine, and then get to sleep. We'll not have you looking weary on your wedding day."

I submit to their aggressive attentions as they unlace me from the delicate gown and strip me of my silk underclothes. Naked, I move closer to the fire for warmth. The duchess considers me for a moment, as if to calculate how pleased Henry will be with the body of his new bride. I lift my arms across my chest and lower my head, discomfited at the sight of my own bare legs, the minnow-shaped birthmark on my upper thigh. I worry that my secrets can be seen, a confession written in fingerprints upon my flesh.

"In you go." The duchess urges me into the tub as Lady Rochford pours in more water from the kettle warmed in the hearth.

"It's hot."

"It has to be hot." Lady Rochford attacks my hair with soap and brush while the duchess inspects my fingernails.

Once they are done, I am dressed in a silk nightgown, and my hair is carefully combed.

"Jane will stay here with you," the duchess tells me as I pull up the covers. "She will be readying for bed shortly. Now you must sleep."

"Yes, Duchess."

When I'm sure they are gone, I slip out from the covers. I open my oak chest and pull out the small wooden jewelry box. Jane was satisfied with the papers she watched me burn those nights ago at Lambeth, but she does not know what I know. The false bottom of the box conceals yet more letters and trinkets beneath—even more precious than those already fed to the flames. Still I know that Jane is right, I cannot keep them. Every night I intended to do away with them as soon as I had a moment alone, but I've been too exhausted to contemplate the endeavor. In weary moments I have entertained the notion of saving a letter or two . . . but no, it is too dangerous. And I had best take care of it now. I pull the letters from the box and sit upon the floor, before the fire.

I was so young then, so young and so foolish. I shake my head over some old pages of music written for me in the flowing script of Henry Manox. The duchess appointed Manox as my music tutor, to teach me the lute and the virginals during my second summer at her residence in Horsham. I can laugh at these relics now: a page of composition, a scrawled letter requesting a private meeting in the chapel at midnight, another professing his undying affections. Manox's words, and later his kiss, sent me spiraling into the blissful dreams of a child playing at love. But it was a kiss, only—I never indulged his begging for more. He was merely a servant, after all. When he dared boast that he might have my hand in marriage, he was reprimanded by the duchess's chamber woman, Mary Lassells, who reminded him of his place in this world—it was not in the bed of a Howard daughter. She was right, and I was thankful for the affair to be over.

This note bears a sharp, jagged scrawl—Francis Dereham's hand—the sight of which makes me cringe. Here are some tokens he bestowed upon me, in our time together: a dried flower, a handkerchief embroidered with a friar's knot. At twelve years old I moved with the duchess to Lambeth, and was eager to be as sophisticated as the other ladies who shared the maidens' chamber. Joan, Lisbeth, Dorothy, Katherine, and Malyn held revelries there at midnight, sneaking in their suitors and feasting upon strawberries and wine. Here is a bit of leftover ribbon, once used to embellish my white linen nightgown; I rub it between my fingers.

Francis, a fair young man with pale blue eyes, attended these secret parties. He drew me into the circle of candlelight and lavished attention on me. He called me his love, his wife—no one had ever been so tender with me before. He promised to marry me, to protect and care for me, but I worried that the duchess would not approve. Francis assured me that the choice was ours: we were already married, he said. Saying the words made it true. Words are powerful in that way—and actions even more so.

The thought of it all gives me a chill; I generally avoid any thought of Francis. It was not an uncommon thing—the other ladies had companions in their own beds. But that does not make it a wise thing, as I've now learned. He was not a fit suitor for me, being poor both in money and stature. A Howard daughter is destined to have a good marriage arranged by her family, and she had best maintain her purity to attract the most worthy suitors. I was too busy basking in Francis's affection to consider what I was risking. It all seemed a delightful game: calling each other husband and wife and acting out our roles on my straw-stuffed mattress. Perhaps Francis sought to gain a better place in the world by staking a claim to me, but it was not my decision to make. He departed on a business venture overseas, and soon after that I was secured a place at court and our relationship—as far as I was concerned—was over. I have not seen or spoken to him since he left. The past is over and done, and I'm glad to be rid of it.

I thrust the ribbon into the flames. One by one the letters and tokens are tossed into the hearth; the fire snatches them up hungrily. I feel a sense of relief as I watch the pages curl and blacken. I am becoming a real woman, watching the dreams of my childhood turn to cinders and ash.

But there is one stack of letters left, each one folded into a small, careful square. This was how Thomas and I communicated, soon after my arrival at court: while walking by me in the hall, or exiting the chapel after Mass, he would swiftly pass a note from his palm into my own. These were the days before a sapphire necklace was ever clasped around my neck, when my heart was still my own.

I pull the ribbon fondly, trying to laugh at myself. How young, how innocent I was . . . though it was all mere months ago, and the thought of my loss is still raw. Thomas is a groom in the king's privy chamber, with an illustrious career ahead of him. Upon my arrival, he was already well known at court as a favorite of the king. No doubt our families would have approved . . . But it doesn't matter anymore, it can't matter. Since then my entire world has changed: few things can send such tremors through a person's life as being loved by a king. Scanning over the lines of text, my eyes begin to blur.

My dearest Catherine, how I so long to hold you
close to my heart and call you my only love . . .

My life will be more than I ever could have imagined—but perhaps it will also be a little bit less. All of this must be put aside now, the words and dreams that led to his perfect kiss, near midnight in the dark garden at Westminster, and all the happiness that kiss seemed sure to promise. This was a different Catherine who received these letters, who responded to that kiss—since then I have been transformed by the king's eyes, by the royal jewels around my neck and a cloth-of-gold gown . . . but who is the real Catherine: the shadow or the light? The smoke or the flame?

I thrust a letter into the flames before I can think twice about it. For a moment the words flash before my eyes, his dark, slanted script burning in the air with ink of fire. I have the urge to pull it free from the flames—but I can't, it's too late, it's done. It's over. But there is more to it than this—I cannot burn the memory of his kiss from my lips, I cannot burn my love for him from my heart, my passion for him from my flesh . . . or can I? Must I, regardless? I have no choice, now. I was only a girl, then. Now I will be queen.

When I shut my eyes, the image only burns brighter. I push the rest of the letters into the fire, then pull a poker from beside the hearth and press them, crackling, into the flames. My eyes sting with heat, my vision blurred in gold and black. I watch until all of the letters are consumed.

The fire's feast is done. I turn and crawl back into bed and close my eyes, trying to think back to my reflection in the mirror, the gold bridal gown. In my mind, the gold cloth is replaced by the flames of the fire, curling the edges of the letters black.

I am different, transformed. The girl I was before is gone; I watched her burn in a flash of flame.

VIII

As I'm dressed, sunshine streams in the window of the chamber, and the gold gown glistens as if I'm being robed in sunlight itself. I imagine how the king, how all of court, will react when they see me, gowned like a royal bride. The thought burns like a small flame of triumph. I stoke this flame, hoping it may be enough to warm me.

"You are a fairy queen," Jane pronounces, "the little girl who catches the eye of the king and becomes his bride. Can you imagine?"

The duchess has been quiet but she cannot hide her smile, no matter how hard she tries. "Of course I can imagine it. I've been imagining this day since first he laid eyes upon my little Catherine."

My little Catherine—then she is proud of me! Perhaps she is even more proud of me than she was of my cousin

Anne. She moves closer and arranges my hair, just as I imagine a mother might help her daughter on her wedding day.

"Or perhaps even before the king saw her," she murmurs. She stands back to appraise me, clasping her hands beneath her chin. When Jane finishes smoothing out the folds from my train, she stands beside the duchess to inspect me.

They had been planning this for me, all along. It makes me feel a bit sorry for the king, his emotions constantly manipulated by his most ambitious courtiers. But the king loves me—*doesn't he?*

A knock upon the door signals that the hall is prepared for the small ceremony. It will be a beautiful, intimate ceremony, nothing like the ostentatious display of riches for his brief marriage to Anne of Cleves. The duchess takes my hand in hers and moves toward the door, but I stop.

"Can I have just a moment?" I ask. The two women blink at me. "Alone?"

"Only a moment," the duchess informs me. "We'll be right outside the door." They leave the chamber reluctantly.

I stand before the mirror looking at a young woman in a beautiful gown. On her head is a glittering gold coronet studded with sapphires and diamonds, and her hair flows in lustrous coppery waves over her shoulders. I barely recognize myself. This gown shimmers like fire. I imagine the fabric purifies me as it touches my skin, cleanses me of sins and burns the memory of those sins from every sinew of my flesh.

When I emerge from the chamber, everyone turns. The lords and ladies, the senior maids of the queen's chamber, the king's chief advisers, all of them drop in a low reverence before me. I walk forward steadily, gracefully.

My eyes snag suddenly on Thomas's face—it's been so long since I've met his gaze. Dark eyes burning against his pale skin, his face drawn; my heart falters. But it is too late for that, too late. He bows his head before me and I move on, smoothly. *I burn through this room, I burn . . .* I see the king standing at the end of the hall, waiting for me. He is closer, more vivid with every step.

"I, CATHERINE," I begin. My voice sounds so quiet. The chamber is filled with bright sunshine, stinging my eyes. "Take thee, Henry, to be my wedded husband, to have and to hold from this day forward, for better for worse, for richer for poorer, in sickness and in health, and promise to be bonair and buxom in bed and at board, till death us depart."

I pledge myself to him; the words are rather easy to say. I smile in relief when I am done with them, and he smiles in return. Then the king pledges himself to me.

AFTER THE CEREMONY, I stand beside the king and sip spiced wine from a jeweled goblet, along with all the rest of our small wedding party. There are musicians striking up a lively tune, and everyone is talking pleasantly and congratulating the king. He laughs and sips his wine, eyeing me over the rim of his glass. No matter who is talking to him or bidding him their best, most gracious wishes, his eyes are constantly trained upon me. I'm sure I'm not the only one who notices.

Thomas moves forward from the crowd. I look at him

blankly, as if we've never met. He returns my look with a practiced courtier's smile. The burning I saw in his eyes moments ago is gone. It is all done now. I am married to the king.

"I present to Your Grace, Prince Edward, Lady Mary, and Lady Elizabeth."

The king's children step forward. His daughters bow slowly, perfectly.

"You look very beautiful, Your Majesty," sprightly Elizabeth announces. She steps forward and offers me a small posy of flowers. "Your gown is the loveliest I have ever seen."

"Thank you, Lady Elizabeth. You look beautiful, as well."

Even before this ceremony, Lady Elizabeth and I were related—sharing a blood tie through her disgraced mother. Now she stands before me, an eager and clever seven-year-old. I warm to her instantly, as I feel she's already warmed to me. Nothing can sever a blood tie.

"Did you arrange these yourself? They are simply lovely. Here." I pull a flower from the bouquet and lean forward to slide the stem over Elizabeth's ear; the yellow bloom looks pretty against her red-gold hair, just like her father's. She smiles up at me brightly and then dips again into a proper bow.

I stand up and turn my smile to Lady Mary. Suddenly I feel as if I've rammed headfirst into a stone wall.

"Good day, Your Grace," she murmurs sullenly, and bows again.

"I am glad to see you in attendance," I tell her. Was that the right thing to say? I sense a quiet rage burning in Mary, a rage she takes little effort to hide in my presence. I turn my attentions to Edward to conceal my discomfort. He is but a little boy, distracted by the sights and sounds around him and ready to toddle off at any moment. Elizabeth holds his chubby hand in hers, and he dares not stray far from her side.

As the day wanes, I become aware of the tone the sunshine makes upon my gold gown: first white-hot sunlight, then a more golden hue, then a rich, burnished copper. I watch the day dwindle to sunset, well aware of what the setting of the sun will bring.

The king takes my hand and leads me to the center of the room. We are a dazzling sight to behold: both clothed in golden raiment and glittering with jewels in the low light. My gaze passes over the assembled courtiers and I picture what they see. I imagine seeing myself through so many eyes, as if surrounded by fragments of different mirrors, different reflections of me.

I bow to my new husband, and we begin our dance. I have never danced with the king before, but we dance quite easily together, though he is so much larger. King Henry is a skilled dancer. He spins me vigorously, my gown spreading out in a cloud of gold around me. The faces assembled move past in a blur.

The dance is done. Tapers are being lit and I am flickering like a flame. The guests slowly depart, and the duchess hurries me to my chambers to prepare for bed.

"It all went by so quickly," I murmur as Jane unclasps the jewels from my throat, and the duchess removes the rings from my fingers. Other ladies have joined us: Lady Bryan, little Edward's nurse, as well as Lady Edgecombe and Lady Baynton, who served Anne of Cleves alongside me. Now they are *my* ladies, sworn to serve me. I am the center of the circle—the candle surrounded by fluttering moths.

The golden gown is unlaced and pulled from my body; I feel a part of my power stripped from me. A silk nightgown is pulled over my head, which slips like the softest of clouds against my skin. The embroidery at the neckline of the gown is done in gold, but the gown itself is so sheer as to be nearly completely translucent.

"Dearest, your fingers are like ice!" Jane exclaims. "That will not do . . . here, warm them in this flannel before I apply the scented cream."

I sit in a chair before the fire and the bejeweled coronet is removed from my hair. Once unpinned, my hair is combed with a wide-toothed ivory comb. Rose-scented cream is smoothed onto my arms and hands. I sit quietly as all of these tasks are performed.

"Here, so you will stop that incessant shivering." The duchess moves forward and drapes a velvet robe of deep claret over my shoulders. The ladies arrange my hair in a fetching manner, then smile and praise my reflection.

Will this be enough? My eyes meet the duchess's in the mirror. Jangling with nerves, part of me wants to ask her what I must do, and another part is afraid she may tell me. I'm abashed at my own panic; it's not as if I've never done this before . . . but my secret knowledge gives me no solace. I want to satisfy the king, but fear seeming too practiced, too knowledgeable.

"Do not worry," the duchess says, squeezing my arm.

"Nothing is sweeter to a man than a virgin on her wedding night."

The other ladies laugh in approval.

Henry sees a virgin when he looks at me. Surely I can transform myself to satisfy his desires? I stare into the mirror and imagine myself a virgin, too. It takes practice and cunning to play a part other than who you are. Court is filled with such people. My nervousness and my cold, trembling hands make my act very convincing.

Tonight I will become new, again. I will become his.

IX 🌿 We each enter the bedchamber from separate entrances—a door on each side of the room leads to separate apartments for the king and myself. The ladies escort me over to the bed, which is draped in sheer curtains embroidered with metallic thread that twinkles in the firelight. They remove my robe and usher me into bed. The king enters the chamber; I can see him vaguely through the shimmering veils.

Once I am properly arranged beneath the covers, the ladies bow to the king and depart. When the door is shut behind them, I glance at him cautiously.

He is similarly robed in velvet, with an embroidered linen tunic beneath, poking out of the neckline of his robe. Mere moments ago he was magnificently robed and festooned with jewels and gold. Now he seems more manly, less godly. I have never seen him this way, looking as a man does when he turns to bed. Lacking as he is the embroidered doublet and puffed sleeves and jeweled collar, I think some power has been stripped from his person, as well. Not many people see the king this way, so intimately. It occurs to me all over again how far I've come, and how there is no going back, now.

He wants me to be his beloved wife, I remind myself. He wants me to love him. A corded belt is securely cinched around his middle. Is he worried about exposing himself to my eyes? I soften at the thought, for I feel the same way. Perhaps we could both remain covered for the night? No, no, that will not do. I turn and give him a shy smile. He sighs and returns it, warmly.

"My sweet wife," he says quietly, pushing aside the veil and pulling down the covers of the bed. As he slips into the bed beside me I look away, focusing on the play of light the fire makes upon the ceiling. We are in bed beside each other, and I'm too afraid to turn and look at him. His breathing is heavy, labored.

His arm touches mine, his warm skin burns through the thin silk of my nightdress.

"Catherine." He leans forward, breathing my name into my neck, his face burrowed in my hair. He pulls me toward him and I'm lying on my back, my body close to his. I think back to the wedding, mere moments ago: like a beautiful pageant with lines I had memorized and didn't even need to think about to recite. All so remarkably easy. Now this is real, without rehearsal.

Be wary of his legs, Catherine, they cause him pain. The duchess's instructions echo in my head, unbidden. *You must distract him from his ailments with his pleasure. Don't be a prude, Catherine. I refuse to accept prudishness from you now.* These reminders serve only to heighten my panic; I feel as if the duchess is standing over the bed, judging my performance, pointing out what I'm doing wrong.

I alternate between closing my eyes and opening them to watch the light and shadow flicker upon the embroidered canopy. My chest begins to ache; I've been holding my breath this whole time. *Breathe, breathe.* I open my eyes—I don't want to appear as if I'm sleeping, trying to ignore him. His massive hands are warm, searching. I dig my fingers into the bedclothes; lie still, lie still and let it happen. Don't think about it. Don't make a sound.

He kisses my neck for a moment and then pulls back to look at my face. He looms over me: a dark shadow in the low light.

"You were made for me. I was sure of it from the moment I saw you, dancing in that pale blue gown."

"You knew, even then?" I whisper, my voice breaking.

"Of course I knew!" He laughs. "With your beauty, your grace. You are exactly what I yearn for. I could not have made you more tempting had I imagined you myself."

He leans forward and kisses me upon the mouth—our first private kiss. I close my eyes and allow the kiss to happen: I am warm, yielding. I was made for him, as if I had been magically put together, an assemblage of parts, like a doll, purely for the pleasure of the king.

As he kisses my neck I can't help but watch, distantly fascinated, as his massive hand covers my breast. A dark ruby upon the king's thumb glints in the light of the fire; it's a large stone, dusty at its core like an eye filmed with age. I know the story of this ring: it was acquired from Becket's tomb, when Henry had the saint's remains exhumed and destroyed, to rid England's church of idolatry. I shiver at the awesome power of this king, at the sight of his hand, with this ancient ring upon it, stroking my own soft breast. I feel exposed suddenly, vulnerable. I only hope that his powerful touch will protect me.

Protect me? Protect me from what? From the king? *I fear him.* I hadn't realized it before now. I hadn't been so close to him, so alone with him to know that I fear him. But I do. And it's too late, now. *Too late, too late.* But perhaps it was too late from the very beginning, from the day he first saw me, first chose me. He has chosen me, above all others. He has chosen me.

His kisses become more insistent and he leans forward, covering my body with his. His weight isn't as oppressive as I feared, upon the high soft bed, but still my breath strains, my heart races. And my hair is beneath his elbow—pulling—oh, then he pulls again, even harder, trying to free us from the entanglement—

"Your Majesty!"

"Catherine!" he cries, brushing my hair gently from my neck and laughing warmly. "You may call me Henry, now."

"King Henry?"

"No, dear, just Henry. In public you must use a formal greeting. But alone, in private . . . and we are in private . . ."

"Henry," I say, my breath whistling by his ear.

He lifts the silk nightgown slowly, by its hem, until I slip from it completely. I lie on the bed naked before him, his hands covering me. I close my eyes. I cannot dare open them. I am so afraid. But I know, just from his touch, what he wants.

As he finally claims me, his breathing turns even more labored. In a few moments he grunts, his limbs rigid. Then he collapses with a great sigh in my ear.

It is over, already. Instead of feeling relieved, I am horrified. This was what he wanted, this was what he desired, to have me in his bed. And that was it? Will that be enough for him? I lie motionless as he pulls away from me, rolling onto his back. Is something wrong with me? Something he hadn't expected? Could he detect, somehow, that which I am most desperate to hide? *The thought of a girl already spoiled by another man disgusts him.* I cannot think of it; I can not think that I've failed already. What will become of me if I have?

He lies beside me, quiet for a long while. I think he's fallen asleep when he rolls over and reaches for his robe. I turn and dare to look at him. His back is curved forward, his shoulders drooping.

"It has been a long day," he pronounces. His voice is weary, cracked. Is he disappointed? Embarrassed? The mere thought of it horrifies me. *What did I do wrong?*

"You don't need to leave," I tell him. I rest my hand in the middle of his broad back. "If you don't want to."

"Do you wish me to stay?"

"Yes." *Yes, please, please stay.* I press my cool palm against his warm flesh. I can't be left here alone with thoughts of the king's disappointment. I have to fix things, I have to make things right.

"Yes," he agrees, "I shall stay." He slides back beneath the sheets. This time I move close to him, pressing my breasts against his arm.

"I hope that you will be patient with your little wife," I tell him, eyes cast down, embarrassed. I am embarrassed, bashful, virginal. "I suppose I do not yet know how—or what—to do. To please you."

"My sweet wife." He sighs.

"I want to please you, my king. My Henry." I rest my cheek upon his shoulder. "I'm afraid it may take me a while to learn how."

He laughs at this, patting my hand playfully. That's right. This is my embarrassment, not his. Not his.

"Do not worry, my dear. You have done well already."

I lift my head and kiss him on the cheek. He laughs again and presses my hand to his lips.

"My sweet, sweet wife," he murmurs. "I love you, Catherine."

"I love you, Henry." My voice is quiet, but it does not tremble. I lie perfectly still, with eyes wide open in the dark. The king falls asleep, and I listen to the thick rattle of his breath. My guilt makes no sound as it settles deep within me, sinking in its claws.

The king is in love with me. But who am I? Who is this girl that the Howards created out of their words, to whom the king has given his love? I am King Henry's sweet wife— Catherine Howard, no more. I wonder if God can see me now, see the treason in my heart. I squeeze my eyes shut, pushing these thoughts from my mind. I am a player upon a stage, even when the stage is a bed, even in an intimate moment such as this, with no costume or mask to cover my nakedness. I must play my part well, *especially* in an intimate moment such as this. I must become my role, and nothing else.

X It seems that my wedding day—a day of triumph for the Howards—was not joyous for all. I've just learned that yesterday was also the day of Cromwell's execution. Thomas Cromwell, Henry's chief adviser.

"Do not feel sorry for Cromwell, my dear." The duchess shakes her head as she pulls a comb through my hair. "He was condemned for pushing the marriage between Henry and that Lutheran German, and rightly so. He would have made the Church of England a Lutheran church, if he had his way."

The duchess puts down the comb and pulls a new hood of pale pink silk over my head—both hood and gown are new. She stands before me and arranges my hair carefully over my shoulder.

"Now we have more important things to talk about."

From the way her eyes flash at me, critically, I know what she means. Suddenly I would rather talk about Cromwell. My face and neck blush scarlet.

"How did the king enjoy his new bride?"

"Very well," I whisper. "I think, very well."

Her eyes narrow at mine as she adjusts my hood, and I blandly return her stare.

"I was nervous," I tell her, "and shy. He liked it." This I can be sure of: I was awoken this morning with the persistence of Henry's kisses. In spite of my qualms, the wedding night was undeniably a success in Henry's mind.

"Good." She smiles. "He is besotted with you. You must be besotted with him. You must be welcoming, flirtatious."

"Yes, Duchess." I sigh. There is always a never-ending list of things I must be.

"Make sure he visits your bed every night, Catherine. It

is imperative. You must charm him, you must desire him. Do you understand?"

I do understand, for this is why he chose me: to feel desired and adored by a young woman, to convince him that he is not old. To his court, King Henry is a powerful monarch, stalwart and sturdy, draped in magnificent jewels. Now I've glimpsed the old man hiding beneath the robes of state, and I know more than is safe to know about a king, let alone to put into words. But it makes me soften toward him, in spite of my fears. A youthful bride is exactly what he needs—*I* am exactly what he needs. I must protect him; we must protect each other.

MY CHAMBERS ARE CROWDED: at least twenty maids are here, buzzing around me in the candlelit darkness, pinning my hair and tying my sleeves and adjusting the farthingale hoop beneath my skirt. I stand still and watch it in the mirror, like a beautiful tableau.

"Oh, Catherine!" The ladies sigh over the layers of rich black lace and cloth of gold. "How exquisite!"

Exquisite, indeed: just last fall I was relegated to the thinnest of cushions and the farthest seat from the fire. Now I'm installed in the queen's chambers at Oatlands Palace, last decorated for Jane Seymour, who did not live to occupy them.

"How wonderful it is to have a young, beautiful English queen!" Lady Browne exclaims. When I was nothing more than a lady-in-waiting, she chastised me for poor embroidery and lackluster manners. Now she smiles proudly upon me.

"Not only an English queen—a *Catholic* queen. It is just what England, and the crown, needs more than ever," Lady

Rochford remarks. Even Jane's usually sober expression has softened tonight, relaxed with wine and revelry.

"It's time, everyone! Are we all ready?" Lady Edgecombe announces. "It's time!"

We rush down the torchlit hall, dozens of velvet shoes tapping upon the flagstones, skirts of lace and silk rustling like waves breaking upon the shore. I'm so excited I can't help giggling, and my laughter is echoed, rippling through the ladies around me, magnified. The light of the torches streams by us in streaks of gold.

"Get in line, everyone, find your place!" I call over the crowd; they all fall silent at the sound of my voice. I snap open my fan, too excited to stand still; the gold lace fan sparkles by the light of the torches. "We have to wait for our cue."

I listen closely to the music emanating from the great hall—yes, there it is!—a high wooden reed plays a dazzling trill. We enter the hall in formation, and the assembled crowd sighs at the sight of us. The hall is golden and sparkling, strung with garlands of red roses, smelling of a balmy summer night.

The ladies and I begin our stately pavane, but at the rapid beat of the tabors, the marauders come out from hiding: all of the king's grooms descend, dressed in black masks and sweeping black capes, scattering us from the dance floor. The crowd roars with laughter, shouting at the spectacle.

This is my moment: I am pursued by five grooms, all waving comically stubby wooden swords, like drunken pirates. They urge me toward the castle—constructed from lengths of red velvet and white satin draped over a wooden frame— standing at the end of the hall. I hurry up the stairs at the back and stand in the topmost tower window. The crowd turns to see me there, glittering in gold, waving an enormous white silk handkerchief as a sign of my distress.

"Save the queen!" the crowd shouts, amidst applause. "God save the queen!"

Now the king arrives—dressed in black silk and cloth of silver, looking like an armored knight—and the crowd erupts with cheering. It has been many years since the king has participated in a masque. *Anything for you, my fair bride,* he told me. Henry does not break a smile, ever the proud knight. He moves forward into the crowd of kidnappers and dispatches them with a few graceful thrusts of his silver sword. Once the last groom falls limp at his feet, Henry overtakes the castle itself, emerging through the red curtain with me in his arms. The crowd, including my ladies, cheer loudly enough to drown out the music.

As planned, the scene concludes with a dance. The king spins across the floor with me in his arms. I feel the tips of my toes clearing the floor as he lifts me into the air. He laughs joyously at the smile on my face.

"You've saved me!" I whisper in the king's ear, breathless. "Like a true hero."

"No, my dear," he whispers, smiling. "You have saved me."

THESE DAYS IN SURREY have been an endless round of hunting expeditions, archery, outdoor games, and elaborate masques to celebrate our nuptials. The king was an athlete of unparalleled skill and vigor in his youth, so I've heard. Though he has aged, I can now see a glimpse of that nature revealed. Henry is a new man, invigorated, and each day ends in the revelry of the night: Henry and I lying atop the massive royal bed with its dark wood and mother-of-pearl inlay.

"Are you enjoying your marriage thus far, my wife?" he asks, his face nestled close to my ear.

"Yes, of course I am, my husband." I giggle at this, in that way that charms and amuses him. "And I can't wait to see Hampton, and all the rest of the court."

My marriage to the king is still a secret, even from the king's Privy Council, though I imagine rumors have long been rampant in London. Tomorrow, after ten days of honeymooning here in Surrey, we will journey to Hampton Court, where Henry will present me to the full court as his queen.

"Ah, yes, Hampton." Henry lets out a long sigh. "I will rather miss our summer retreat. This season is best spent in the country. It is quiet, secluded. Court is full of eyes and ears," he murmurs ominously. The fear must be evident on my face, for he laughs aloud and wraps his arms around me.

"Do not look so frightened! I will protect you, Catherine. Do not worry."

"I need not worry," I tell him, my arms encircling his neck, "as long as I have you to protect me."

"My sweet wife." He sighs, holding me tighter.

"Henry," I whisper in his ear. "I like saying your name, when we are alone."

I am becoming accustomed to this: the two of us together, alone in the royal bedchamber. I feel safe now in Henry's arms, protected by his love and affection. With the king's arms around me, I have nothing—not even the eyes of the court—to fear.

XI 🙠
Hampton Court spreads out before me, resplendent, beneath a pure blue sky. The glorious red-brick façade shines golden red in the sunshine.

Upon our entrance, courtiers drop to their knees in obeisance. Whispers, like the rustling of a hundred crows' wings, follow in the wake of my every step as I'm escorted to the queen's apartments: a presence chamber, a drawing room, and finally my bedchamber, where the tall windows reveal a view of the royal gardens, riotous with color. All of the ladies of my new household—too many to count—hover around me, kiss my hand, and pledge their oath of service. I relish the sight of Lady Ashley, bent in dutiful reverence before me. But I'm sure their whispers will rise and fall as soon as I depart. I was once a maid in the queen's chambers, I know what it is like. What they don't know about me their whispers will invent.

The king arrives to escort me to the royal pew in the Chapel Royal, for Mass. The chapel is flooded with multicolored sunlight from the stained-glass windows, lighting the curved vaults of the gilded ceiling. Looking down upon the upturned faces of the assembled court, I imagine I see varying degrees of shock and admiration rippling over their expressions as they gaze upon their new queen.

I've done it, I think, triumphantly, the choir of male voices rising as Mass begins. *They can all see that I've done it. I've won the heart of the king.*

A HOST OF SILVER TRUMPETS blares a fanfare as Henry and I enter the great hall; the sound shimmers in the air before us. There are hundreds of people here—the entire court is assembled for a banquet in my honor. The king leads me to the front of the hall, where we are seated side by side beneath the cloth of state: a crimson velvet canopy embroidered with a Tudor rose. All the grandeur makes me think about my coronation. How will it feel when the crown is set upon my head?

We are presented with platters of venison, beef, roast swan, salt cod. The peacock royal is roasted and its skin then reapplied, so that it appears the bird is merely squatting upon the platter, alert, his jewel-bright tail feathers spread in a fan behind him. Even the loaf of bread brought to us is elegantly wrapped in bright orange silk. And for dessert: a marchpane mold of our entwined initials—*He&C*—painted in gold leaf.

My eyes wander around the great hall, taking in the high stained-glass windows, the carved ceiling painted in blue, green, red, and gold.

"It is the story of Abraham," the king tells me, motioning to the elaborate set of tapestries lining the walls. "I had it commissioned." Scenes of the biblical tale are depicted in vivid color. In the tapestry closest to us, Abraham gazes at his infant son.

"They are breathtaking, my lord." But it is more than that; I can see why Henry identifies with Abraham, who was also in dire need of a son and heir.

"As breathtaking as the gooseberry tarts?" The king

laughs, urging another tart onto my plate and putting his arm around me.

"You know well how to keep your wife happy." I bite carefully into the tart, chewing in rapture. What he doesn't know is how long I went without such indulgences.

"Indeed, I do—what pleases my wife pleases me the more."

At the wave of Henry's jeweled hand a huge assembly of musicians and acrobats comes forward to entertain us with their antics. I clap my hands in delight over the proceedings, and Henry laughs all the more for my enjoyment. He pulls me close to him, stroking my cheek lovingly with his jeweled hand. The eyes of the court are upon us, appraising the king's love for his new wife. The cold stones, ruby and emerald, brush against my skin, sending a rush of relief and triumph through my body. There is no one to ignore me now.

Gazing upon the crowd in the great hall, I'm distracted by a pair of dark eyes, watching me. Thomas stands in the corner, his eyes lit by the flickering candles. When he catches my gaze, he does not look away.

The night flowers are blooming, you should see them, he said, the first time we spoke. I had often noticed him standing in the corner, watching me; he was never one to join in the dance. He was different from the other lords—reserved, even a bit solemn. But there was something so earnest in the way he spoke, the way he looked at me, as if he were laying his feelings bare upon his face. *The garden is most beautiful at night.* I remember the low timbre of his voice, the warmth of his lean, long-fingered hand.

His dark eyes smolder; my flesh turns warm. I look back

to the fools and minstrels before us, eager for distraction. I smile, gently: the measured, noble expression of a queen.

I HAVE MORE than seventy attendants of various ranks and positions ready to do my bidding, though I can never be quite certain what all of their roles involve: the lord chamberlain, the master of the horse, chaplains, waiters, ushers, maids. The maids are responsible for the considerable task of dressing me each morning: arranging the farthingale hoop around my waist and tying my sleeves in place. There is even a cupbearer, whose task is to keep full my goblet of wine. From the outside looking in, one would think I had nothing with which to concern myself.

Nearest to me I always keep Lady Rochford, who is adept at court etiquette and the proper behavior of a queen. Our heads are often bowed close together, her mouth demurely hidden behind a lace fan. She constantly counsels me on how to address the various members of court, how to act at public occasions, even how to speak to my royal husband. I've come to dread the anxious fluttering of her fan, knowing that it signals some obscure impropriety.

Only in my own chambers, in the company of my ladies, can I find some peace. I spin into the room in my new gown: bold blue silk with long, drooping sleeves.

"How beautiful, my queen!" Lady Ashley, Lady Christina rush forward, quick to lavish praise on me. The duchess walks forward to inspect me, her steely eyes running efficiently from my copper hair to my velvet-shod feet.

"It's rather French, isn't it?" she comments, perhaps a bit warily.

"Say what you will." I turn to the mirror to inspect myself. "The French fashions are by far the most becoming, and I'm sure the king is appreciative."

"We can all see that is true," the duchess remarks with a prim smile.

"Look," I urge, thrusting my sleeves before her, "this bears the new trim."

The duchess takes my arm in hers, and her face instantly brightens. My motto has been embroidered in gold thread around the sleeves of the gown: *Non aultre volonté que la sienne.* No other will but his.

"Well done," she says. "I am sure the king approves." Her eyes communicate more than she dares say aloud, that it is reminiscent of Jane Seymour's motto, "bound to obey and serve." I have followed the duchess's advice to use Jane as a model. That is, in all ways except for my wardrobe: the sleek French hood is simply far more elegant than the traditional boxy English headdress the late queen preferred.

For my royal emblem I have chosen a red rose, encircled by a gold crown. It is a symbol of my royalty, and an allusion to my impending coronation. All of court has heard the king call me his "rose without a thorn." This symbol is being painted onto stained-glass windows, entwined with our initials. Designs have been rendered for a set of elaborate jewels: rubies to represent the petals of the rose, and a gold wire twisted into a crown set with diamonds.

"In all my years I've never seen our king act quite this way," Lady Edgecombe remarks, her eyes lowered to the embroidery in her lap. "Not with his other queens."

"He certainly loves nothing more than to indulge his young bride," Jane adds. "I think it quite romantic."

And I think it quite necessary. What better way than these gowns, these jewels, these newly decorated apartments, to put Henry's love for me on display? To convince all of court of the validity of their new queen?

"Still, perhaps it would be wise not to take such advantage of his majesty's generous affection," Lady Edgecombe remarks, "or else the coffers will soon run dry."

"I find it difficult to believe that you would act with such prudence were you in my position, Lady Edgecombe." My cheeks burn at her insolence; I am queen, why should I refuse any gift offered by my generous, loving husband?

"I beg your pardon, my queen," she mutters begrudgingly, and returns to her embroidery.

"I have new samples for you, Your Grace," Mistress Elle announces, lumbering into the room, arms laden with bolts of cloth. "Bright colors, straight from the palace gardens, just as you requested." I follow her to the window seat to inspect the rose pink, crimson, and saffron silk. Mistress Elle holds a length of yellow silk beneath my chin.

"It is the color of summer," she comments.

When I turn to look in the mirror I'm struck by a sudden memory: stories of Anne Boleyn enchanting the king by dancing in a bright yellow gown. I pale at the sight of my face. I am the best loved of all of Henry's wives—everyone says that he indulges me far more than any of the others. Why will their memories not leave me in peace?

"The king will find you quite lovely in this, I'm certain," Mistress Elle adds. Do I detect a hint of a sinister smile on her face? The king found Anne Boleyn quite lovely in yellow silk, with her long, flowing black hair. I am eager to reprimand her, but cannot think what to reprimand her for.

"It is a weak color," I remark in disapproval. Lady Edge-combe looks up from her embroidery; usually I like every-thing I see, and want a gown made in every color, every fabric. "I prefer a richer shade, like the crimson."

"Of course, my queen." Mistress Elle nods obediently, no glimmer of mockery visible on her face. Had it been there, or have I imagined it?

XII ❧

At Hampton, Henry is often sequestered with his advisers, clerks, and members of his Privy Council. I spend the daylight hours entertain-ing myself with plans for my wardrobe, or redecorating my chambers, or taking walks in the company of my ladies around Hampton's lush gardens and beautiful courtyard. Today it is too hot for a walk outdoors. We wander the vast stone hallways, admiring the large, brilliant tapestries de-picting gods and heroes of ancient myths. There are times I miss my solitary rides, or the private lute playing I enjoyed as a lady-in-waiting, tucked away in the royal gardens. Now I may do whatever I please, but never alone.

My footfalls echoing along these halls, I think of the yel-low silk. I'm well aware that Queen Anne adored Hampton and spent much time here. It had been Cardinal Wolsey's palace, and the king gifted it to Anne upon the cardinal's death. I pass beneath a twined *He&A* carved into the gateway of Hampton, feeling for a moment that her ghost watches me from overhead. But I try my best to banish these un-pleasant thoughts, for Hampton is a beautiful place and I cannot help but love it here.

"What is down this hallway?" I ask the others. A dim gallery stretches before us, lined with portraits. I press on into the darkness, as if heedless of lingering ghosts.

One particular portrait gives me pause. With a flutter of my hand, a servant rushes to light some candles from the flames of a nearby fire. As a torch sputters forth in flame, a faint gasp of recognition ripples through the ladies as the portrait is revealed. It is the Golden Prince—my Henry when he was first crowned king, when he was but a few years older than I am now. He stands tall and slim and strapping, an image of youth and vitality. But I instantly recognize the bright blue eyes, the curved pink mouth, the red-gold hair the same color as the wisps upon my lord's head. *Is this my husband?* Perhaps. More accurately, this was Katherine of Aragon's husband, the young king the Spanish princess married so many years ago.

"He was the most beautiful prince a country could hope for," the duchess had told me about the young King Henry, her voice uncomfortably wistful. "He was a strapping athlete, with the heart of a poet." Her eyes had turned glassy, staring off over my shoulder. "Think of that when you look at him, Catherine. That is what he wants you to see." And now I'm gazing at the eyes of the Golden Prince himself: just as handsome as the duchess had described, in that first blush of youth and power.

We stand here quietly for a moment, all of us silently appraising the form of the Golden Prince. When I turn and continue down the dim gallery, I feel those bold blue eyes watching me pass. Now I have one more ghost following me down these halls: the ghost of the beautiful prince my aging king once was.

THE SUMMER HEAT increases, the air torpid and thick. The king has been busy during the day and night with official matters of state, so I am told. My days are spent in the company of my ladies, wandering the palace gardens where the royal gardener's creations—a roaring lion's head carved from a bush of red roses—have begun to wilt in the glaring sun. We find solace from the heat in my chambers, spending hours on embroidering altar cloths and other subdued tasks. But by the evening I'm restless, ready for the celebratory banquet, my legs prickling with the need to dance.

It isn't until I'm seated beside the king that I notice how weary he seems. Not the same rejuvenated Henry riding at the head of the pack during our honeymoon in Surrey, this Henry is breathing heavily. And something else: his left leg has been tightly bound beneath his hose, the foot elevated upon a pile of cushions. I note this out of the corner of my eye, but do my best not to acknowledge it directly. His face seems older than it did just days ago, sagging in the heat. The face of the Golden Prince rushes back to me, unbidden. I am relieved by the antics of the fool, here to distract us from the discomfort of an oppressive summer evening.

When the dancing begins, the king nudges me.

"Go on, Catherine," he urges me. "Join in the dance. Show them the way it should best be done."

"Not tonight." I shake my head and take another sweetmeat. "I would rather stay here beside you, my lord."

"Oh, come now." He sighs. "You know how I like to watch you. Look." He gestures over to a corner of the hall where his grooms stand around, sipping ale and watching the ladies dance. I flutter my eyes over them only briefly, cautiously.

"Take Culpeper over there, your cousin, see?"

I look over at Thomas, though every part of me wants to resist. He looks very handsome standing there, smiling.

"He never dances, your cousin. I think he doesn't know how. Too clumsy on those long legs of his." Henry tilts his head back and laughs.

I prefer watching you. Thomas's voice echoes in my ear. Then he had pressed my fingers to his full, soft lips.

"You should show him how," the king says.

I open my mouth to protest, but Henry waves his hand in a swift swirl in the air over his head. Thomas sees the motion and immediately walks to the king's side and bows; he does not look in my direction at all.

"How may I assist, Your Grace?"

"You may dance with my dear queen."

Thomas blinks at him for a moment, then recovers his smooth courtier's smile.

"A great honor, truly. But surely you can find another dancer who may better match the queen's heightened skill. I'm afraid I am not a worthy partner."

"I know." Henry laughs, clapping Thomas on the back. Everyone around us joins in the laughter, though I doubt they all heard the joke. "I think she could teach you a thing or two. You'll not charm any ladies standing around sipping ale, Culpeper."

There is nothing else to do. I stand and smile graciously at Thomas, and offer him my hand. As we take our places, I look past Thomas and smile at the king. The song begins—

a strong volta—and Thomas and I execute the flirtatious kicks and turns across from each other.

Thomas isn't a natural dancer, but I can see that he's trying very hard. His courtier's smile is gone, and his face is a picture of resolve. But I try not to look at his face, I try not to feel aware of his eyes upon me. Then the moment comes when he must lift me—I feel his large warm hands enveloping my tiny waist, lifting me off the ground, twirling. The drums beat; I suck a gasp of air through my teeth. He places me on the ground and I can feel that my cheeks are pink. I struggle to put on the courtier's mask again, the measured facial expression, hoping that my flush will subside.

When the dance is done, I offer Thomas my hand, and he dips into a deep bow.

"Thank you, Your Grace, for the honor of this dance."

"You may thank my lord for the honor, for he bestowed it on you," I tell him, smiling at the king all the while. My smile makes my cheeks hurt; my eyes are stinging, starting to water.

"He's a tall one, that Culpeper." The king laughs as I return to my chair. "He lifted you a clear three feet from the floor. You looked as if you were flying, my sweet bird."

"It rather felt as if I was," I admit. "Rather dizzying."

I pick up my goblet of wine and drink.

"WILL THE KING be joining us today, my queen?" Lady Ashley inquires, walking beside me to the archery lists.

"The king is detained with matters of state," I inform her, just as the king informed me. "The life of a king is not simply an excuse for revelry."

Beneath my cool demeanor, I am stung: the round of banquets and masques celebrating our marriage has ended, and we've had to return to life as usual at court. I strive to please my husband, but it proves difficult when his mood is so profoundly affected by things beyond my control. Matters of state aside, the king's swollen legs plague him; even during a private supper in his chambers, his manner is strained, and he hasn't the stamina to lavish attention upon me as he once did. Henry is a powerful man, but not the god many think him to be.

"Then we must enjoy revelry with our queen, in the king's absence." A young lord bows gallantly, proffering to me an elegant bow and arrow carved of nut-brown wood and gleaming in the sunlight.

"I'm afraid it's been a while since I've tried for a target," I demur.

"Ah, you've certainly hit your target—for you have pierced my very heart."

The ladies giggle at his dramatics; just as he had hoped, no doubt. They are all my pretend suitors, these handsome young courtiers, bestowing pretty words of devotion to their beloved queen. I enjoy spending time with the younger, less dour members of court.

"I will help you, my queen." Thomas steps forward, smiling slightly. His eyes crinkle at the corners when he smiles.

"Thank you, Thomas." I offer him my hand, just as I would any other flattering young lord. "What skill I have on the dance floor I lack with bow and arrow."

"I seem to recall you're a fair shot."

He walks me to a spot across from a clean target and instructs me how to hold the bow properly, the slim arrow resting lightly upon my fist.

"That is right—perfect, my queen, perfect." He holds his hands out toward me in support, but he is clearly hesitant to touch me. I am no longer a lady-in-waiting, after all.

"Pull the arrow back a bit more, my queen," he says. His fingertips barely brush the underside of my arm; the ghost of a touch. I pull back, feeling the muscles in my arm and shoulder pulled as taut as the strained bow.

"Now—release."

The bow springs, the arrow glides forward in a graceful arc; but it bounces off the target instead of finding its home.

"You are a fine tutor, Thomas." I smile. "Pray, show me how it should be done."

I hand him the polished bow, my fingertips dangerously close to his. He pulls an arrow from the quiver at his belt and steps forward. I stand near him as he eyes the target and lifts the bow, his shoulder rolling beneath his fitted velvet doublet. Pulled taut, the bow strains against his chest. Then the release: a strong shot, and when I hear the arrowhead puncture the canvas target, I laugh aloud, leading the applause.

"Well done, Thomas! Well done."

"Thank you, my queen." His voice is quiet, intimate. He catches my eyes with his. I blink toward the sun, washing my face clean of any expression, before anyone sees the look in his eyes mirrored in my own.

XIII

My ladies and I are veritably surrounded by lords in the gardens, in the hall: reading me poetry, lauding my beauty, professing their undying love. Of all of them, Thomas is the most quiet, the least boastful, offering self-deprecating asides instead of lofty poetry.

"I cannot compete with the poets here at court, I'm afraid." This he tells me in the garden, beneath a pear tree, the branches drooping heavily with fruit.

"And why would you need to compete with them?"

"To impress Your Majesty, of course," he says. "What else would convince you of my complete devotion than a verse, in rhyming couplets?"

"Ah, yes. It was a delightful poem." I wave flirtatiously at another lord, the author of said poem. "I must agree. I do not know how you will convince me of your loyalty if you can not write in rhyme."

"Indeed, there is only one path left for me." He sighs, resolute.

"What is that?"

"I will play the jester." His face is serious, brows knitted. "Bright red hose and tinkling bells on my hat. Would that please you?"

I laugh aloud at this notion; the ladies echo with a chorus of giggles.

"Ah, my very own fool," I cry. "My little sweet fool."

I avert my eyes, suddenly, from his face.

"No, that is not necessary, Master Culpeper," I say, gliding past him. "I am afraid you would make a very dreary court jester." The ladies laugh at this, for a long time.

Tonight I will send a gift of a ruby ring to Thomas, in secret. Monarchs often reward subjects for their loyalty; it is all a bit of courtly romance, nothing out of the ordinary. But I have made sure to instruct him not to wear it in public. Better to be discreet.

In private, I press my lips to the ruby before dropping it into its velvet pouch.

"YOU HAD BEST BEWARE, Catherine," Jane whispers as she readies me for bed. "Must I remind you that you are no longer a lady-in-waiting in the queen's chambers, carrying on a flirtation with your chosen suitor?"

It was more than a mere flirtation, I want to tell her, but I don't dare it.

"I treat him as I do all the others, Jane, you know how it is. Would it not be conspicuous if I treated him differently?"

"You do treat him differently, though you don't know that you do. I see the way you look at him, and likewise how he looks at you."

Then perhaps mine is not the only heart to suffer? Perhaps Thomas also hides the truth behind his practiced smile?

"The king laughs when I flirt with his grooms," I say, feigning sudden interest in polishing my sapphire ring. "He thinks it all a lark."

"But he is not the only one watching you, Catherine. Everyone is watching you. Everyone sees what they want to see."

"What does that matter, now that Henry has married me?"

"It always matters!" She grasps me by the arms and shakes me vigorously. "There are those who oppose you, Catherine. They oppose the Howards and are eager to see something amiss in your behavior. You must be certain not to show them anything they could use against you."

"Who? Will you at least tell me that?"

"The Seymours, for one. They've long been Howard rivals. And anyone who supported the king's match with that Lutheran from Cleves will likely not want a Catholic queen on the throne. The duchess, and Norfolk, will be wary of your enemies. We are here to help you, but you must do your part."

"I don't see that I particularly need your help." I'm tired of being constantly told what to do. Now that we are married, the demands of my family have only increased.

"Is that what you think?" She arranges my jewels upon the velvet cushion of my jewelry box, carefully swirling my necklace into a coiled nest.

"Are you saying that you could have done it, that you could have charmed him?" I challenge her. "And if you think you could have, then you are a fool not to have tried."

"You are the fool if you think you got here on your own. The Howards dressed you, created you, prepared you for your role, and then put you in the king's way at every opportunity. The last thing we want is to see you squander your position now. No, you did not get here on your own, and you will not stay here on your own terms."

"But I am the one to have to give things up, aren't I? All the rest of you reap the benefits of my position, but I am the one who has to swallow my heart?"

"Don't even dare talk about it, Catherine." Her whisper is harsh, biting. "Look at you—you have everything. Everything! How could you possibly want for more?"

"All I ever wanted was taken from me," I say bitterly. "You don't understand."

"I understand that you are a *child*," she snaps. She looks at me with narrowed eyes. I feel tears burning in mine, and I bite my lip to stop it from trembling. She sighs, and settles upon my bed. She rests her hand on mine.

"You are young," she says, gentler this time, "and having everything makes the one thing you can't have seem more important and desirable than all the rest. I do understand. More than you know."

Jane's eyes shift away from mine; she blinks. I wonder if she's thinking of her husband, George Boleyn, whom she helped to condemn with her own words. Perhaps there was more that she wanted from him, but did not receive. Perhaps he was too enamored with his sister to pay his wife any mind. And now he never will.

"But now you must understand, Catherine. You are queen, and you must behave as a queen, for all our sakes."

"I should behave myself for you," I say tartly, "in thanks for putting me where I am today? I did not choose this."

"I did it, the Duke of Norfolk, the duchess. Even Thomas helped put you in the way of the king. We all did this—we all made you queen."

I blink at her, my vision blurred.

"Thomas helped?"

"Yes, he did." Jane's gaze is level with mine, unfaltering. "Thomas was eager to do whatever he could to help you win the king's affection. He is your cousin, after all. As you rise, we all rise with you."

"Thomas wanted the king to marry me?" But of course he did. That is how it is in this family; power and ambition trumps all—even love. I am not as blind to this fact as Jane may think. I close my eyes but there I see the letters—Thomas's letters, the pages curling red and black in the flames. It still pains me that I had to be rid of them, and now I feel like a fool. Perhaps those words I so cherished meant little to him. Perhaps I meant little to him. But no—no—I saw that look in his eyes. I saw . . . but what does it matter, how can it matter, now?

"I will beware." I sigh, feeling defeated. Innocent flirtation was the only way I could live my old dreams, but I suppose that makes it less than innocent. I gaze at the jewels spread out upon the dressing table before me and rest my fingertips against a ruby necklace, too small for me to wear.

"What brought Anne down?" I ask, barely audible. I want to hear about the witch from Jane. She was there, she saw it all.

"Oh, Anne." Jane sighs, as if just remembering her. She smiles at me wryly in the mirror. "Anne was her own worst enemy."

As I walk the halls of Hampton Court without the king at my side, Henry's past blooms derisively in my view. A glimpse of a carved pomegranate, a wrought-iron *H&J* abandoned in a pane of glass—more artifacts of my husband's previous wives. Ghosts watch me as I lie in bed beside the king at night, whispering words of love into his ear. I worry I may say the wrong words and unwittingly remind him of another lover.

I must find comfort in the king's love and protection. I am his queen; all of England prays for me in every church in the kingdom. *God protect our dear Queen Catherine.* I repeat this prayer, silently, when the eyes of the ghosts burn their brightest.

But I fear that some spirits will not heed any blessings from God. Of all the ghosts who crowd upon me in the queen's apartments at Hampton, I fear the ghost of my own cousin the most.

"I heard stories of the king's passion for Queen Anne."

"The first Queen Anne."

"Yes, of course the first Anne! The second he could not bear to share a bed with!"

My ears perk up at this giggled conversation. The ladies are seated on cushions before the vacant fireplace, facing away from where Jane and I sit at a carved oak table. I lower my eyes to the cards in my hand and listen.

"He could not get enough of Anne Boleyn."

"The witch? Perhaps that was part of the enchantment."

"Enchantment or no, the king visited her bedchamber every night, without fail. Sometimes he visited during the day, and led her to his own chamber. Even when they fought—and she fought him quite cruelly—still his desire was not abated."

"Not even on a day such as this?" One girl sighs languidly. I feel perspiration collecting on my upper lip.

"Definitely not on a day such as this."

I drop a card on the table, my eyes still lowered.

"Is that true?"

Jane shuffles her cards before answering. "Yes. Yes, it is true."

I drop my hand and walk quietly to the privy chamber,

the inner sanctum in the royal apartments, to which only Jane and a few senior ladies are allowed entry.

I'm ashamed at myself for not reprimanding those girls for speaking the name of the witch in my presence. She must have been a witch, to have charmed the king the way that she did. He risked everything to be with Anne. He separated from the pope to be with her, and was excommunicated from the church. He banished his wife and shunned his own daughter in order to make her his, and planned a glittering coronation before the former queen was even dead. He made all of England swear to honor her as queen, and their issue the rightful heir to the throne.

Now I am his wife, but no coronation date has been set. He has not visited my bed in a fortnight. We have been married only a few months, and already I feel my power slipping away from me, sapped from me in the stifling summer heat.

I hear the door open and I look up to see Jane enter the room.

"What did she do, to bewitch him so?" I blurt out. "How did she do it? I need to know."

"Don't say such things, Catherine."

"But he risked all to be with her. She had power over him."

"No, she didn't, not really, as evidenced by her sad end."

"But before then, she did have power over him. All of court could see it."

"What about your power, Catherine? Are you saying King Henry is slipping away from you already?" she inquires sharply. I turn away, not wanting her to see my anger. "It is not in your best interest to keep secrets, Catherine. I must know everything. That way we can plan our strategy."

The thought of strategy makes me want to laugh—a dark laugh, void of joy. They've married me off to an old, ailing monarch who barely has the stamina to indulge his own passions—what strategy could help me now?

"It is the fault of the weather—the heat," I inform her. "That is all. It has nothing to do with me."

"True enough," Jane says, sitting beside me on the bed. "Anne Boleyn matters no more. She hasn't mattered for a long time. Only you matter now. You are the Howard upon the throne."

"I am the Howard upon the throne," I murmur, listless. The heat in this chamber is stunning; I feel it pressing upon me from all sides.

"You have to get pregnant, Catherine. That is all there is for it."

I drop onto the bed, weary, powerless. How can I have any hope of getting pregnant if the king is too ill to visit my bedchamber? How charming, how lovely, how enticing do I have to be to pull him out of the mire of illness and age?

"I don't know if I can do it," I tell her.

"You haven't any choice."

XIV   The heat has driven the court on progress; a change of scenery often serves to rejuvenate Henry and eases the swelling of his legs. We've just arrived at Grafton in Northamptonshire, and shall remain here through early September. The roads were dusty, and we've now seen weeks without rain. But there is good hunting here, which has already done wonders for Henry's disposition. He was more energetic today than I've seen him in a while, and it gives me hope that his health will improve. I pray for this, both for his sake and for mine.

"The rain will come soon, to relieve us," Jane assures me, sensing my nerves. The air in my bedchamber is heavy, still. Only candles are lit around the bed, and I'm wearing the lightest silk nightdress, the outline of my naked form easily visible as the moonlight slants in the window.

"The linens are fresh and cool," she tells me, smoothing her palm over the coverlet. I'm relieved to have left Hampton for another miniature court, though the court on progress is considerably larger than the small party we had at Oatlands Palace. Still, I'm hoping that this handsome, intimate country manor will inspire the king to visit me.

The door opens, and Henry enters. Jane bows and hastily takes her leave. I'm standing by the window, letting the pale light filter through my thin gown.

"Catherine," he breathes; I can see that his steps are labored. "Are you tired?"

"It was a wearying day," I say cautiously, "but I'm glad that you're here."

"I am as well." He moves forward and embraces me, but only briefly. "But I think I must bid you good night. You look lovely, as always, but tired. You need your rest."

The king's eyes are red, the lids drooping.

"Of course, my lord. I will be better rested tomorrow."

And with that, he takes his leave. In spite of the heavy air, a chill runs up my spine. There will be no hope of another heir for England if the king is not well enough to visit my bed. I look out the window over the garden, where the roses droop upon their vines in the heat. I close my eyes and pray for rain.

I blow out the candles, then take to my high bed and slip between the cool sheets, in search of a dream that may distract me from my concerns. I find here, in the dim shadows of blue and gray, an old dream about Thomas.

We are in the garden together, and the sky is pitch-black and splattered with stars. I rush into his arms and we share our first kiss. I dwell on this one moment again and again, adding in further kisses besides. In my dream, Thomas is bold and I respond to his touch with reckless eagerness; we have nothing to lose, or to fear. In my dream, I am simply Catherine, without any further claims upon my heart aside from the one that dwells there, swells there now: *Thomas, I love you, I want to be with you, I want to be yours forever . . .*

Jane will scold me for this, somehow. She knows everything about me. The courses of my monthly blood and the nature of my nightly excretions into the chamber pot are common topics for chatter among the maids in my household, there is no doubt. There is much speculation about my acts with the king when we are alone together in the royal bed, and what those acts may come to, and when we may see those results. My dreams are perhaps the only private thing I have left to myself—for there is no way the ladies can pull them from me, though I'm sure they would try if they could. I've always had a penchant for dreaming. I can't completely change everything about myself simply because I am queen.

"DRINK THIS."

I open my eyes to find the duchess standing over my bed.
I am not particularly surprised; what details of my life she
is not privy to I'm sure Jane supplies. I've spent the last few
nights with the king, now that the progress has begun to re-
vive him. Quickly on the heels of either success or disaster,
there is the duchess, eager to appraise the situation with her
critical eye and tell me what next to do.

She holds out a goblet and pushes it into my hand. The
liquid within is cloudy, with a strange, musty odor of dirt
and dried herbs.

"What is it?"

"Drink it. It will help you."

"Help me what?"

"Help you become pregnant, that's what." She turns to
Lady Rochford, already pulling out my gown for today's
wear. "No, Jane, the ice-blue one. It's very hot today. We
must keep Catherine looking cool, serene."

"We were only married this summer," I remind the duchess, alarmed by her impatience. "I haven't had much time."

"You will never have enough time, Catherine, remember
that. Immediacy is vital. You were in his bedchamber last
night. Yes? And then you came here to sleep?"

"Yes. The king told me he would be waking early in the
morning for the hunt."

These days and nights at Grafton have made all the difference in the king's health and disposition. We've adopted
a more relaxed existence on this progress, adjourning to the
king's parlor in the evenings for a recital—I on the lute and

Henry on the virginals—and we dine in private before adjourning to bed. Still, the heat is detrimental; the king is not restored to the robust energy he displayed on our honeymoon in Surrey. When he looks at me, he sees his reclaimed youth. When I look at the king, I see his mortality. We are like two sides of a strange, distorted mirror.

"Indeed," the duchess murmurs thoughtfully. "And your monthly blood, has it arrived yet? How do you feel?"

A familiar ache twinges in my belly at these words, but I haven't the heart to tell the duchess about it.

"I'm not sure, yet. I can't be certain."

"Drink up," she says succinctly, pushing the glass toward me.

I struggle to sip the grayish drink. Back at Lambeth I used to fear pregnancy. Though I followed the advice the ladies gave me to protect myself, there were nights when Francis was too persistent to dissuade. Anxious days were spent pondering what would become of me if I were with child; Francis's promises of marriage did nothing to quell my fears. Now my entire existence is hinged upon becoming pregnant, and the habitual lateness of my monthly blood continues to fool me, cheat me into thinking that I have achieved my singular objective.

I am sure that Henry thinks of it even more than I do. I sense in him a great desire for affection, as if he has long been starved for this type of intimacy. And underlying all of his pleasure is that hope, that prayer. When he rests his hand tentatively upon my belly, I feel fully aware of all that is expected of me, though I know not what else to do to make it come about.

"There is more we must discuss," the duchess continues,

adjusting the collar of my linen shift with brisk efficacy. "You must ask him about your coronation."

Though I wish to dismiss the subject, it does worry me. I am royal consort and have assumed the title of queen upon marriage, but have yet to be officially anointed as such. This will be imperative in order to secure my place upon the throne, and to secure my progeny within the line of succession. With deep resentment I recall the soaring triumph (brief though it was) of Queen Anne seated upon her royal barge, the gentle swell of her belly visible beneath her glistening gown.

"It is more difficult than that."

"What is difficult about it?"

"I cannot ask him until I know that I am pregnant."

"I think you had better ask him about it sooner than that. There is no use wasting time, Catherine. He was well prepared to hold a coronation for that German lass just a month after their wedding, if only she had lived up to his expectations."

"The king has very high expectations."

"As well he should, Catherine. He is the king. My question is this: if last winter he was so eager to have a queen that he planned to crown a German, why is it that he is taking his time in crowning you?"

"I do not know," I tell her. "Perhaps it is the heat. Perhaps he will change his mind in the colder weather."

The duchess sighs briskly, her nostrils flared.

"Think, Catherine: if you were to be crowned and bear a son, your triumph would be greater even than that of Queen Jane, who was never officially crowned. Your triumph would be the greatest of all the queens." Her eyes turn glassy for a moment, as if gazing at the brilliant tableau she has just conjured in her mind.

"You must broach the subject with him. You know what I mean—cajole him a bit. Be flirtatious. Surely you've learned those tricks by now."

"Yes, Duchess."

"Use your feminine wiles, Catherine. They are very powerful if used deftly, very powerful, indeed. And besides, they are all that you have."

"Yes, Duchess."

"And remember: *every night*. He must visit you every night. Do whatever you need to do to make that happen."

I am only a young girl, I think to tell her. *I am not a magician. I am not a witch.* I can make the king feel young again, but I cannot actually make him young.

XV Today we ride south to Bedfordshire, and plan to stay at Ampthill for a fortnight. It seems a large task to move so many people. A significant portion of my household and the king's accompanies us on our summer progress, as well as an assortment of advisers, cooks, and additional servants. Still, I need do startlingly little. My role in this performance is all show, while my clothes, my jewels, my belongings are prepared behind the scenes.

A line of carts is drawn up before the manor, and the grooms of the stables walk among them and pass their hands over them to make sure our belongings are properly secured before we depart. The young men tug on rough ropes and tighten fat knots; their hands are dark brown with dirt and thick with calluses. I look down at my own hands—small, soft, and pale against my blue riding habit. The horses are tacked and ready, my silver mare bridling at the front of the group beside the king's enormous hunter. The mare is a beauty; a groom brushes her flanks and her pale gray coat glistens in the early morning sunshine. The king chose her for me—a good, reliable horse for a long ride.

"You miss her, don't you," a low voice says, so close to me that I start at the sound of it. Thomas sidles up beside me, admiring the mare. I feel embarrassed, suddenly, awkward in his presence.

"Who?"

"Your little Molly, that brown horse you rode when you first came to court."

"My pretty, perky Molly." I sigh. "She's asleep in her stable at Westminster. Not a proper horse for a ride such as this."

"But you still miss her."

I'm hesitant to admit this in earshot of the beautiful horse the king gifted to me. And why should Thomas be the one privy to my secret thoughts?

"Yes," I tell him. He smiles and offers a low hand to cup my foot and help me onto the saddle. I pause, but only for a moment. Once mounted, I arrange my habit in a pleasing fashion for the ride.

"I understand," Thomas says, handing me the reins. "It's natural to miss something you love, no matter what it is. Even a little brown horse. Sometimes a replacement just isn't the same as the original, but you'll get used to her."

He smiles and squints up at me in the sun, patting the neck of the mare. I return his smile—placid, revealing nothing. That is all Thomas will get from me.

The king has arrived, mounting his hunter. I'm glad that

Henry is looking well, and I'm glad that he was well last night. I am tired this morning, and my ladies shared knowing looks in speculation over the cause of my weariness: Was I kept awake late into the night by the king? Or am I already with child and in need of rest? I can only hope the latter is true.

Last night I lay beside Henry wondering why I wasn't asleep, only to realize my eyes were wide open in the darkness. And I woke this morning with an odd feeling, which clung to me even as the ladies dressed me and my trunks were carried out for our journey. I feel a dim recollection of things imagined in my sleep; the residue of dreams clinging to me when I know it would be best not to dwell on them.

I am aware of the futility and the peril of dreams, but they prove difficult to restrain once given free rein in your mind.

AMPTHILL IS A LOVELY PLACE, offering Henry further opportunities for hunting expeditions. I've heard the ladies in my chamber whisper that Katherine of Aragon was sent here for part of her exile, after she was banished from court. I felt wary of what ghosts might reside in these halls, but I think the summer sunshine, the music, the mummers' dances, and the fool's tricks have swept any ghosts from their hiding places. The king sat all last night with his arm wrapped around me at dinner, and even placed kisses upon my forehead, cheeks, and lips, for all to see. Hopes for another heir for England have been renewed.

All manner of games are played in the gardens at

Ampthill—it is truly a summer haven. There is archery and tennis, as well as fishing and hunting. Today, Henry has urged me to join him on a hawking expedition. We attend Mass together and then make our way out to the mews, where the cages of hawks and falcons are kept.

"You look very pretty today, Catherine," Henry remarks, smiling.

"Thank you, my lord. I did not know what a person should wear for falconry. I am glad to hear I've chosen rightly." I *have* chosen rightly: the gold and copper highlights in my hair burn bright in the sun in contrast to the creamy lavender silk of my gown. I twirl for the king, and he applauds in appreciation. We mount our horses in the company of councillors, grooms, and the royal falconer and make our way to a hillside overlooking a glen filled with trees.

Thomas is with us, for he is an expert falconer. I find myself wishing he had not joined us, to allow my confused heart some diversion. He helps the king put on enormous leather gauntlets, and sets the hooded hawk upon his hand. The falconer removes the leather hood to reveal the hawk's round, piercing golden eyes. I wince at the sight of those long talons gripping the king's wrist.

"Do not worry, Catherine, she cannot hurt me." Henry laughs and gently strokes the bird's sleek, russet feathers. With a launch of his arm the bird takes flight, soaring and dipping and swaying over the canopy of shimmering trees. For a moment she seems to vanish entirely, blotted out by the sun's brightness.

"That's my girl," the king exclaims approvingly. The hawk is diving, beak down and wings pulled back, a dark stream against the blue sky. A moment later she has disappeared into the leafy greenness below us.

Moments pass, and the king sends out a whistle—a line of high, sharp notes—and the hawk emerges from the greenery, her great wings flapping, streaked with gold in the sunshine. There is something grasped in her enormous talons, which Thomas skillfully grabs just as she releases her hold in order to settle again upon the king's arm. Henry offers her a small piece of meat from his hand, and she works it in her curved onyx beak.

"Come now, Catherine. It is your turn. All you have to do is hold her, and I will do the rest."

I edge forward cautiously. The hawk is looking at me keenly. Her eyes are yellow fire.

"She will not ruin my dress?"

"No, no, don't worry about your dress. Here, these will look quite lovely on you." He gestures to Thomas, who holds open a large gauntlet for me to wear. The leather is thick and has an earthy smell. I look away from Thomas as I put my hand in the glove; inside it is soft and warm. I hold out my arm as the king has done, and take between the fingers of my other hand a pinch of meat. The hawk hops lightly from Henry's arm to mine, snatching the meat from my grasp. I jerk back at this, but Thomas holds out his hand to steady me.

"That's right, that's right," Henry says. "Now with one thrust upward, she will take flight."

"I—I don't know how." The bird is light, a delicate weight on my arm. But her curved beak seems dangerously close to my face, and I can feel her thick talons shifting with her movements.

"You can do it, Catherine." Thomas whispers. "Just one motion, graceful, like a dance."

Thomas moves toward me, as if to cup his hand beneath my elbow. I push upward suddenly to escape his touch, and I feel her push off from my glove, unfolding her wings like the sails of a great ship. She glides off into the sky before me, her wings spread wide as she rises and swoops low in a great circle.

"Oh, did you see that? Did you see it? Oh, how wonderful," I breathe.

As the hawk continues her circles in the air, Henry and the other grooms have turned to admire another bird perched upon the falconer's arm. I turn back to watch the hawk dive and spin over the trees.

"She is beautiful," Thomas remarks. I turn slightly, just enough to look at his face: his eyes fixed, his mouth set, resolute. *Did you put me in the king's way?* I wish I could ask him. *Is this how you wanted things to happen?* I feel his hand graze mine: his long fingers against the back of my hand, fingertips brushing my knuckles. I stand perfectly still, as if carved from stone.

"Catherine!" The king calls my name. "Come look at this beautiful creature. No doubt you'll want a dress to match her feathers, my sweet wife."

The king laughs; everyone laughs. I walk over to appreciate the chocolate-brown falcon perched upon Henry's wrist. My legs are trembling so violently I worry they will crumple beneath me.

I hear a shriek in the distance. I look up in time to see the russet hawk dive toward her prey.

———

SUNSHINE STREAMS into the bank of arched windows in this tiny chapel, illuminating dust motes floating in the air. In spite of the heat outside, today the light seems pale, chilling, penetrating my skin and bones and alighting upon the secrets of my soul. I kneel beside my husband, mirroring his pious movements with my own, but inside I feel naked before God's judgment.

I can't stop thinking about the touch. It was an accident, of course, and means nothing. Or, at least, it should mean nothing. Had Thomas meant to touch me; does he still have that longing? I imagine the moment again and again. The very hand that holds my rosary beads burns with a hidden shame.

Confession is not an option: my husband is the supreme head of the church, and could be privy to such secrets. No, there is no sanctuary reliable enough that I may unburden my soul. I can only pray that God will listen and accept my mute plea: *It was unintended. I will never do it again. I will cease thinking of it, altogether.* But I know that God has seen it all, has seen the dreams I nourish in my head and the love I harbor in my heart. My soul is translucent as glass, and perhaps as fragile.

I cross myself at this thought.

AFTER MASS, the thought of returning to my chambers repels me. The confined rooms will no doubt allow my mind to wander to places it is not allowed to go. I announce instead that I shall take my horse out for a hard ride, and walk directly to the stables.

"But it is hot out today, Your Grace."

"The roads are very dusty."

"Your pink silk will be ruined."

"Then be of some use and fetch me my riding habit," I snap, and continue on my way to the stable. By the time Jane returns with my habit, my horse has been tacked up, ready for mounting.

"You need not come with me, Jane. I'll not be long." I think she will be relieved at this, but instead her brow crinkles in concern. I swing myself easily into the saddle. I'm in no mood for a rebuke or a warning—I need to venture out, to not be watched for a while. I set off at a gallop before she can formulate a response.

The meadows around Ampthill are vast and sloping, all of them crisscrossed with narrow roads and footpaths. I urge the mare down a path toward the trees, where we feel the relief of relative coolness beneath the leafy bower, protecting us from the sun's glare. By the time we're deep in the greenest part of the trees, I realize I'm panting, my lungs constricted and my throat dusty and dry.

The mare slows to a canter over the soft grass, but I hear a pounding of hooves behind me. With a sharp tug on the reins, my horse wheels around. Thomas is before me, mounted on a dark brown hunter. I gasp—a sound of terror—at the sight of him.

"Your Majesty," he says, pulling back upon the reins. He swings one leg over and drops gracefully to the ground. "I apologize—I didn't mean to frighten you. I didn't know you were here."

"I—I was taking a ride," I tell him, looking down at the horse's silver mane fluttering in the wind. Thomas steps closer, warily.

"I pray that I have done nothing to offend you, my queen."

His eyes linger upon my face. They are so dark, those eyes, nearly black, and piercing. His face is even paler than usual. I know what he is thinking about: the touch. Perhaps it haunts him, as well.

"I would like to die if I thought I had offended my queen."

"Those are pretty words," I chide.

"They are not meant merely to be pretty." He reaches out and rests his hand upon the neck of the mare, dangerously close to my leg. "They are true."

A loud shriek pierces the air high above us: a hawk circles the trees, hunting for her prey. I look up, craning my neck to see where the hawk swoops over the trees, her wings outstretched against the blue sky. The branches tremble; the sun flickers over my face. Between the branches, the top of the hill above us is revealed. A group of courtiers stands there in the distance, accompanied by the royal falconer. Can they see us here, in the trees? My vision reels: a young lord leans over and whispers to one of the others—a lady, no less, who cranes her neck elegantly to listen. Then the branches move again, obscuring the tableau. I only hope they cannot see us. I fear what they would be able to see.

Wordless, I give the horse a sharp tug—Thomas flinches, pulling his hand from the mare's neck. She turns abruptly with a snort, and we ride away.

Now I realize what I've done. I was supposed to burn my life, all of my life before my wedding day, as if none of it had happened at all. When I put those letters on the flames I thought that I had triumphed over memory.

But burning the letters has only given them more power. They've risen from the ashes of that fire like a brilliant phoenix, a symbol of my loss and regret. Memory distorts with time, like air rippling over a fire—what is gone becomes only more precious, becomes a yearning, a perfect dream. Every word of those letters, every moment I shared with him, has been memorized in the language of a dream, continuously visited, revisited. The letters are gone but only haunt me more; I close my eyes and remember the words by heart. I have nothing of the girl I used to be, aside from those old dreams. I have become a ghost of myself.

XVI I lie upon the royal bed beside the king. Spent and exhausted from the exertions of making love to me, Henry fell immediately to sleep. I only wish that I could so easily find respite.

We will be leaving Ampthill soon, and I am glad of it. We are traveling next to the More in Hertfordshire, another manor once owned by the late Cardinal Wolsey. We will spend much of October there, and then make our journey to London for my first official entrance to the city as queen. I watch the moonlight filter through the curtains into the dim chamber. The air is heavy and warm, no fire blazes in the cold hearth.

The king's arm shudders against me, and I leap from the bed in fear. The room is dim, the floor cold beneath my bare feet.

"Edward . . . he is . . . Arthur. He is—it is Arthur," Henry mutters. It must be a nightmare, but I can hear the distress in his voice. I think to call the men of the king's privy chamber, but the words stick in my throat: Thomas would answer the call. I look down over my naked body, my hair flowing over my bare breasts. I creep closer to the bed and climb upon it, my legs folded under me.

"Edward," Henry wails. The panic in his voice frightens me.

"Henry, please wake up, my love, please." I try shaking him gently, my hands on his arms.

"Edward! Edward!"

"Henry! Please wake up! It's only a dream."

His eyes fly open suddenly. He stares at me as if he's never seen me before.

"It's only a dream," I repeat. "It's only a dream."

"Oh." His eyes roll around in the dimness, he tugs distractedly at the bedclothes. I pull back a bit, trying to seem relaxed. I don't want him to see the fear in my eyes, nor do I want to see the fear in his. He rustles for a bit and then sighs, lying quietly in the darkness.

"History repeats itself, Catherine," he says, and the bitter edge in his voice chills me. "Do you understand that?" He sighs again and rests his hand upon my knee. I press my hand on top of his.

"What history?"

"My history, England's history. I had a dream about Arthur, again." He rubs his face with his hand and yawns broadly.

"He was always so thin as a young boy, so pale and weak. Sickly."

Our eyes meet in the darkness. *Pale and weak*—the same words he has used to describe Prince Edward.

"History repeats itself," he whispers thickly, "England needs another heir."

"Do not worry about the past, my lord." I rest my hand on his shoulder. I want to soothe him, but suddenly I do not know how. I find a sexual encounter so much easier to navigate than an emotional one.

"I will do whatever I can," I tell him. "You must know that. I will do everything that I can."

I am the only one who can end this particular nightmare for our king. If my child is a boy, he will wait in the line of succession just behind Prince Edward, the son of a Seymour. If Henry's fear of repeated history comes true, then the crown will pass to the second son, just as it did to him. My son could be King of England. I could bring joy to the Howards with this. And to Henry. And to all of England.

And, perhaps, to myself: a baby of my own to sing to, to hold against my breast.

IN HONOR OF my first official entrance to London as queen, the lord mayor and all the guilds of the city row out in barges draped in banners to join us in our procession down the river. The sun is high and glittering brightly on the water, sparkling off the jewels on Henry's fingers and the rubies embedded in the bodice of my gown.

The heat has subsided over the past few weeks, but today the sun is bright and hot as we slide languidly over the Thames. I lift a spiced pomander to my nose to cover the river's stink. People crowd at the shore, throwing drooping wildflowers upon the still water as we pass. They wave at Henry, and they peer curiously at me. Cannons fire from the Tower of London, followed by the crackle of gunfire in salute as we pass by.

"We'll stop first at the Tower," Henry tells me, putting his hand upon my arm. My stomach sinks, leaden. In my mind the Tower is associated with evil things.

THE ROYAL APARTMENTS in the Tower of London are more sumptuous than any I have seen before, clearly designed for momentous occasions: weddings, coronations. The ceilings are high, the rooms cavernous. In the center of the bedchamber stands an intricately carved bed, draped in lush red velvet and piled with plump cushions. Queen Anne no doubt rested in this same bed, her dark head propped upon a velvet pillow.

"My darling, are you chilled on a day such as this?" Henry laughs. "You are shivering. Don't worry, I will see fit to keep you warm." He wraps his arms around me; I become tiny in his embrace. I feel my breath constrict, my chest tighten.

"I've something to show you here." He gives me a last squeeze before taking my hand in his. "I've been longing to show you my collection."

In the Lion Tower are cells filled with monkeys, wild cats, and all manner of exotically colored birds. Two leopards peer out from the shadows beyond the wooden railings, watching us as we pass. I gasp aloud at each cell as we approach it, gripping Henry's arm in fear and excitement. My nervous giggling is echoed by the cacophony of bird voices; Henry startles the animals in their cages with his hearty laughter.

"They will not hurt you, dear. Come, I will show you my prize." He steers me toward the last cell. I jump back in fright, and Henry roars with laughter.

"No need to be frightened. He's harmless as a kitten. Besides, I'm here to protect you."

I clasp Henry's hand and step closer to the cell. Within, a great lion lounges in the shadows. His eyes glimmer in the dimness, his enormous dusty paws stretched out before him. He stretches, brandishing his claws, emitting a powerful yawn. Then he shifts closer, and I can see the face of the beast.

"He is beautiful, Henry," I whisper. The lion's fur is tawny brown, his handsome face striped in black on either side of a wide nose. But the feel of the animal's golden eyes upon my flesh makes me shrink closer to Henry's massive shoulder.

"He was not such a kitten when he first came here, I'll tell you that. Roared the moment anyone came near—he could drive a man mad with his roaring. But now I've got the best of him." He chuckles at this, satisfied. I turn away from the cage, but can feel the lion watching me.

"Let's retire to your apartments, Henry. We will return to our music, and I shall sing for you," I offer sweetly, a bit seductively. I know he can't refuse such a proposal, and I'm desperate to leave this place, full of shrieking birds and hissing creatures, and most of all to leave this lion in peace.

THIS OCTOBER has brought with it a great deal of rain, pouring down upon us between spurts of bright sunshine. The wall of heat that presided over the summer has finally broken, and we all feel the relief of temperate days and cool nights. Fires are lit in the fireplaces, mulled wine is poured, and the cracked earth beneath the withered garden is finally quenched.

We've moved on to Westminster, knowing that a further

change of scenery will continue to invigorate Henry after the drowsy summer. My new apartments have served to inspire afresh my dreams of velvet cushions and silk drapes and jewel-encrusted clocks that tick aloud the time. These are to be my chambers, and I care not to be crowded by evidence of previous inhabitants. I am grateful for the distraction of selecting my new décor.

As the rain pours down outside, the halls are clogged with a variety of courtiers, merchants, villagers, and advisers, all of them with petitions for the king. I've met the Privy Council for the first time, a formal meeting with an intimidating group of stiff old men who offered me pretty words and pandering smiles. But those smiles did not always reach their eyes: they were all inspecting me, analyzing me, as if trying to discern from the color of my hair or the sparkle of my eyes what my effect will be on the king, and how long it may last. I feel that I should know the answer to this myself, but I do not.

In some cases, loyalties are plain enough: Archbishop Cranmer once worked closely with Cromwell, as did Thomas Wriothesley, easily marking both of them as enemies. But the king's council is led by our ally, Bishop Gardiner, and my uncle Norfolk is lord treasurer. There are others, but I can't keep straight the names and titles of all of these men, and have little understanding of what they do in service to the king—or, more likely, in service to themselves. There is always a hidden motive; being a Howard has taught me this well. In spite of Henry's obvious adoration of me, I sensed their desire for me to leave, thinly veiled beneath dutiful bowing and gracious words.

I departed with a smile, knowing that my petitions to the

king—the Howard petitions, brought to him through me—
have already been granted, as all of these men clamor for
the king's attention. This month has brought still greater
wealth to the Howards, as I've been granted an array of
land and manors once belonging to the late Thomas Cromwell, as well as all of the property once granted to Queen
Jane.

TODAY, IN THE MIDST of choosing new colors and fabrics with which to decorate my chamber, I receive a visit
from my family.

The duchess had informed me of their visit, but I still
feign a certain amount of surprise. I bid them to enter the
main chamber of my apartments, where they may see me
surrounded by bolts and swatches of fine fabrics. I'm glad
of the cool weather, for it permits me to wear my new gown
of royal purple satin, trimmed with silver embroidery. The
duchess accompanies them, and they all bow before me: my
brothers Charles, Henry, George, and my half sister Isabel.
Even jealous Isabel bows dutifully before me; a practiced,
gracious bow. I must admit that I rather enjoy it.

"Oh, come now, stand. I am your sister, after all." I move
forward to Isabel and take her hands in mine.

"I hear that father arranged a profitable marriage for you,
before his death." *But not so profitable as the marriage I arranged
for myself, is it now?*

"Yes, indeed, Your Grace, but I come to request a place in
your household so that I may serve my queen."

I can see her usual dour expression hiding behind her attempt at a courtier's smooth smile. I wonder if she still has
Papa's lute—she took it from me when we were children,

more out of spite than genuine interest. If I ask for it now, she will have to give it to me, in order to remain in good favor.

The boys are much more attentive and flattering to me than ever they were when we were young. As the youngest of ten children, I was afforded little attention at home. I always sensed that Isabel and the other girls were envious of my placement at court. I can only imagine how they feel about me now.

"I should like to see you in crimson velvet, Isabel, perfect for the days of Advent." I flash my eyes at the duchess and smile. "No need to worry, sister. I'll have Mistress Elle cut the dress for you, and I'll pay for it from my own coffers."

"Your Majesty is most generous," Isabel says, sweeping again into a deep bow.

"I enjoy being generous," I tell her, "even to the most humble of my servants."

When she stands, the smile is frozen onto her face.

XVII

Isabel has been stationed in my household, and I've managed to place George in the king's privy chamber. I can't help but think of my father in the blush of my success; my father who had always hated court and never won the king's favor. Wouldn't he be proud of his little Catherine now? Father had always imagined that my pretty face might be used for the benefit of the family—a fact that won me Isabel's immediate disdain. But now she treats me with the same effusive kindness and flattery as the other maids in my chamber, though with her the act is far less convincing.

"The king has turned his sights away from the dissolution

of abbeys and monasteries," I tell the duchess over our evening game of cards. We sit in my luxurious royal apartments at a highly polished card table near a roaring fire.

"There is little left to dissolve," the duchess remarks, "but it is good he has set his sights elsewhere. The church requires protection from many threats. Many of those religious houses do much good."

"And many were corrupt, and deserved to be dismantled." That is what Henry says; to think otherwise is heresy. "The king told me about holy relics that turned out to be chicken bones, fake tears on a statue of the Virgin Mary. It was sacrilege."

I like talking this way with the duchess. It makes me feel very womanly, very worldly. And I hope to dissuade her from our usual topics, for once.

"And now England has a Catholic queen," I remark, setting a card upon the pile between us. "Surely that will aid in healing the church's wounds." I wonder if the duchess loves me better than she did Anne, if only for this reason. Many accused Anne of sympathizing with Lutherans and supporting the heretical "new way" of thinking. It was during her queenship that the dissolution began.

"It will do England little good until you are crowned queen, for all to see."

I say nothing, but turn back to my cards. Why is it that she can't be happy with what I've done thus far? Why must she always demand more?

"I am doing all I can," I assure her, as I always do. "You know that I am."

"Yes, I know." She presses her lips together primly and

shifts in her chair. "But is he?" she whispers, not lifting her eyes from the cards in her hand. My eyes dart around the room, but the other ladies are chattering loudly in the adjacent chamber.

"Do not say such things," I breathe. Doesn't she remember how such words condemned Anne? "Do not even think them." But I fear my urgency reveals more than I had intended; all that I know about the king that must be hidden, protected.

"I see," the duchess says quietly. I don't want to know what she's thinking. She sets her cards down on the table with a decisive snap.

"You've won again," I say brightly, eager to change the subject. "You always win."

"That's because I anticipate your move, Catherine." Her steel-gray eyes are leveled at mine as I scoop up the cards. "I know your move before you know it yourself."

AFTER THREE SOGGY WEEKS, the rain has finally ceased. Since then, this golden autumn has inspired Henry to begin a newly active routine, the likes of which he hasn't attempted since his jousting days. He rises each morning between five and six and attends Mass at seven, then mounts his black hunter for hours of hard riding, his horse often tiring before he does. The change in Henry is obvious to all. Nothing like the tepid hunting he periodically had the energy to indulge in over the summer, his expeditions are now elaborate, and he drags home more game than the court dared imagine. The activity is clearly beneficial, for he's already begun to shed some of his excess weight.

I, too, am relieved by the advent of the cool weather. In

spite of my royal jewels, I fear I am much like everyone else at court, praying that the king is in good health and fine spirits. Tonight, he smiles at me, resting his hand upon mine. The king's loving gaze is all that matters—his and no one else's.

After supper, we retire to the royal bedchamber. As he slowly removes my bronze dress, the fabric crinkling in the dimness, I realize that I have grown used to this. The fire is still high, and Henry admires my naked form in its golden light. When his eyes are shining upon me like this, I feel an undeniable surge of power.

"I think I should like to plan an entertainment for my husband," I tell him, stretching my arms and legs. He will certainly not refuse me, now.

"Why does your husband deserve such an entertainment?"

"Because he is my husband, and I like nothing more than to see him happy." *And I am tired of sitting around a bunch of whispering ladies, bent over their embroidery all day. An entertainment would give me something to do, to plan.*

"You can see me happy right now." He smiles as he bends forward to kiss me. But I *will* plan an entertainment. I think of it as he makes love to me. It will be good for us to enjoy fine music, perhaps to dance and let everyone admire us. Let them all see how well and how happy the king looks, married to me.

"I sleep late in order to rest from our nights together," I tell him moments later, my head resting against his heaving chest. "I'm quite certain the ladies whisper about my laziness."

"Let them whisper." His low laughter rumbles. "They do

not understand how I crave you—the way I once craved fruit tarts or dumplings."

"Then I am your fruit tart, now?" I ask, sitting up on the bed so that he can see the way my long hair falls loosely over my bare breasts. I must use my power now, while I have him here, watching me.

"You are my favorite indulgence."

I appraise his form with my eyes, allowing him to see me looking at him, appreciating his improved physique. The king is still an old man, but he is trying. At least I will be responsible for inspiring him to look and feel younger; he was married to Anne Boleyn when he began to grow fat.

"And you are my Golden Prince," I tell him.

"And you are my rose without a thorn."

I find it both enchanting and daunting to be considered perfect by another person. It makes my secret faults all the more visible when I look inward upon myself. But in Henry's eyes I am perfect, and that is what is most important. I nestle beside him, curling my body to his. I will wait for him to fall asleep before departing for my own bed. But he nudges me slightly on the arm, a gentle prodding.

"Sing me a song, sweet bird." His voice is surprisingly mild, almost childlike.

"You have many more talented singers at court than your silly bride." I laugh.

"Silly nothing!" he says gruffly, and rolls over to face me. "You have the sweetest voice I've ever heard." He is quiet for a moment; I listen to the pace of his breath to anticipate if he's falling asleep.

"I overheard you in the garden one day, before we were

married. You were singing a song—something about a white kitten, and a moss patch." He nudges my arm, impatient. "Sing that for me."

"That foolishness? You want me to sing *that* for you?" It was a tune I wrote as a child, sitting in my tattered gown on a patch of moss behind my father's house. The thought of it embarrasses me in ways that even lying naked in the king's bed cannot manage.

"Yes, I do. Please, I do."

There is no denying a king his wish. I sing gently and quietly, as sweetly as I can, my voice tremulous and thick. I notice a tear forming in the corner of Henry's eye—I find it frightening to be so close to the raw emotions he keeps concealed from all others.

After a moment of quiet, I pinch his arm playfully.

"That is the song of your silly wife." I sigh. "You'd best not tell anyone, or they will think me a fool."

"No, no," he says, placing his enormous hand over my small one. "No. It is sweet, and clever. You are sweet and clever. I hope you will sing it for me again, soon."

Sweet and clever—clever! I feel a strange rush of affection for Henry. It makes me somehow happy and sad all at once: it's not love, but it's something. A pleasant warmth. No one has ever called me clever before.

WITH HENRY DEEP in slumber, I make my way back to my bedchamber. It's late, and upon entering my apartments, I'm surprised to see a fire still lit in the main chamber, a group of girls chattering excitedly around the cheerful blaze.

"Queen Catherine! Queen Catherine!" they cry jubilantly as I enter, falling neatly into their reverence. "Please sit with us, before the fire."

"What is going on here, a late-night revelry?" I settle upon a lounge beside Jane, all eyes turned toward me.

"Mistress Alice was telling us about her paramour," Lady Christina remarks. "A mysterious young man who has a way with letters."

"Letters?" I inquire.

Mistress Alice—a pretty girl with golden-brown hair and a blue silk gown—stands before the small assembly. She acts out a scene, her animated movements silhouetted in the light of the fire: she holds out her hand for a young man to kiss, as if he were standing before her, right now. After a graceful bow, she lifts her hand for all to see: there is a letter nestled neatly in her palm. I would know it for a letter even had they not told me—it is folded into a small, perfect square. The ladies squeal with delight at her performance. Alice sits heavily upon her chair, her head falling back as if she might faint.

"But she will not tell us who it is." Another lady sighs. "If you ask her, Your Majesty, then she will be duty bound to tell you."

I smile at this though my head aches, my mouth suddenly dry.

"I will allow Mistress Alice to keep her secret," I say, most graciously. I lift myself from the couch and bid them all a good night. Jane follows me.

"She seems much in love," I murmur to Jane as we move away from the brightness of the fire.

"She does, indeed. We may have a betrothed maid in our

household, any day now. I can only imagine what effect that will have on her embroidery."

I cannot speculate on her embroidery. I turn and watch in silence: Mistress Alice's hair tumbles loosely from its pins; her eyes glisten in the firelight. She seems full of love, of life, of everything.

I sit in my royal chamber in a silk gown and fur-lined robe, feeling empty.

XVIII

For over a week I've filled my days with every detail of tonight's entertainment: choosing musicians, planning a musical program, selecting the menu, and instructing the servants as to which gold platters and goblets will be used to adorn our tables. I plan to wear my dark purple satin gown, which is being further embellished with jewels along the neckline.

I've needed this, desperately. While Mistress Alice sits upon a satin cushion, gazing dreamily into the fire, I've needed to be busy, to be elsewhere, and not be witness to her joy. Suddenly this mere maid I took little notice of has a strange power over me: the sight of her causes in me an actual, physical pain. Whenever I see her hands, I imagine a note nestled there: *I regret I cannot spend more time with you, my lady, but I hope soon to walk in the garden with you by my side . . .*

In spite of my delight in ordering precisely the banquet I crave—the dried fruits to be served, the elaborate cakes to be constructed—I am constantly aware of a clinging fog dimming my satisfaction. Thomas will marry someone else. Why had it not occurred to me fully before now? After all, I married—but what choice did I have? While I was doing my duty, he seems to have fallen in love. This thought leaves a deeper wound, a scar that I conceal behind a jolly laugh and a new stomacher embroidered with silver thread. Perhaps this, and a gem on every finger, will be enough to distract me from myself.

"Oh, it's so beautiful, Your Majesty." Mistress Alice sighs as the ladies help ready me for the entertainment. Her covetous fingertips touch the diamond-and-amethyst necklace, dark and glittering against my pale skin. I generally revel in the envy of my ladies-in-waiting, but this time it feels empty. I would give her these jewels right now if it meant that I could be free, that I could have Thomas. This is the price I pay for the ambition of my family, and for the love of the king.

The great hall is lit with candles and torches, and the scent of cinnamon and cloves pervades the warm air. Spiced wine is sipped from golden goblets, and when the musicians begin their lively melodies, everyone joins the dance. I feel better when I'm dancing, lighter. After hours of twirling in the midst of the throng, I need to lean against the wall for a while to catch my breath.

Beyond a silk curtain, two ladies whisper to each other behind fluttering fans.

"Bewitched, again," one says. I stand back, shielded by the red curtain.

"He is just as he was with the Great Whore."

"Shh, mind what you say!"

"But if everyone says it, it's hardly a scandal."

"Yes, it's true," the other lady demurs, fluttering her fan before her. Their faces are hidden in shadow, but it is clear they are facing the head table, gazing at Henry.

"And this one her cousin! Do you think she is cut from the same cloth?"

"Spoiled and greedy at the least . . . I pray the king will not be made a fool, again."

"Always with these wives he chooses. These obsessions, I should say. A proper wife cannot be found in such madness."

"She is only a girl, a silly girl. Certainly not fit for the throne."

"I doubt she will ever find herself upon it," the lady observes archly. "I see no rush to plan her coronation."

Bewitched, again. But I am not like Anne. I make him happy, without the use of Anne's witchcraft. I will not end up like Anne. I look up to see Henry seated at the head table, leaning back lethargically upon his throne. I wish there was a way I could tell Henry about the whispering of these women, a way that I could phrase it so that he would merely laugh at the notion that I may be like Anne . . . but I know it is not possible. I dare not say her name, and neither does he.

The entertainment draws to a close. I rush along the edge of the crowd in order to sit beside Henry, to bid our guests good night. In my hurry I strike my shoulder against that of a courtier, jostled by the crowd.

"I beg your pardon, Your Grace." The young man bends low. When he lifts his head, I see his face lit golden by the candles around us.

"I'm sorry," I mutter, forgetting myself. *I'm sorry, Thomas.* His name burns in my throat, but I dare not say it aloud.

"The fault is mine, Your Grace." He smiles, his eyes crinkling.

"I suppose I should congratulate you," I say brightly, smiling.

"Congratulate me?"

"Indeed. I've heard a great deal about love letters delivered to a certain lady in my household." This smile makes my cheeks ache. "I hope that you will be happy together."

"Love letters? I regret to say that I did not pen them. If your ladies talk about me, it is most likely about my lack of skill in dancing."

He jokes, but he is looking at me steadily. It reminds me of the night we met, our eyes locked upon each other, unwavering.

"You've not been giving letters to Mistress Alice?" I ask. I smile blandly, as if we are talking of nothing important.

"Ah, it is Lord Robert you are thinking of—another groom in the king's chamber. I showed him my trick, you see, how to slip a note to a maid, without anyone seeing."

He smiles endearingly.

"Then I was mistaken," I tell him, lowering my head graciously.

"Do not apologize, Your Majesty." He bows deeply, humbly, before me. "I offer all of my love and honor and protection to my queen." He says this deftly, easily, a pretty bit of gallantry. But when he looks up at me his eyes are serious, he is not smiling. There is no denying the look in his eyes, or the dangerous lightness in my heart at the sight of it.

I dare not linger for long. I smile carefully at Thomas and step away from him to sit beside the king. Henry sees me and takes my hand in his. Henry kisses me. Henry tells me that he loves me. Everyone moves past me in a blur. Suddenly the music is ended, the entertainment is over, and all of our guests have departed. I feel full and empty at once, and I don't know which feeling frightens me more.

It is a warm night in the garden and Thomas walks toward me. The roses are blooming, glorious, monstrous, their heads heavy and drunken on weary vines. He walks up to me smiling, and I leap into his arms.

Thomas kisses me, one perfect kiss. And then another. The garden is dark and we lie upon the dewy grass. The dew turns my blue dress black and stains his satin doublet; the grass smells like summer and is soft against my arms, my cheek. He loosens the stays on my corset. The touch of his hand upon my bare flesh sends a tremor along my spine.

I wake, suddenly, in a dark room. It was a dream—all of it a dream. Through the sheer bed curtains I see a fire barely flickering in the hearth. I blink for a moment, disoriented. It was early summer in the garden, but here I'm shivering; my naked flesh prickles with cold. I tug at the bedcovers to pull them up to my chin.

The king lies beside me in bed, asleep: a large, old man. I watch him, expecting his eyes to fly open and stare at me, accusingly. Surely I have lost all control of my mind, of my dreaming, if I can dream about another man when lying beside my husband, the king. I force myself to breathe steadily, quietly, and settle carefully back into bed so as not to wake Henry.

The heart, the mind are treasonous. Even with my eyes

open the images of the dream run through me. I listen to my racing heartbeat. It is dangerous to dream, to sleep. Old ghosts are inside me, all the time, fighting their way out.

TODAY THE SKIES are clustered with gray clouds. I stay in my chambers after dinner and admire my jewelry, whiling away the hours before Henry requires my company.

"A letter for you, Your Grace." A page arrives and offers me a letter with a low bow. I take it and set it upon my lap, distracted by the waves and flickers of the fire in the hearth. It is a lazy day, and nearly done. Perhaps I'll take a nap. But first I open the letter.

> *Dear Queen Catherine,*
> *As your friend, I wish you all the wealth, honor,*
> *and good fortune due upon your happy appointment*
> *as queen. I hope that you can recall the unfeigned*
> *love that my heart has always borne toward you in*
> *our years together at your grandmother's Lambeth*
> *establishment. I write to you now with a solemn*
> *request, that you may offer me a place in your*
> *royal household, for the nearer I am to my queen,*
> *the happier I shall be. I am visiting my family*
> *in the country and will be less than a fortnight in*
> *arriving from the time this letter is sent. I hope*
> *that you will be as happy to see me as I am to see*
> *you, and we can enjoy each other's company as we*
> *did in years past.*
>
>

Your faithful servant,
Joan Bulmer

A friend from my past—but I have no past. Have I not sufficiently burned it from my heart with those tokens and letters consumed by the flames? But apparently fire is not enough to cleanse the soul. According to the date on the letter, Joan will be arriving in just a few days to take a position in my household. There is no way I can refuse her. I have the urge to throw this letter into the fire, but I stop myself just in time. The ladies peer at me carefully over their embroidery hoops. I must conceal all.

"You've not received unpleasant news, I hope, Your Majesty?"

"No"—I smile—"an old acquaintance of mine will be arriving shortly. She will become a lady-in-waiting. It has been a long while since I've seen her."

"That is good news, indeed."

"Yes," I agree, folding the letter into a small square and securing it into the belt of my gown. It is imperative that a queen not show fear. How has Henry managed this constant measuring of his emotions, all his life? Or perhaps for Henry it is different—his emotions become law. I sit quietly, lazily, just as I had before reading the letter. I yawn.

"I think I shall retire for a time," I tell the ladies. "Just a short rest before readying for supper."

As soon as I'm alone in my privy chamber, I pull the letter from my belt and thrust it into the hearth. Relief rushes through me as it's caught up by the blaze, but it is short-lived. She is coming; there is nothing I can do to stop it. It does not matter if the letter is burned. The letter is the very least of my problems.

TODAY I MEET with Lady Elizabeth, for she expressed an interest in hearing me play the virginals. While Mary has only been sour and distant since I married her father, Elizabeth has been eager to spend time with me. I only hope that this young girl—highly educated and well schooled in the ways of the court—will not easily detect the deficiencies in me as a royal consort.

After our recital in the sunny parlor, the golden autumn sunlight stretches across the polished floor. A servant comes to stoke the flames in the hearth, and Elizabeth and I sit together in the warmth of the fire. She is clearly an intelligent child, but also a bit melancholy, as if full of questions and yearnings she dare not put into words.

"What is it like to be queen?" she asks me, her voice quiet.

"Well, I am new to being queen. But I've found it quite good so far. I certainly enjoy living here with your father, and with all of our other companions. And I love having new gowns, and planning entertainments. I had no idea how much I would enjoy it, for I had never been given the opportunity to plan one, before."

"Did you not always have new gowns?"

"Not quite like these." I smooth my hand reverently over the rich brocade of my skirt.

"And you have your ladies with you all the time, is that right? And they must do as you bid them?"

"Yes, of course." I smile at this notion, thinking of Joan's impending arrival. Perhaps I would be doing Elizabeth a favor by telling her the truth: as queen, you must hide all true emotion. You must consistently act in a way opposite to how you feel.

"I loved the party you arranged—it was my favorite of this year! And your gown was so beautiful. What else do you need to know to be queen?"

She does not ask me how one becomes queen, of course. She is well acquainted with the concept of the line of succession. No doubt she has understood her own predicament for a long time: third in line for the throne behind her half siblings Edward and Mary and, like Mary, still not restored to her title of princess.

"You need to be the type of person others naturally respect and revere."

"For to be queen is to be close to being the Virgin Mary on earth, for you are the only other woman to whom men bow down, to receive all the love they don't give to their mothers or their wives."

Her words fill me with a fear I dare not show on my face.

"Yes, I suppose you're right. That is why purity and goodness are such important qualities in a queen, for they are of paramount importance to men." I feel Elizabeth's blue eyes burning into my face as I speak—Henry's eyes. I wonder if there is a bit of her mother in her, as well, but I dare not think long on this. The thought of her mother makes me shift uneasily in my seat.

"A virgin queen," Elizabeth murmurs, her wide eyes reflecting the raging fire. "That is what the Virgin Mary is to them. That is what they want in a true sovereign, if she's a woman. Kings are different, of course."

"You are right." I smile, and pat her hand playfully. "Kings are different."

XIX ❧ Joan Bulmer arrives. The same smooth brown hair, fair face, and elegant manner I once envied now strikes me with a strange eeriness; the very familiarity of it out of place in this new life of mine. But any reservations I have are well hidden. I greet her with the enthusiasm due an old friend.

"Look at you, Catherine," she whispers in my ear as we embrace. "You look a queen, you truly do."

"And you look like my Joan—my dear, sweet Joan!"

"How long have you known our queen?" Lady Edgecombe inquires.

"I have known her since she was a young lady, living at the dowager duchess's establishment at Lambeth." Joan says neatly. Lady Edgecombe nods in approval. And perhaps it is as simple as that.

Joan is cheerful as always, and we walk arm in arm together in the gardens, discussing the masques being planned for this winter. All the while I'm aware of the other maids of the chamber who follow our steps in an orderly group. I can only hope that pulling Joan close to me, as a maid in my privy chamber, will encourage her to use some caution in talking of the past.

The sun is setting in streaks of pink, yellow, and orange across the sky. It's time to ready for tonight's banquet, to welcome foreign ambassadors visiting court. My chamber is full of laughter as Joan and Lady Rochford help to dress me, to arrange my hair and place the jewels upon my fingers and clasp strand upon strand of pearls around my neck. I bestow upon Joan a small brooch in gratitude for her service to me, and her smile is broad and genuine. Perhaps old ghosts need not haunt me after all.

But seated beside the king during supper, I feel panic rising in my chest, threatening to close my throat. The sight of Joan seated among the other ladies seems quietly threatening, obscene. In the midst of my panic I smile, I laugh when laughter is expected, I nod and turn my head gently from the right to the left to survey the members of court assembled in the great hall before me, as any good monarch will do when presiding over a meal. But with each sweep of the room, my gaze snags upon the image of Joan seated at a banquet table, talking with the other ladies.

Joan is out of place here, belonging to a different memory: she is lounging upon a bed in the maidens' chamber, wearing a white nightgown and sipping from a goblet of wine. We are all eating strawberries, a whole bowl of them swiped from the dining table and brought to our room at midnight by a small host of young men. Francis Dereham is here, watching me with his pale blue eyes. He lifts a strawberry to my lips and smiles as I take a bite.

I blink, trying to clear the image from my mind. I wonder if when Joan looks at me, the same visions intrude: the maidens' chamber, me with Francis. She can't say anything about me, about Lambeth. Should I ask her not to? No, no, I must not even address the issue. She will only implicate herself if she says anything about me. And why would she want to risk her coveted position in the queen's household?

———

THE AUTUMN DRAWS to an end, the wind chills, the moon wanes, and my monthly blood comes again in the same on-slaught as in all the months of years previous. *What is wrong with me? Why am I not pregnant?* There have been times when I've imagined that I am: in the morning, waking up groggy and remaining tired all day. Or lying awake some nights, unable to sleep. I felt sure these were signs of pregnancy, but then the blood came to show me my mistake.

The ladies, I know, make fine gossip over the cloudiness of the urine in my chamber pot, the dullness of my eyes, and any other aspect of my disposition that may cause specula-tion that I am with child. I can also feel Henry watching me, waiting for news. He's begun to measure all of my be-haviors—or perhaps he always did so, and I've only begun to notice it—be I tired or restless or anxious or excited on any given day, he combs through them for a possibility of pregnancy. And what of our frequent lovemaking? What is missing from our nightly pleasures that they do not have the desired result? Regardless, it seems clear that a lack of pregnancy is my fault alone.

"Joan seems a devoted lady-in-waiting to you, Catherine," Jane remarks as she dabs color on my lips in preparation for my private dinner with the king. Her tone conveys more than she says aloud; I'm sure the duchess has told her all about my affair with Francis Dereham while at Lambeth. For a girl without a past, I have a great deal I need to hide. "I think it best that you keep her close to you, to be assured of her loyalty," she tells me.

"Tonight is an important night for you, Catherine." The duchess suddenly sweeps into my privy chamber. Doorways do not stop the duchess, nothing does. She settles a ledger of sorts upon my writing desk and starts leafing through the pages.

"Your blood finished two nights ago, is that correct?"

"Yes, I suppose that's true."

The duchess eyes Jane for a moment before returning to her pages. Once my hair is properly arranged, I approach the desk.

"What's this?" I ask. The pages reveal some form of calendar with notes scribbled on some of the days, along with pictures showing the state of the waning and waxing moon.

"I've been keeping track of you since your honeymoon, Catherine," the duchess informs me, not looking up from the book. "Lady Rochford and I have been. It's apparent that you wouldn't think to do such a thing."

I look closer: *tired all morning, frequent urination, heavy bloodstained sheets in morning, fell asleep after Mass, bed with king, bed alone.* It's all about me, all of it. Every night I've been with the king recorded on the calendar, every ache and pain in my body written down, even my mood: *weary this evening, snappish.*

"I had no idea you had such a thing," I utter. The duchess glances up at me, craftily. Why is it that I am the only one to feel awkward? She blinks her pale eyes and sets her finger upon today's date in the book, her fingernail touching a perfect circle drawn upon the page.

"There will be a full moon tonight, Catherine. That is a good sign. It is all a good sign: your blood, your mood, the weather. You must be with the king tonight. It is imperative."

"It is not really my choice." None of this is my choice. "It depends on Henry." The duchess furrows her brows at this, but I dare not say more. I can only imagine if she added those notes to her book: *King too tired, legs swollen and aching, temper irascible, difficulty moving, difficulty performing.* It feels dangerous just to think about it.

"When the fates align, Catherine, you must do your best to fulfill your duty."

"I always do my best."

"Then tonight you must do better."

"YOU SEEMED QUIET tonight, Catherine," Henry remarks, pulling me by the hand to his bedchamber. "I think this might lighten your mood."

The door shut behind us, he hands me a narrow wooden box. Inside: a gold necklace strung with emeralds and pearls.

"Oh, it's beautiful, Henry! It will look lovely with my green velvet dress."

He stands behind me before the mirror, leaning forward to clasp the jeweled strand around my neck.

"Lovely," he pronounces. Just looking at myself in the necklace, I feel suddenly lighter. Even with all that I now have, I never tire of receiving new gifts.

"I wish I had a gift for you!" I gasp, in gratitude. Then a flash of sorrow cuts across the king's eyes. I watch his reflection as he blinks, looks away from my face. I turn to look at him and put my hands on his arms.

"You know I am trying, my lord. Please do not worry. It will happen soon."

"I know, I know," he murmurs, pulling me closer. "I do not doubt you. I do not doubt you." There seems to be more behind these words than he is willing to say, but I don't press the issue.

"You cannot deny it, Catherine, you've heard the tales: I am the cursed King of England."

"That's simply not true," I tell him. "You are the most beloved king this country has ever had."

"It's not just about England," he growls. "It's much more than that. God is unkind to me. He punishes me."

I can't help but bristle at this notion. I've heard that Henry has a complicated relationship with God: any misfortune that befalls him, he is certain must be due to God's direct displeasure. I've heard of Henry's self-pitying rants, trying to discover what sins he committed to deserve the sadness he has been forced to endure.

"There must be something I've done—some sin against God that I continue to pay for to this day. I thought I had found it, in divorcing my brother's wife and putting aside that sin. But then I was cursed anew, marrying that witch, that grotesquery."

My cousin—I must erase the thought from my mind. I don't want him to suddenly remember our relation, or else he may consider me yet another sin.

"But these things are not your fault, my lord," I say soothingly, putting my hands on his shoulders, telling him what he wants to hear. "None of this was your fault, I'm sure God can see it."

"Then why does He try me so? Can you answer me that?" He waves his hands, his anger suddenly expansive, his face flushed. My skin prickles in fear: he's never raised his voice like this to me. "In all these years, with all these wives I've been granted but one son—one son, Catherine! And his mother taken from me so soon after his birth."

I flinch at this mention of Jane, as if slapped across the face. But Henry is too steeped in his own self-pity to notice.

"The crown is not safe as it should be, and even my own people up in the north plan to rise against me, again. What did I do to deserve this?"

He sits heavily upon the bed, his cloth-of-gold doublet and jeweled fingers glittering in the low light. In spite of my fear, I stand before him and take his hands in mine.

"You think that God has cursed you?" I ask, squeezing his hands and smiling. "But my lord, can you not see how you are blessed?"

"Do not mock my fears, woman!" he snaps. I jolt back at the sound of his voice. "You've been queen for mere months—you know not what a lifetime of kingship can do to a man's soul." He rises from the bed abruptly and stands, staring into the fire. I want nothing more than to run from this room, but I know that I can't.

"I do not mock you, Your Grace. I only strive to be the type of wife of whom God will approve." Or are the sins of my past yet another curse against Henry, piled on with all the rest? "Will you not let me comfort you?"

I move forward again, tentatively, and place my hands upon his arms, resting my head against his back. This has worked in the past, many times, pulling him out of a glum mood or worry about politics . . . all I have to do is to get him to turn around and look at me. I press myself against him, my breasts flat against his back. But he will not turn.

"I live with fear, every day, Catherine. I am a target for them all—everyone eager to do away with me and climb on to my throne."

"No, my lord, everyone loves you. How can you say—"

"Words of love keep no one safe!" he rages, turning and breaking from my embrace. He glares at me for a moment; I'm horrified by the anger burning in those bright eyes. "They will say one thing to my face and yet another behind my back. They could slip poison into my food, or burn my palace, or pay an assassin to visit me in my sleep. Do you understand me, Catherine, when I tell you the danger of being king?"

"Of course," I whisper, my voice cracked. "Of course I understand."

"You are a fool to think this crown keeps me safe! You are a woman—nay, a girl. A girl I have dressed as a queen. You will never understand."

He turns to glare into the fire, as if I'm no longer present. Indeed, I feel as if I have vanished from the room completely. Somehow, the sight of his back turned to me is more frightening than that flash of anger in his eyes.

"You are dismissed," he grumbles.

"I bid you good evening, my lord." I perform the proper obeisance, though he does not deign to turn and look at me. I exit the king's chamber, trying to muster a fake courtier's smile for the benefit of the guards stationed there. They are all gracious, dutiful; I have no doubt that they listened to every word. The ambition of the Howards has led me directly into danger. If the crown offers no safety to Henry, then certainly it will offer no safety to me.

I WEAR MY GREEN VELVET gown today with the new emerald-and-pearl necklace, perfectly complementing the row of pearls embroidered in the neckline of the gown and the trim of my green hood. As much as I would like to avoid him, I've invited my husband for an evening meal in my presence chamber, hoping that food and entertainment will cheer him. I had hoped that the sight of me thus arrayed in his recent gift would cheer Henry, but I can tell that his mood is still grim. There is much that this king harbors in his great, old soul. While his body grew misshapen from illness and lack of exercise, his soul was ravaged by lies and mistrust.

All day, the halls of the palace have been rife with whispers about the rebellions in the northern regions. Watching the fool's antics, I can see the stress of these rebellions settling in the king's spine, his shoulders drooping and his back hunched forward like an old man's. But suddenly his spine straightens in his chair, his shoulders roll back. His blue eyes alight with interest.

I follow the path of Henry's gaze to see a pretty Seymour girl before us, recently added as a maid to my household. She is petite, with honey-colored hair, wearing a gown of brown velvet trimmed with gold, the square neckline accentuating her ample bosom. She looks a bit like me, or perhaps how I once looked: that wary gaze, that tentative smile I wore when I first approached the king.

I open my mouth to say something to divert his attention, to bring his focus back to me. But my horror keeps me mute. She's just the king's type, of course, that's why the Seymours placed her in my household—just as the Howards placed me in the service of Anne of Cleves.

"Mistress Mary," he says, in his charming, sweet tone. The sound of it roils in my gut. The girl before us curtsies gracefully, bowing her head and lowering her eyes. No doubt she has been well schooled by Jane Seymour's brothers, Edward and Thomas. Perhaps they are expecting that I will be pregnant soon and want a lady ready to distract the king while I suffer the confinement of the birthing chamber. Henry seems surprisingly innocent of all of this—perhaps he is a pawn in this game, just as much as I was. Just as much as this Seymour girl, standing before us.

"I trust you find your new position to your liking?" the king asks.

"Indeed, Your Majesty. The queen is a kind mistress, as you are a kind and generous master." Her eyes flash up at his only briefly, before her final obeisance. I smile and nod at the girl, and she steps aside. This is the smile I imagine Katherine of Aragon pasted upon her face when met with the king's lingering gaze over Mistress Anne Boleyn; or Anne of Cleves's smile when her new husband first took a fancy to me. I take a sip of wine, my throat suddenly dry.

For the rest of the night I laugh aloud, I applaud, I sparkle. I am fun and youthful and merry, hoping that the king will admire my slim waist, my firm full breasts straining from the bodice of my gown. I breathe a sigh of relief when I see his eyes upon me, but just as quickly they flash back to the lass in brown velvet dancing before us. Is it possible that

Henry has become bored with his bride? They still say that he is more affectionate, more indulgent with me than with all the others, but clearly his adoration of me does not stop another lady from catching his eye.

I must become everything to him—it is my only hope. I must become pregnant to save Henry, and save myself.

XX The duchess sits before a roaring fire in my chamber, tapping a deck of cards efficiently against the polished table. She motions for me to sit across from her.

"You must fix it, Catherine," she remarks succinctly, as if we were talking about a torn hem. "You have created this mess and now you must fix it."

She is talking about the Seymour girl, who sits in the main chamber at this very moment, her golden head bent over the embroidery on her lap.

"I am trying, Duchess. It is difficult. I know not what to do."

"Difficult to keep his attention?" she murmurs disapprovingly. "You've not been married long, Catherine. I thought you would have known better how to handle him."

Her words sting me; I look down at my cards.

"Are you listening to me? I would never have supported you if I thought you would not be able to handle him."

"I am trying my best."

My voice cracks with emotion; the duchess lifts her hand in warning. We sit quietly for a moment, waiting for the chatter in the adjacent room to grow louder before we continue.

"All is not lost for you, I think. But you must remember how it was, in the beginning. You must remember the power of seduction." Her eyes flash at mine, a mischievous smile tugging at the corners of her thin lips. "It is what got you here, after all. You must not be lazy, simply because he is not spending his every hour seducing you. Perhaps it is time that you seduce him."

"They say that if I don't produce an heir soon, he may choose another bride."

"Indeed, they also say he may take back that Flanders Mare."

"Please tell me if you know anything."

"I know only what you know, my dear—only what those fools in the banquet hall babble about when they have taken too much ale. What I have heard is not the question here. It is up to you to control the situation."

"Control the king?"

"In the bedchamber, at least. Think, Catherine. The masquerade of a virgin is over. Now you must give him more, you must desire him. You must please him so that he desires no one but you—at least until you are with child."

My eyes wander over to Mary Seymour, her golden hair bathed in the light of the fire.

"If you can't keep him away from that Seymour girl, we'll have to find someone else who can."

"Someone else?" I look at the duchess, but she is suddenly absorbed in rearranging her cards. I want to reach over the table and shake them from her grasp. "What do you mean?"

"If the king is in need of a mistress, there is always your cousin Mistress Norris."

"You wouldn't—" Before I can finish, the duchess flashes her pale gray eyes at mine; they are unrelentingly cold, like ice. It seems clear that yes, indeed, she would.

"If you can't keep him from planting his seed in another Seymour, there had best be another Howard girl in his bed to distract him."

"But then, what will become of me?"

"I don't know, Catherine," she observes coolly, placing her cards upon the table in a fan. "What *will* become of you?"

TONIGHT I WEAR my pale blue silk gown with a simple blue hood, the same I wore when I first caught the king's eye. I eschew the royal jewels for the tear-shaped sapphire—the king's first gift to me. Gazing at myself in the mirror, I realize just how limited are the ways in which I know how to please him. I must use what power I have perfectly: I bow deeply, humbly before him in his parlor.

When I stand, the king is smiling at me. I'm both relieved and confused. The last time we were alone, I was witness to his rage. He has not visited my chamber since. Will he say something about our argument? Or has he already forgotten it? Seeing my lute in my hand, he waves me over to my usual chair. Uncertain, I sit beside him and begin to sing:

> "Pastime with good company
> I love and shall until I die
> Grudge to lust, but none deny
> So God be pleased, thus live will I
> For my pastance,
> Hunt, sing, and dance,

My heart is set, All goodly sport
For my comfort:
Who shall me let?"

"Delightful, Catherine! You know I love hearing my com-
positions sung in such a sweet voice." His eyes sparkle in
that way I've seen before. I had worried he was still angry
at me. Now I wonder if I even take up that much space in
his mind. He is a king, and has more important things to
think about.

He touches my hand warmly. I put the lute aside as he
tugs me forward, pulling me onto his lap, where he kisses
my face, my neck.

"I have missed you," he breathes.

"And I have missed you."

"I have been—busy." He looks up at me, his face close to
mine. His gaze is warm, familiar. His pink mouth is softened by his smile. But still, I can remember the look of vivid
rage I saw but days ago—I worry that I may not be able to
forget it.

"I understand, my lord."

"Sweet bird," he whispers in my ear, "how I've missed my
sweet bird."

But I know my work is not complete. Tonight is different
because I know it must be so. The duchess was right; the
masquerade of a virgin is over. It is no longer enough for
me to lie there and passively submit myself to him. I must
offer the king something different: a young woman desirous
of him, and him alone.

Luckily, he responds to my boldness with a vigor I hadn't

thought possible. When his passions are spent, he grips me tightly in his arms—almost too tightly, pushing the air out of my lungs—gasping and rasping in my ear: "You are mine forever, Catherine. You are mine only, mine forever . . ."

I recite the same words of my love and lust in his ear. *You are mine, Henry, you are mine, forever . . .*

But I am not such a fool to believe that this works both ways.

THE KING'S PASSION for me renewed, I have spent every night of the last fortnight in his bedchamber, often staying till morning. The duchess is pleased with me for evidently upholding my half of the bargain. Meanwhile, Henry is eager to do anything for me, as if I will become pregnant as a reward for his many gifts.

"What is your heart's desire?" he asks, once his passion has been sated. "Jewels? Fabulous gowns?"

A coronation, I think, *more grand than that for Queen Anne.* But I know better than to overplay my hand.

"You've given me beautiful jewels and gowns." I sigh, contented.

"Yet you do not seem to lose interest in more," he jokes.

"I've never experienced a true royal Christmas," I tell him, innocently enough.

"Ah, I see. It is revelry that delights my young queen. Very well. Where will this royal Christmas take place?"

"At Hampton Court," I tell him.

A shadow passes briefly over his eyes. Perhaps Hampton still harbors the ghost of Cousin Anne for him, for I can sense her in the halls when I am there. Still, I love Hampton and my dream of a sumptuous royal Christmas there is simply too tempting to keep secret. And perhaps this, the first Christmas of our marriage, will finally defy the ghost of Anne in Henry's memory.

"Of course, my dear," he says, squeezing me close to him. "Hampton it is!"

Let the walls of Hampton echo with such celebrations that our revelry frightens all ghosts from the shadows! Let the vision of me, dancing in a gown of red and gold, burn through all of the memories of his past wives, and lay all of those old ghosts to rest.

XXI

Over a hundred guests have arrived to participate in the Christmas festivities at Hampton Court. In honor of their arrival, and to mark the beginning of the celebrations, a magnificent hunting expedition sets out. The snowy woods are filled with heavy hoofbeats. Appareled in velvet and furs, I ride my silver-gray mare toward the front of the pack, behind the king. The woods are pale blue and gray with snow; the trees' icy limbs glisten, silvery in the bright winter sun. It is a marvelous day, and I feel myself growing short of breath, even a bit light-headed as we head faster and faster through the trees, over the open meadow in pursuit of our prey. Horses snort, dogs bark. When the dogs rush forward, I carefully pull myself from the cavalcade, positioned atop a hillock of snow.

I'm in just the right place to see the king emerge from the stand of trees with his prize: an enormous buck slung over the back of his groom's horse. I smile at Henry; his cheeks are pink with excitement, like a young boy's. I applaud his success, amazed at the violence of the spectacle: men in glittering doublets and heavy furs mounted upon giant horses pounding over the underbrush and hauling the carcasses of animals out among the snowy trees. It is a true display of power in its most primal, bestial sense.

TONIGHT IS THE first formal banquet, followed by midnight Mass in the Chapel Royal to signify the beginning of the twelve days of Christmas. I wear a red velvet gown that I know Henry loves, my cheeks still pink from the cold wind.

"Catherine, you are youth incarnate," Henry pronounces upon my arrival. He takes my jeweled hand in his and presses it warmly to his lips. I can feel everyone—all of the court, all of our guests—with their eyes upon us, appraising the scene. Surely they can all see how well the king looks, for he has lost a great deal of weight in these past few months. Surely they see the lively twinkle in his eyes, the vivid color in his cheeks, and must remark to one another that the king's new bride is doing well for him. I *am* doing well for him—a good wife, a good queen.

Lady Anne of Cleves approaches the head table. I have not seen her since my days as a lady-in-waiting in her chamber, and for a moment I am speechless. But when she looks up at me, not a flicker of ill feeling taints her expression. She immediately drops to the floor at my feet in an elaborate bow.

"I show my respect to you, my queen," she says in halting English, "as I would to no other woman in England."

Unable to find the proper response, I grasp her hand in mine.

"We are both so pleased that you are here," I tell her. Henry rises as well to give her his good wishes. Indeed, Lady Anne looks far more joyous than she ever did when she was queen. I take her hand and lead her to the dance floor. Henry can only laugh at the sight of the two of us— his previous and his current wife—dancing together to the sprightly music.

I dance late into the night, enjoying all the while an abundance of food and wine and continuous music. Garnished brawn is served—spiced boar meat with fruit and jelly sprinkled with flour, like a fine dusting of snow. There are games for the children, and they delight in the confections on display: cakes shaped like Henry's royal residences, complete with turrets and cannons. There are sugar figurines of King Arthur, Charlemagne, Alexander the Great, and others, painted in red, blue, and green, the armor made of silver or gold leaf. Henry sits back upon his chair beneath the cloth of state, enjoying all the dances, the tableaux, the entertainments presented before him. Children race through the hall dressed in white satin, glittering white wings of gauze tied to their backs. These tiny angels dance before the king: the court is heaven, and Henry is God. Henry tilts his head back and laughs.

"Will you not dance with me, my lord?" I ask, nearly breathless from dancing.

"You are doing quite well on your own, my dear. I will join you a bit later."

I open my mouth to protest, but stop myself with a smile

just in time. The king has stayed seated all night. It is unlike him to abstain from dancing during such an elaborate celebration. I think to peer at his leg for any signs of a bandage, but I dare not reveal my suspicions.

It is the end of the banquet when the king stands, and I detect a vague wince pass over his face as he does so. Still, he knows well his royal duty, and a great part of it is performance. He holds out his hand to mine for a dance. Though he manages all of the steps admirably, the dullness in his eyes betrays his distress to me.

"I shall take my leave of you now, sweet wife," he says, bending low to kiss my hand. The king's hand is trembling, and there is a mist of perspiration on his upper lip. The sight of him thus frightens me—what happened to the vibrant, energetic king I saw earlier today at the hunt? What could have happened between then and now?

"I shall join you, my lord," I announce with a flourish of my velvet gown, bidding all of the company present a good night.

Henry walks quickly down the hallway with me in tow; I have to hurry on my short legs so as not to be dragged along. But this is clearly not the gait of a passionate man looking forward to bedding his bride, as he may want it to appear.

"Henry," I whisper, in hopes of slowing him. We are in the hallway near his bedchamber. "Henry, are you quite well?"

"I am fine, my wife, do not worry." He bows again over my hand. I have the feeling suddenly that he wants to be rid of me. "I'm afraid we must part ways. I have business to attend to, even at so late an hour."

"Are you sure you do not want me to stay? We could walk together to the Chapel Royal."

"Indeed, you had best let your ladies tend to you before the service. I will be attending a Mass in private, but will see you for further festivities tomorrow. Until then."

I rise on my tiptoes and kiss him gently upon the cheek.

"Until then, my love." But what kind of love am I, if I can't even console him in his pain, if he does not even want me to try? Henry disappears into his chamber and closes the door in my face.

I turn swiftly from the door, my cheeks burning. Here I am standing like a fool before the king's door—his useless little wife. I do the only thing I can think to do. I hurry back to the hall, scanning the crowd, searching for the face I've been so long avoiding.

"Thomas," I say, hurrying up to him. He bows deeply at my approach.

"I was just heading to the king's chambers," he tells me, his head still lowered. "He departed rather abruptly. I'm afraid I lost him in the crowd."

"Yes, please go quickly."

He looks up at me, his dark eyes wide with alarm.

"He mentioned he has many things to tend to tonight, and may be in need of your assistance."

"Of course, my queen."

As he passes by me, the sleeve of his doublet accidentally brushes against the velvet sleeve of my gown. It is a brief caress, a fleeting warmth—and then he is gone.

HENRY KEPT UP a tiring façade of good health at dinner today, but it is clear that he is unwell. Though I took his hand in mine and inquired quietly as to how he was feeling, he answered with the same false cheer he bestows upon everyone. He does not see how foolish it makes me feel to be kept in the dark about his ailments, which must be apparent to the majority of his guests. He is treating me as little more than some simpering handmaiden of court, to be shown the same silly charade as all the rest—not as his chosen wife and queen.

While the king is resting in his bedchamber, I am busy with the final fitting of my gown for the masked ball, to be held on Twelfth Night. I am to be Cleopatra, robed in shimmering gold. The ladies slip the slim gold sheath over my head, then flutter around me affixing a gold crown and gold bracelets.

"Let me see! Let me see!" I crow excitedly. But when they step back to allow me a full view of myself in the mirror, the image is not what I had envisioned. The cloth of gold is stiff, and binds my bosom awkwardly. The skirt hangs straight against my legs and does not sway gently as I walk. Perhaps if I were a foot taller, and thinner, with paler skin and darker hair, then the gown would look beautiful, statuesque. The image conjured in my mind is of Anne Boleyn, smiling, her black eyes sparkling in the firelight.

In spite of the coddling flattery of the ladies, my disappointment only deepens.

"No!" I yell, waving my hand to silence the lot of them. "It is not right. I will need a new dress, a new costume altogether." I pull the crown, in the shape of a golden asp, from my head. It tangles in my thick curls. I growl in anger; Joan rushes forward to carefully pick my locks free from its grip.

"What about the goddess Aphrodite, with her golden apple?" Lady Rochford suggests.

"No. Someone dresses as Aphrodite every year."

"What about an animal, like a butterfly? A set of beautiful gauze wings could be made for you."

I turn at the sound of this voice—it is Mary Seymour's. I eye her carefully, the firelight playing in warm light and shadow upon her face. I recall suddenly that Jane Seymour, when queen, had forbidden her ladies from wearing French fashions, for the French hood simply looked too becoming on one of her maids. I can understand that, now: it wasn't simply envy, it was self-preservation.

I can't be some stupid winged insect, I want to yell, to pull her hair like a child. *I need to be the most beautiful. I need for him to look at me, and not at you.*

THE DAYS OF CHRISTMAS continue with a variety of daily events—tilting, hunting, hawking. I attend these, cheerful as always, as if matching Henry's false merriment with my own. Perhaps he thinks I am too spoiled a girl to play nursemaid to him, perhaps it is an injury to his pride for his youthful wife to discover his infirmity. But what about my pride? If I cannot act the part of lover to him, I would like to at least attempt to act the part of wife.

Today, too weary to join the hunt, Henry attends the bearbaiting demonstration. A great ring has been constructed near the palace gardens, with seating arranged all around. We pile into the seats, covered with furs in the chill weather, and watch as an enormous brown bear lumbers to the center of the ring.

"He is a grand one, is he not? And raging already,"

Henry remarks, applauding as the bear is chained to a post, his neck cuffed in a thick metal collar.

When the dogs are released into the ring, the roar of the crowd drowns out the roars of the bear. People crowded into the front rows stand, cheering. The dogs rush toward the beast, their teeth bared, barking sharply in the cold air. The bear rears up on its hind legs to display its enormity before us: he is powerful, but powerless. Frightening but also threatened. I cheer, my eyes darting with the movements of the dogs, who leap forward to bite at the bear's neck and belly. The bear sweeps one dog aside with a massive paw—it lies motionless in the dirt, its skull crushed by the blow.

"Ah, he got him! He got him! With only one blow, did you see that? With only one blow!" Henry opens his mouth and laughs. The bear opens his mouth and roars. I feel a shiver wash over me, and stick my hands back into my fur muffler for warmth. Two dogs leap forward and tear the bear's throat and the brown fur turns slick and black with blood. The beast falters, falls. It is all fascinating, but I cannot help but wince as I watch it happen. Henry is watching intently. I peer at him, carefully: his eyes are wide, unblinking, as he watches the bear go down.

"They were too much for him," he remarks, almost to himself. "They were all too much for the old beast." He laughs again, and everyone seated around us laughs with him, but the laughter seems hollow, forced. I am shivering beneath my furs and eager to sit inside, before a fire. I'm eager to leave this ring, where the enormous corpse of the bear lies prone before us, warm air lifting from his torn flesh in a cloud of steam; a ghost hovering, visible in the bleak midday sun.

"Will you accompany me to the parlor, my lord, for a goblet of wine and a seat by the fire?" An attractive offer, added to the flirtatious lift of one eyebrow. But the king demurs, lumbering a bit awkwardly from his seat. I hold out my hand for him but he ignores it, waving instead for a groom.

Thomas sidles up beside him. His dark eyes flash at mine, only briefly.

"Being king does not wait on ceremony, my dear Catherine," Henry says, laughing jovially. "I have important matters to attend to, but I will join you in celebration this evening."

"Of course, my lord." I smile, a bit wistful. "I shall see you this evening."

All of this playacting at cheerfulness wearies me, even bores me. I think this is why I'm so looking forward to the masked ball—it is an opportunity to be released from myself, for a while. I can understand why Henry enjoys masques for this very reason, though I doubt that at over six feet tall there is any costume that could begin to conceal his identity. Still, the dream is there—the dream of being new, of being different for one night. A brief respite from the often tiring performance of whatever role life has given you to play.

XXII

Finally, my new costume is done; I have just enough time to ready myself before the masked ball begins. Tonight I am Helen of Troy, the most beautiful woman on earth: half mortal, half goddess. My gown is constructed of yard upon yard of dazzling white silk, stitched at the edges with metallic gold thread. The silk fits becomingly across my full bosom, draping loosely below my collarbone. The loose skirt flutters like angels' wings, a long trail of silk following behind me. Bands of gold are twisted around my bare upper arms, gold rings set upon my fingers. My hair is elaborately braided on top of my head and clasped in a delicate crown of gold wire twisted around glittering diamonds that I am sure will catch the candlelight in the hall, the sparkling reflected in my eyes. My mask is a delicate mesh of gold wire webbing, studded with small diamonds to match the crown.

The moment the cool wire of the mask is pressed to my face, I have transformed. I look in the mirror as Joan secures the mask, the pins concealed by my hair. I've made sure my eyes are still visible in the mask, for Henry has often said they are among my best features. Those hazel eyes blink back at me now, through the elaborate twists of gold flecked with diamonds, but they do not seem like my eyes. I barely recognize myself; the feeling is altogether intoxicating.

As I sweep into the great hall I can see the breath escape Henry's lungs at the sight of me. *Yes, that's what I want!* Yes. Henry wears an elaborate tiger face striped with black and gold, a majestic mask with his blue eyes peering out from the black-circled eyeholes in the center. And those blue eyes are trained on me—all eyes are trained on me. They devour the curves of my body, my breasts and waist and hips seductively visible as I walk toward the king, the light silk swishing against my legs.

A dazzling array of musicians, acrobats, tumblers, and

dancers perform for us, dashing in and around the crowd, clasping the hands of young ladies and pulling them into the dance. Finally, the Abbot of Misrule appears, his entrance greeted with a cacophony of cheers and applause. He has been chosen to host the night's festivities: a member of court wearing a jester's bright colors, with jingling bells on his hat and pointed shoes, a brightly colored harlequin mask stretched across his face.

"Come, all creatures striped and feathered and furred and winged! Come, all gods and goddesses, all heroes and warriors! All must join the dance!"

The drumbeats are loud, the music raucous. I have just enough time to carefully lift my long train and drape it over my elbow before I'm thrust into a vigorous dance. I spin and spin—so fast that it's dizzying. I try to catch the king's eye, to see if he is watching me. The dance moves quickly, and I move from one partner to the next, swirling in a sea of masked faces.

People I know from court are generally easy to identify (isn't that Uncle Norfolk, appareled like a knight?) regardless of their costume. But there are so many guests here whom I've only just met—so many mysterious eyes peering out from behind feathered and sparkling masks.

"Helen of Troy," a young man remarks, taking my hands in his. He is wearing a glittering mask of red-and-black satin, his cape also red and black. The mask has a beaklike nose, the top edges pointed like devilish horns. I look into his eyes and see that they are pale blue, and staring at me boldly.

Those eyes are familiar.

"Don't you recognize me, Catherine? I think you would know me anywhere." His hand grasps my waist a bit too tightly. I turn my face away and smile to conceal my alarm.

"Mask or no mask," I say, smiling but firm, "you should refer to me as queen."

He laughs at this and spins me around, the great train of my silk gown fluttering like a cloud around me.

"Ah, but you are my Catherine. Don't you remember, my little minnow?" he teases. "You know my name."

"You are the devil," I play along, though my voice is cold. "And if you name the devil, he ceases to exist."

At this, he laughs loudly, giving me a vigorous spin. "Not this devil."

He clutches me now, too tight, too close. His face is mere inches from my own, those blue eyes uncannily pale and bright.

"Perhaps you don't remember me? You have a tendency to forget matters of the heart." His voice is a low growl, teeth clenched. "Here is a reminder: you promised I would never know your heart to swerve."

"I am afraid you are mistaken. You have confused me with someone else," I whisper, but he can hear my desperation. "You do not belong here."

"That is no way to welcome an old lover." He smiles cruelly. "I will return, Catherine." He mouths the words carefully. "I will give you time to change your mind."

As soon as the music ceases I break from his grasp and pull away from the dance floor. I wave at a servitor for a goblet of wine, which I sip quickly to calm my nerves. Henry makes his way over to me.

"My dearest Helen, you are even more beautiful than the legends claim."

He bows formally over my hand. He is acting the part of King Henry, not my Henry.

"I beg that you may save a dance for me, later tonight."

"Of course," I say, bowing delicately. But I know that he will not dance with me, I know that he is incapable of dancing. Henry steps back, observing the celebration. He is standing carefully, taking the weight off his bandaged, ulcerated leg. His formality makes me feel even more alone, when I feel I need his protection more than ever. I don't know how to talk to him. I don't know what to say.

I look to the dance floor and see the devil's mask sweep by me again: a leering smile, the blue eyes focused directly on me. Where is Joan Bulmer? Has she seen this devil? Does she recognize his eyes from those midnight parties at Lambeth? I can't take the thought any further—I must be imagining things. The devil is dancing with Mary Seymour, appareled in gold like a queen herself. Both of them laughing, dancing, laughing. I stand still in the midst of the crowd, my gown glowing like fresh white snow. Those pale eyes follow my every move—there is nowhere I can go, nowhere I can hide.

"Revelers!" the Abbot of Misrule calls over the crowd. "It is warm within, but cold without. And what is a celebration of Christ's birth without the rush of winter upon our flesh? To the gardens we go!"

We all follow him in a throng, the children first, a great rush of glittering masks and jeweled doublets and thick velvet robes. The air is bitingly cold but refreshing against my skin. Jane rushes up to clasp a gold cape around my shoulders, and I press forward in the midst of the crowd, plunging into the garden maze, a swirl of cloth of gold and white silk trailing after me.

I rush to the center of a particular circular hedge, craving just a moment of escape. No one will seek refuge here: they are sure to be too caught up in the goings-on of the celebration.

Too late, I realize that I am not alone. A black-caped figure stands before me. I gasp loudly, and he turns: a brown-and-gold hawk face looks back at me. I instantly recognize the dark eyes that sparkle in the midst of the mask. I let out a deep sigh and step forward, reaching my hand out to him.

"I'm so glad it's you." Only after the words are out do I realize how they sound. He reaches out his hand and grasps mine, tightly.

"And I feel the same," he whispers, his voice shivering with cold, "more than I dare say."

He bows his masked head and presses his lips, moist and warm, against my hand.

My heart is treasonous. My heart is a danger to me.

Henry's laughter booming in the distance shocks me from my reverie. I turn and rush away, without a word. I can hear the Abbot of Misrule calling in the darkness, calling all the revelers back indoors. By the time I reach the hall, I'm shivering, the gold cloak pulled tight around my shoulders. The hall is warm, fires burning in every hearth. I stand as close as I dare to the flames, sipping from a goblet of wine.

We begin our unmasking, one by one, first Henry and then me. We politely gasp as everyone reveals themselves, though it's often easy to predict who is hiding under their costumes. When Thomas unmasks I dare not turn my gaze away, I dare not move or breathe. I stand and smile, like a joyful and appreciative queen. Henry has his kingly look plastered upon his face as well; he looked healthier and more robust when wearing the tiger mask. I watch warily— I want to scan the crowd, but I dare not appear agitated. I wait for the red-and-black devil to appear, and unmask himself.

The unmasking is done, and no devil came forward to reveal his true identity. I don't know whether to feel relieved, or even more haunted.

XXIII

I watch through a pane of puckered glass as caravans of guests depart; snow slants across the window, blurring the scene in a veil of white. As I bade my good-byes I felt lighter, in spite of my trepidation of what the future might entail. I had hoped that the Christmas celebrations would be a way to display Henry's love and devotion and desire for me, but when he fell ill I felt overlooked, wholly unnecessary. If physical love is all that I have to offer him and he is too distracted or ill to appreciate it, then what will become of me?

I don't forget the duchess's words about finding another to take my place. I don't forget the pale blue eyes I saw at the Twelfth Night masque. Though I may be overlooked by Henry, I am not so insignificant to others. I will always be in danger, and I must endeavor to protect myself at all costs.

Danger follows me, even into dreams: since Twelfth Night, my sleep has been restless. I yearn to close my eyes and find peace, but instead I see the maidens' chamber at Lambeth: the candles burn low, the wine has been drunk, the late-night treats devoured. Francis takes my hand—his pale blue eyes shine in the dimness—and leads me to my bed, in the corner of the room. The ladies giggle and pinch me in jest as we pass them.

These dreams startle me awake; I stare at the ceiling, trembling in fear.

As is customary, Henry and I will exchange gifts on New Year's Day. I've had a very handsome gold goblet engraved with our initials, as well as a quilted cap with a feathered plume to cover his thinning hair.

"Did you enjoy your royal Christmas, my queen?" he asks. We are lounging before the fire in his chamber. He has already put the quilted cap upon his head, but has yet to bestow any gifts upon me. I nestle close to him in hopes of not looking too eager. There are but few ways I can gauge how happy the king is with me; gifts are one of them.

"I did, indeed. But I am glad our guests have departed." I indulge in a yawn. "It is rather more restful to be here with you, finally alone."

Henry smiles at this, content. Now that we are alone, Henry seems more my Henry again, though he is clearly weary from all the recent exertions and his bad leg is still bandaged beneath his hose. I consider inquiring about his health but think better of it, though a bit sadly. If he wants to keep me at arm's length, there is nothing I can do to force my way into his confidence.

"I have a gift for you." He reaches over to a nearby table

and produces an impossibly small wooden box, and places it in the palm of my hand. It must be a ring. Perhaps a ruby? An emerald? I open the lid and peer inside.

A gold coin is nestled upon a tiny bed of velvet. One side is carved with Tudor roses, the vines twisted into lover's knots around the initials *He&C*. On the other side—my emblem of the rose crowned, with an inscription carved around the edge: *Henricus VIII: Rutilans Rosa Sine Spina*. The Rose Without a Thorn.

"I've had it struck in celebration of our happy marriage, and in tribute to my beloved wife."

"It is beautiful, Henry!" None of his other wives had a coin minted in honor of their marriage, so far as I have heard. There is no mistaking this triumph! "It is so beautiful."

AFTER THE DIZZYING celebrations I'm rather relieved that the court is settling back into its old routine. I've even picked up embroidery as a quiet way to while away the hours after dinner, and I often invite a musician to come and sing to me as I sit by the fire with muslin and needle in hand. Late in the afternoon the needle often slips from my grip, and I merely curl up before the warm fire for a nap.

"How has she been feeling?" I hear a voice whisper; I feign sleep and listen to my ladies.

"She's been tired as of late, more tired than usual. It seems a hopeful sign."

Even with my eyes closed I can see the prim smiles passed from one face to another. I dare not stir, knowing that they are all watching me.

It does seem a hopeful sign, but not hopeful enough. Lady

Rochford wisely keeps her remarks to herself, knowing what she knows. Henry has taken to my bedchamber only twice in the new year; his leg is on the mend, but he is still weary.

"What if he has found another woman to take to his bed?" I whisper. It is late at night, and she folds the bedcovers carefully over me.

"Do you think that he is capable, even if he had a mind to do so?"

I don't answer this, pressing my lips together anxiously.

"What if there is something wrong with me?"

"You are a young girl yet, there is still time. The royal physician reported nothing amiss."

"At least not to me," I say darkly. Henry ordered the physician to examine my womanly parts—indeed, the most embarrassing experience I have ever undergone. Clearly my husband worries that there may be something wrong with me, for it is understood that the fault cannot lie with him. Matters of state, war, and religion are the domain of a king. All of the responsibility of pregnancy lies solely with the woman.

At least, no one would dare suggest otherwise to the king.

A YOUNG PAGE enters my chamber with a bow. "I have a letter for you, Your Majesty." It is late, and Jane is preparing me for a private supper with the king. Tonight I will look seductive and virginal in my cream silk gown, my hair flowing loosely over my shoulders. As Jane carefully arranges my curls, I break the seal of the letter—no doubt a petition from yet another distant relation.

But as soon as I scan the first lines, I know this is an altogether different sort of letter: *We beseech you, Your Majesty, that we may be humbly included in your presence, able to celebrate the good fortune of so dear a friend . . . Sincere wishes from your most humble servants, Katherine and Malyn Tylney, Dorothy Baskerville, Elizabeth Holland.* The ladies of Lambeth, all of them eager for appointments in my chamber. My vision blurs for a moment; I can see Joan just in my line of vision, placing my jewels in their proper boxes.

A flash of memory rips through me: that devil I saw at the Twelfth Night masque. Those pale blue eyes staring at me from behind the mask of red and black. That voice that sounded so familiar—Francis Dereham's voice. Surely it must have been a nightmare, that was all, the kind you have when you're awake and have danced too hard and drunk too much wine. But this letter in my hand—this is real, is solid. I fold the piece of parchment and hide it in my nest of drawers when I'm sure Joan's back is turned.

I have no choice, of course, just as I had no choice with Joan. I will take them all in, all of them. I will pull them close to me. I will honor them, in the hope that they will return that honor by keeping my secrets silent, safe.

HENRY HAS BEEN more attentive and affectionate over the past month, but now he must leave Hampton for a meeting with the Privy Council, in London. It is the first time we will actually be apart since we were married. When I bid him good-bye there is a real urgency in my embrace. I know well when I am closest to sanctuary: when the king's big arms are wrapped around me. I need that safety now, more than ever.

"I hate to be away from my pretty bride, not for a day, not for a night," he murmurs in my ear. Did he say the same to Queen Anne, to Queen Jane?

"I will be here, thinking of you, waiting for your return." I kiss him on the cheek to assure him of this, and he laughs. He squeezes me affectionately, smoothing his hand over my hair. But his advisers are waiting, and the king must depart.

IT IS MIDNIGHT in the maidens' chamber. The ladies of Lambeth are all dressed in white nightgowns with ribbons in their hair. Katherine moves through the room lighting dozens of candles while the rest crowd onto Dorothy's bed and whisper excitedly.

There it is—the tap on the door. Malyn responds, ushering the young men in—Francis among them. Wine is poured, a bowl of strawberries set upon Dorothy's bed.

In the midst of the laughter, Lisbeth starts singing. She is seated upon her bed, the firelight behind her bright upon her golden spiral curls. Joan and Malyn begin to dance, their nightgowns whipping briskly around their exposed ankles, the linen thin with the firelight shining behind them. The men applaud their efforts, lifting their goblets of wine in a toast.

"It's your turn, Catherine," Lisbeth says, smiling. "Francis is here to dance with you."

All eyes turn to look at me, and I look down at myself. I'm not dressed in a white nightgown. I'm dressed in the gown of gold I wore on my wedding day, the royal jewels around my neck.

"No," I tell her, "I can't. I don't belong here."

"Of course you do, Catherine." Lisbeth smiles. A young man sits behind her on the bed; he wraps his arms around her and kisses her upon the neck. She closes her eyes and begins her song, again.

"This is exactly where you belong, Catherine." Suddenly Francis is beside me, pulling me close to him. "You are my wife, after all. We are already married." He is pulling me over to the corner bed, the bed that we shared. I am fighting him, and all the other ladies are laughing.

I wake with a gasp. The room is dark: my chamber, in my royal apartments. It is late at night, a fire roaring in the hearth before me.

"Are you all right, my queen?" the ladies murmur. "You fell asleep."

"I am fine," I tell them, breathing deeply. "It was only a dream."

"Of course it was only a dream. You are safe here." A lady rests her hand upon mine and urges me to lean back upon the cushioned chair. I look up and meet her eyes: it is Lisbeth, smiling at me.

Now I remember. Yes, of course, I remember. They are here, already. The ladies of Lambeth are all here. I try to keep my expression clear, unaffected.

"Here," Lisbeth says, patting my hand, "this will calm you."

She closes her eyes and begins to sing. The song of the maidens' chamber. The song of my past. The other ladies smile, their eyes glossy in the low light.

———

IN THE KING'S ABSENCE, the circles of intimacy in my household have simultaneously grown in size and constricted tighter around me. The outer ring includes my older sister, content to work on her embroidery and not particularly interested in the game of court life going on right under her nose. In addition to Isabel are the others appointed to their posts by outside forces, including the pretty Mary Seymour, to whom I have been outwardly kind and generous, though I am careful to keep her hidden behind taller women when we walk, and choose dances that she struggles to master. The next, smaller circle consists of the senior matrons long acquainted with service in the queen's chamber—to a variety of different queens—who keep strict control over the younger maids.

The innermost circle, the maids of my privy chamber, now consists of the ladies of Lambeth, as well as my maid of honor, Lady Rochford. Joan, Lisbeth, Dorothy, Katherine, and Malyn smile at me sweetly and sometimes—I imagine—a bit knowingly, as if over an amusing secret. We link our arms on walks in the galleries and halls. They dine with me in my presence chamber, and perform the prettiest dances when the meal is done and the chamber is lit with candles.

Jane sleeps in my chamber with me, and the others sleep in the two adjoining rooms. These are the first faces I see in the morning, the first to know if I am feeling well or ill. I sit in a chair as they flutter around me, putting rings on my fingers and arranging my hair, tightening my corset stays until I can barely breathe. They accompany me to Mass. They are the first to tend to my needs and also the first to receive my gratitude, most often in the form of gifts. They will bathe and perfume me in preparation for my nights with the king, and will be the first to know if my blood has arrived, or if the sheets upon my bed require changing. They will be the first to know if I sleep alone at night, or if I sleep at all.

Wherever I walk, they follow in a sumptuously dressed, obedient flock, like the feathers of a peacock's tail, sometimes crowding in a neat crescent behind me when I linger before a painting in the hall, other times at a safe distance as I talk to the Duke of Norfolk, to offer the illusion of privacy. But this is certainly an illusion; just because they do not speak does not render them incapable of hearing.

"You surround yourself with mere children, Your Grace, you must know that," Lady Edgecombe informs me. "If not for Lady Rochford, I know not how this household would run."

"They are not children," I inform her, carefully. "Just yesterday you praised Mistress Lisbeth for her dancing, and Mistress Malyn for her embroidery."

"They are inexperienced in the ways of court, and I fear will be of little help to you."

"They are a comfort to me," I answer her, and smile. And she believes me. We all play our roles very convincingly.

"I REGRET TO INFORM YOU, Your Majesty," Lisbeth intones, her bright green eyes fixated on her reflection in the mirror as she arranges her golden curls, "but I'm afraid your household is dreadfully dull."

"Lisbeth! Watch yourself," Joan reprimands, but I know better than to act a haughty queen to Lisbeth.

"Does a life of luxurious propriety not suit you?" I inquire.

"No, and I don't think it suits you either. Embroidering altar cloths, Catherine? Are you Queen Jane, all of a sudden?"

Her words sting me.

"Oh, don't be so cruel to her, Lisbeth. Show some respect to your queen!" Katherine cajoles, but it is partly in mockery—whether of Lisbeth or of me, I cannot decipher.

"You cannot tell me that you admire the prim, pious, permissive perfection of the jewel of the Seymour clan?"

"It's certainly not the fun that Anne had at court," Dorothy adds, her voice low. At this remark, their eyes dart toward one another, wary smiles playing at the corners of their mouths, eager for my reaction.

"I think it best not to partake in the type of fun Anne had at court, for it was all short lived," I say, my voice an imitation of the duchess's stern tone. But I soften it with my own smile. "Still, your comments are duly noted."

The ghosts of my past are now flesh and blood in my privy chamber, holding my hand and plaiting my hair and turning the coverlets down on my bed. How does one please a ghost? How does one keep the past from haunting the present?

To the delight of the newest members of my household, I hold a Saint Valentine's celebration in my presence chamber. I invite a host of musicians, and the ladies practice their newest dances before an audience of young male courtiers. The unwed ladies write their names on billets; with eyes closed, the young lords draw the name of their partner for the evening, pinning her name to their sleeves. The night is spent dancing in pairs, drinking wine in the secluded darkness of the chamber. The candlelight flickers; the woven faces of lords and ladies peer from the tapestries, spying on the unfolding scene.

I would never have dared to indulge in such an event in the king's presence, but the happiness of my ladies is integral to me, now. They know too much about me. I need to know what makes them content in order to ensure their loyalty. At the very least, I can remove myself from the flirtation and play the serene monarch, surveying all assembled. Luckily, there is no one here to tempt me otherwise—he has accompanied the king, a dutiful servant.

I know well what makes these ladies happy: they flirt candidly with young lords, and then challenge one another to execute the most difficult new dances before an enraptured audience. The courtiers are clearly enthralled by these new additions to my household, and enthusiastically applaud their efforts. I prefer to stay seated, denying my feet their urge to join in the dance. In spite of the fine music and noble company, the entire evening strikes me as frighteningly, obscenely reminiscent of our late-night parties in the maidens' chamber.

"A lovely turn, lovely!" the lords cry at the end of their performance.

"Our queen is most gracious, to prepare such an entertainment for her household." A young courtier bows reverently before me.

"Our queen loves nothing more than to be entertained," Lady Edgecombe remarks, her eyes cast down to her embroidery. She clearly does not approve of my inviting male courtiers to my chamber, but what could possibly happen with her, and other senior ladies of the household, present?

"I suppose you would only approve if I spent my days and nights stitching shirts for the poor," I comment. "But why must I devote my time to such things if I have a lady such as you to do it for me?"

The ladies of Lambeth laugh loudest at this; Lady Edgecombe purses her lips.

"Our Queen Catherine is a romantic, a dreamer," pronounces another of my pretended swains, "and I have just the gift for her:

" 'The flaming sighs that boil within my breast,
Sometime break forth, and they can well declare
The heart's unrest, and how that it doth fare,
The pain thereof, the grief, and all the rest.' "

"Oh, how beautiful. Did you write that?"

"I am afraid I have no talent such as this. It is a poem by Sir Thomas Wyatt which I share with my fair queen."

"Sir Thomas—I shall invite him to court! I would love to have a true poet nearby, to recite to me his verses."

"Then you'd best choose another poet," Katherine sniffs, "for Wyatt's in the Tower again."

"Whatever for?"

"Treason—a religious matter, of course," Joan remarks. "They think he's a Lutheran."

"It's more than that," Lisbeth says slyly. "The king's been against Wyatt for a long time, regardless of his religion."

"What do you mean?" I ask, but Lisbeth offers only her sultry smile.

The young lord bows his head humbly. "If you do not think it impropriety, my queen, I will explain: the heart's unrest Sir Thomas suffers in his poem was due to his affection, years ago, for a certain Lady Anne."

"Oh, I see."

Another young man smitten with Anne's love spells. It makes me sorry for him, to have lost years of his life in the Tower for a woman not worthy of such pure feeling, such beautifully written sentiment.

"You should free him, Catherine," Malyn urges dreamily. "Petition the king and free the poet. Oh, wouldn't that be romantic?"

"Yes, Catherine—free the poet!" Lisbeth announces, her hand resting on her paramour's shoulder. "That would make all of your ladies happy. And you do want us happy, don't you?"

I choose to ignore the underlying threat in Lisbeth's voice. I request the words of the poem to be written out for me. I can only wonder what Sir Thomas might write for me, if I were to see him freed from his imprisonment. This would be a greater work than any altar cloth, surely. Perhaps taking up the cause of a poet might prove I am more than the silly girl some courtiers still presume me to be.

XXIV

"You had best calm the celebrations in your chambers, Catherine," the duchess informs me. Nothing stays secret from the duchess long. "The court has begun to gossip about raucous parties in the queen's chambers. Must I remind you that you are not a maiden anymore? You are a queen, and must attempt to behave as one."

"It has nothing to do with me," I say, bitter at her eagerness to scold me. "It has to do with Lisbeth, and the others. I have to entertain them, make them loyal to me."

"You cannot indulge their every whim. You know well the type of fun your ladies enjoy. Are you going to re-create Lambeth for them, here? You are a queen, Catherine, not a blasphemous, wanton child."

"I don't see what else I can do—I have to keep them happy. I have to keep everyone happy!"

The duchess folds her hands primly over her gray silk, motionless as a statue; her face is hard, as if sculpted from cold marble.

"You've made a fine mess of things now, haven't you?"

I turn on her, livid. "You told me to welcome them to my household!"

"I told you that because it was your only alternative. Now these girls—this pack of wolves—have infested your privy chamber. And now they'll have you do their bidding, indulging their every fantasy, however inappropriate. You are queen, you cannot let them make you their slave."

I am already your slave, I want to tell her, but I wouldn't dare.

"You have opposition here, Catherine. People are watching you, waiting for you to make a mistake. You do realize that, don't you?"

"Yes, of course I do."

"The Seymour family, and anyone with heretical tendencies, would be eager to remove a Catholic queen from the throne by whatever means—especially before you've produced an heir."

An heir, an heir . . . why is it the one thing which I haven't yet accomplished is the most vital, even after all I've achieved? Still, I'm relieved when the duchess doesn't mention anyone else—those pale blue eyes I saw peering out of the devil mask at Twelfth Night. I must have been mistaken. I can't mention it, for saying it aloud would make it too real.

"You look tired, Catherine." The duchess sighs. "That won't do. The king is returning tomorrow, and it's imperative that you look your best." She confers with Jane about preparing a bath for me, but the thought of submitting myself to their insistent scrubbing and vicious comb makes me want to slump to my knees in weariness.

"I am tired," I blurt, suddenly near tears. "It's wearying, having all of these people to please, not knowing what they might do or say against me."

The duchess moves forward. For a moment I consider trying to embrace her, but as much as I may desire it, it is impossible; the duchess is unyielding. She grasps me by the arms and shakes me so vigorously that I gasp in fear.

"This is all your own doing, because you acted a child and a whore and spread your legs for some boy to enter you, with a whole host of women witness to your sin. You ruined yourself, Catherine." With one last shake she thrusts me upon the bed.

"You are still a child, but we found you a way to the throne of England. Now your past has come back to haunt you, as dark pasts generally do. And now we all must be wary of what messes you've made. I'll not be bothered with pity for you."

WHEN HENRY RETURNS, I fall into his embrace without reservation.

"I've missed you, my lord."

"Ah, Catherine, how I have missed you."

Will he detect the change in my household, the change in me? He holds my hand during the banquet to celebrate his return, and we watch the ladies dance. As the music ends, Lisbeth flashes me a daring smile and a wink, just as she did years ago before adjourning to her bed with her latest lover. The sight of that lascivious smile here in the hall, with the king at my side, is yet another alarming reminder of what my life has become.

In light of all of this, I think I could benefit from some additional popularity and appreciation from my courtiers.

"He has been missed at court," I say sweetly, pretending innocence of the reasons underlying Thomas Wyatt's imprisonment. I have calculated just the right moment to bring this petition before the king: we are lounging privately in his chamber, and I am arrayed in rich wine-colored velvet that lends a heightened color to my cheeks.

"He is an unworthy man for court," Henry growls. I dare to laugh lightly at this, and he shoots me a dark look.

"You don't understand why I value such a poet, Henry. Please, let me explain it as well as I can." I slide closer to him and take his hand in mine, my cheeks warm and blushing and my eyelids fluttering. Very effective. "You are a poet, Henry. Just like Sir Thomas. You have poetry in your head all the time, but your wife has no head for letters."

He opens his mouth to disagree but I press on, smiling bashfully.

"But I crave poetry, all the same. Release him, and you will be offering poetry to those who have no gift for it themselves."

Through Henry's sigh, I can hear a hint of resignation.

"Let's talk no more of it tonight," I tell him, pressing myself close to his arm. "I missed you when you were gone. I'm glad that you are here now, with me."

I KNEW I HAD HIM, and I was right: all it took was my earnest pleading, then flirtation and indulging the king's sexual desires. The king's resolve against Wyatt gradually softened, and he was released in the middle of this month. Henry enjoys indulging my whims, and the decision has met with great approval at court.

"My sweet, compassionate wife," he says, embracing me as we enter the hall for dinner, "nothing gives me more pleasure than to make you happy."

I've also arranged other releases: old-maid Helen Page and my own cousin John Legh had been imprisoned for petty crimes. I am indeed a caring and generous mistress, and no one can dare say otherwise. It is only late February and yet everyone seems so cheerful you would think that spring had already begun. I bask in a special approval from Henry, and all the rest of the court. The surge of appreciation and popularity reflects upon Henry as well; it comes at a good time, distracting people from news of unrest up north.

Meanwhile, the plight of yet another prisoner has come to my attention: Margaret Pole, the Countess of Salisbury, has spent years locked in a cold cell in the Tower. She's at least seventy years old and has been nothing but a devoted servant to the king; it is her family that is the problem. Pole is the last of the Plantagenets, who also have a claim to the throne—one that supersedes the Tudor claim, though few are bold enough to state it. The king has long feared that the countess's son, Cardinal Pole, may use his own mother to usurp the throne. After refusing to support the king's divorce from Katherine of Aragon, Cardinal Pole fled England and the king imprisoned his mother so no one could use her as a pawn for power.

This woman is a victim of the ambitions of her own family, imprisoned for sins she has not committed. The king often fears the wrath of God—I cannot imagine that God will look kindly upon a king who has locked up an old woman and left her to rot. If I could see the release of the countess, that would be a queenly act above all others.

I broach the subject first as merely an act of basic kindness and charity: to clothe an old woman properly for the coming winter. Henry softens at this meek appeal, and allows me to request a list of garments be made for the countess and delivered to her cell: a wool kirtle, a satin nightgown, a furred petticoat, a warm cloak, and four pairs of wool hose, all paid for—with the king's permission—from my own purse. But is this really enough? What if I could do more, and save this woman from suffering? If I could secure her freedom, I would be looked at differently by all of court, and might gain some much-needed respect.

"She is an old woman, Henry," I prod, carefully. We're seated before the fire in Henry's chambers, the firelight flickering in random patterns upon the carved wooden walls. I know when my ability to charm the king is at its height: alone, together, by candlelight, wearing a gown with a low, square neckline.

"Her imprisonment is a king's concern, Catherine."

"I know, you are right. But the plight of one so lowly as the countess is also God's concern."

"Do not lecture me, wife." His blue eyes flash at mine— it's clear that I've lost already. So quickly. Perhaps I had no hope of winning at all.

"Would you like to hear some music, my husband?"

And so I am the simpering maid, again, the pretty plaything. It seems the only permanent role my husband desires for me to play.

XXV

I sit before the fire in the dining hall to await the king's arrival at dinner. It is a beautiful day out, cold but bright. I hope that a hard ride might ease his troubles, for I've heard the king is angered by more rumors of rebellion in the north. The people there consider themselves devout Catholics, and have rumbled their dissent ever since the king separated from the pope in Rome and put himself at the head of the Church of England. There have been reports that the rebels intend to start a war as soon as the weather warms enough for battle.

What succor can I offer a king who faces an uprising of his own people? I do all that I know how to do, taking extra care in preparing myself for our dinner.

But instead of my king, a comparatively tiny page appears.

"His Majesty is attending to affairs of state today, and regrets that he cannot dine with his queen."

I open my mouth to ask when the king will be free from his duties, but after another bow the page quickly disappears. I'm struck by the harsh succinctness of the message—not the usual words that Henry would send to his beloved. Is he angry with me? Has he simply forgotten me? My cheeks burn with fear at the thought.

AFTER DINNER WITHOUT my king, I learn that there is to be no banquet for tonight's Shrovetide festival, usually a night of great feasting and dancing before the days of Lent.

"Had the king told you anything, Catherine?" Lisbeth laments. "Wouldn't he have told you if he wasn't planning a banquet, or a masque?"

It is dangerous to guess the mind of a king, I want to tell her, but I know that I cannot. The sight of Lisbeth's pout makes me boil with anger. She is a nothing but a selfish child, and now I must contend with her disappointment when I have far more important things on my mind.

"Then we will have to celebrate tonight in your chambers," Katherine remarks. It is all a game to them, all of this. "Don't you agree, my queen?"

A small group of lords dine in my presence chamber, to the delight of my ladies. All of the courtiers smile and greet me graciously, and the musicians do well to impress me with their talents, but I can see what lingers behind every smile, every pretty word: they are wondering what is wrong with Henry, why the king is not presiding over a grand feast, seated beside his queen. I try my best to smile so as not to let on that I know as little as they do.

———

As the ladies ready me for bed, I listen only vaguely to their steady stream of chatter. It is a lost day, and I feel likewise lost. When Jane enters my chamber looking anxious and pale, I wave my hand to dismiss the others. They remove themselves quietly and close the door behind them.

"Jane, what is happening?" I clasp her hand in mine and pull her close.

"I spoke with your cousin." She squeezes my fingers. "This information is from him: the king is dreadfully ill."

"What is wrong with him?"

"It is the ulcer on his leg that pained him all during Christmas. This time it has closed over completely, causing a dangerous imbalance of bad humors. He was raving this morning like a madman, and then turned black in the face."

"Raving? What about?"

"That he has an unhappy people to govern—a people he will shortly make so poor that they will have neither the boldness nor the power to oppose him."

"The northern rebellion." I sigh, somewhat relieved.

"There is more—he's blamed the Privy Council for the execution of Cromwell, saying they used false accusations to persuade him to execute the most faithful servant he ever had."

A coldness settles deep inside of me, a freezing of the soul: the king could regret such an action, a decision of life and death?

"This is dangerous talk, Jane."

"Indeed, and since then it has become worse. As of this evening, the king has been altogether unable to speak."

"The king is ill, and speechless? Do they know how to cure him?"

"They fear for his life, Catherine. And I fear for yours."

"For mine?" I let my gaze break from her intense stare.

"There has been talk of poison, my queen. And if he has been poisoned, there are those who will blame you."

"Me? Why would I dare such a thing? How would it benefit me?"

"A dowager queen is afforded a great deal of luxury and honor, if not power. And if you were already with child—"

"What does Thomas say? Does he fear for the king's life?"

"It is hard not to fear for it, to see him in such a state. You must be careful, Catherine." I see her eyes glance down toward my belly in my white gown. Though small, it is round—the same roundness I've always had, though perhaps a bit magnified from all of my indulging on rich food and drink. But I know well that no infant prince resides there. I move beneath the covers to conceal myself from her gaze.

"I will see the king tomorrow," I say calmly. "I will see him and make my own judgment. Thank you for this information, Jane."

I squeeze her hand and bid her good night. I lie in bed wide awake, watching the flames slowly die in the hearth. When they are burned to cinder and ash, I shiver, nestling deeper beneath the covers, searching for comfort and sleep.

SEVERAL GOWNS LIE discarded upon the bed—this one too garish, this one too somber. It's important that I choose the right one. It is the only thing over which I have any control.

"The dark red sarcenet," I announce, twisting my petticoat around my hips and stepping into the waiting gown.
In the mirror I look bright and warm and cheerful. I don't
look like a woman going to visit her elderly, ill husband. But
I am.

"I would like to see the king," I inform the guards at the
king's apartments. One of them opens the door, but does not
bid me enter.

"I am sorry that the king cannot see you at this time, my
queen." His obeisance is effusive, pandering.

"Does the king not wish to see me, or is he unable?"

"He is dealing with important matters of state which I am
afraid must be catered to immediately. I assure you that he
longs to be by your side."

I look past the guard's elbow and spy the other men
standing in the distance. One is tall and thin, wearing a
dark blue cape. He turns to the door just as I look and I see
a familiar face: I think it is Edward Seymour, the brother of
the late Queen Jane. The guard closes the door farther, so
that only his face is visible in the crevice.

"I am more than willing to wait, if that would please the
king. I would be most grateful to see him, if only for a short
walk within the palace." I smile thoughtfully up at him, daring him to add to his lie. How dare this mere guard lie to
me, the king's chosen?

"I'm afraid that he will be unable to do so at this moment,
but we will call upon you as soon as he is available."

I think it best for now to hide what I know. I walk back
to my chambers, the quilted sarcenet rustling against my
legs like a thousand whispers.

———

"IT HAS BEEN three days," I whisper to the duchess, my eyes blurring until I cannot see the cards in my hand. "I have heard nothing. They will not let me see him. And I think I saw that Seymour brother in his chamber."

"Edward Seymour?"

"Yes. Why should he be allowed entrance, and the king's own wife be barred?"

"He must have an ally within the king's chamber. He is a Seymour, Catherine. And some say a Lutheran," she hisses, "and therefore an enemy of yours. Tell me—is there any possibility that you are you with child?"

The duchess must know the truth of this; she intently scruntinizes the calendar of my bodily functions. I feel as if she's daring me to lie, to see if I can manage to do so effectively. I look around, carefully; we are alone in this corner, but I'm wary of how close the other ladies are, seated with their embroidery or chatting by the fire.

"No—don't answer that," she says, as soon as I open my mouth to speak. Her eyes flutter away from mine. "You could be; it's too early to know. There is always the possibility."

But there is no possibility. I think to explain the fatigue the king often suffers, preventing him from visiting my chamber, but I remember how such words damned Queen Anne. I press my fingers to my lips, afraid of what may escape.

SIX DAYS. No word.

"I must speak to him myself," I whisper to Lady Rochford, before the others descend upon my bedchamber to ready me for the day.

"But they've barred his chamber, Catherine. If I knew how to get you in, I would tell you—"

"No, not the king. I need information."

She nods slightly. Pursing her lips in resolve, she quietly absents herself as the others arrive to dress me in green brocade.

AFTER SUPPER I don a fur cloak over my gown and Jane and I take to the garden for a late-night stroll. Jane leads me to a particular secluded corner, where a cloaked figure awaits in the shadows. When he turns, Thomas starts as though in fear at the sight of my face. As I approach I can't help but notice how pale he is, his face drawn and tired.

"Thomas, tell me what's happening."

"I've wanted to tell you, but they've told me to keep it secret. By this time all of court knows he is ill."

"How ill? How did this happen?"

"He is *very* ill, Catherine." His dark eyes wince in fear at these words. "He may be dying. I know it's treason to say so about a king, but I think little of treason when it may well be true."

I step back and lean against a hedge, my breath suddenly short. Thomas moves closer, his voice barely a whisper, his head lowered over mine.

"He has not spoken for days, as if struck dumb in some way. I asked him if he would like you to visit and he reacted violently, as though driven mad by pain. I think he is embarrassed. We all know how he has endeavored to hide his weakness from you."

"But if he is dying, will no one tell me? Am I to learn of my husband's death along with all the rest of the court?"

Thomas shakes his head.

"Did someone do this to him?"

"I do not know that, there is no way to know until it's over. But there are those eager for the king to die so that young Edward can take the throne."

"Prince Edward is only a child."

"Yes, but a lord protector would be appointed. That is where the true power would lie."

Edward Seymour—if he were lord protector with little more than a babe upon the throne, then he would, by proxy, become King of England. I shudder at the thought of Henry being surrounded by those who wish him ill. The power of a king puts poison in men's hearts, and I'm afraid of that same poison attacking me. *If only I were pregnant!* They would not dare harm a queen who harbors an heir to the throne in her womb! But I'm not pregnant, and the king is unable . . .

If only Thomas could do this for me. The thought shoots through me like a bolt of lightning; everything seems too sharp, too bold all of a sudden. I fear I may faint.

"You must be very careful, Catherine," Thomas whispers, his voice hoarse with urgency. "You must be careful of who surrounds you, who listens to your conversations. There are spies all around—please, promise me that you will guard yourself." Thomas grasps my hand; the feel of his touch sends a shock through me, but I dare not shake him off. His warm hand enveloping mine makes me feel safe, if only for a moment. "It would pain me if you were hurt, in any way." I need not look into his eyes to know that this is true.

Jane and I depart, arm in arm, my hood concealing my hair and face.

"Is it a fine night out, Your Majesty?" Lisbeth asks cheerfully as we enter my chamber.

"Quite cool, but fine indeed. I can smell the coming of spring."

The ladies giggle happily at this. Life is a masque, and I must play my part well. Katherine pulls off my cloak and Lisbeth tugs at the stays of my corset to ready me for bed. Joan pulls the curtains back from my bed and turns down the bedclothes. As a nightgown is pulled over my head, I hear a shriek.

I struggle to force my head through the neck of the gown, eager to see what all the gasping is about. I walk over to where Joan stands beside my bed. Tucked under the bedclothes, an arrow lies upon the white sheets. Its sharp tip is covered in blood, staining the linen with a gruesome red smear. I reach out to remove it but Joan jerks me away.

"Catherine, no!"

Dorothy approaches the arrow instead, all the other girls looking on. She lifts it carefully and inspects the tip.

"Animal's blood, certainly," she says, "deer, most likely."

"Who would do such a thing?" Joan exclaims.

I can't help but look to Lisbeth and the rest of them, in search of the evidence of treachery. Their faces are pale with distress.

"Get rid of it," I say. "Just get rid of it. And there shall be no talk of it outside these chambers."

While Dorothy disposes of the arrow, Lady Rochford grasps me by the shoulders and looks deep into my eyes.

"We must be more careful with you, my queen. We must be always careful."

I nod, watching as the linens are promptly changed. I feel uneasy settling into bed where the arrow rested its bloody head just moments ago. There are such things as signs and omens, and people often claim to see them: mystical things, of course. This was not a mystical vision but a savage, intentional act. I fear it is an omen, nonetheless.

XXVI It has been seven days now since the king's illness began. For the last three days I've stayed veritably hidden from the eyes of the court. My ladies deem it safer for me to take my meals in my own chambers while the king is sequestered in his. Every day I watch as Lady Rochford tastes my food before permitting me to eat. I'm considering asking the other ladies to do so as well, as a test of their loyalty to me.

In spite of the lively fire and the feast laid before me, my feeling of imprisonment in the gilded cage of queenship is now more palpable than ever before.

The duchess visits, ostensibly to cheer me, but her news is grave. Henry suffers visibly, and has yet to regain the power of speech. Numerous physicians have prescribed a variety of cures, but little change has been made in his condition.

"I spoke to Jane," she murmurs lightly, hovering over our gaming table. "She has told me that your monthly blood has just ended."

"Only Jane knows, I made sure to keep it secret."

"If the king were well, this would be the perfect time for you to be made pregnant. There are already rumors that you are with child."

"There are always such rumors. Would that they were true."

"It is imperative that they be true." Her steely eyes penetrate mine. "There have been other rumors, you know—rumors that the king is concerned that you are barren, unable to have children. The king cannot wait forever," she says grimly. "Catherine, your life is at stake."

"What am I to do?" I feel myself on the verge of panic. "What can I do, if he is ill and not able to bed me?"

"There are those who do not want a Catholic queen, you understand. Not even a Catholic dowager."

"I know that."

"Perhaps you would do best to think of yourself, think of your future, and put thoughts of the king aside, for now. He cannot help you now—he cannot even help himself. You are in dire need of a royal heir, in order to protect yourself with the king's power in the event of his—" Her voice drops, barely audible. ". . . that he does not recover."

"What are you suggesting? Any lie I tell of a pregnancy will be discovered soon enough."

The duchess thumbs through her cards quietly. We turn back to our game, but I can't concentrate, my thoughts swimming so erratically that I can't see the cards before my face.

"There are those you can trust to help you, Catherine."

"I don't know who I can trust."

"You can trust me, and Jane. And you can trust your cousin Thomas. We will all assist you if you decide to take action."

"Take action," I murmur, the meaning of the words unclear.

"On your own behalf," the duchess answers. "You may

need to act on your own behalf to protect yourself. There are many jealous of your ascension to the throne."

"Yes, I know."

"And they will do whatever they can to uproot you. The Reformation party considers you an instrument of Satan—I have seen those very words printed in their religious tracts. They fear your influence on the king."

"I never talk of religion with the king." I think of the bloody arrow upon my bed; I can feel it pressed against my spine.

"It is not only about you, but the entire Howard family. There are many eager to tumble those of us who have climbed so high."

I have climbed very high, indeed: suddenly I feel as if I'm standing on the edge of a giant precipice, looking down.

"That is true," I tell her. "I know it is true."

"Then you must be with child, Catherine. That is the only way you can be safe. With a child in your womb, no one will dare threaten you. It is the only way."

Suddenly I feel as if I've tipped forward off the precipice, the cold wind rushing by my face.

"What are you suggesting?"

"You know what I'm suggesting—no doubt you've already thought of it yourself."

I flutter my eyes away from hers, an unwitting admission.

"Take action on your own behalf," she says succinctly, and leaves it at that. She wants me to betray my king, my husband. Are things that dire already, that she would suggest an act of treason?

TONIGHT, THE DUCHESS visits my privy chamber as Lady Rochford prepares me for sleep. All of the other ladies have been sent to bed. The duchess places the book upon my dressing table, crushing a silk handkerchief beneath its weight.

"It's been ten days since the king's illness began, and still you do nothing?" she asks sternly.

"Do nothing? What am I to do?" But the moment I say it, I regret my words. The duchess points to tomorrow's date on the calendar.

"Tomorrow, a perfect opportunity for you to become pregnant."

"I can't do it," I say, breathless, rising from my chair. "Do you know what you're suggesting? If discovered, it would be the death of me!"

"It could be the death of you, regardless!" the duchess declares. "This all has little to do with you, Catherine, this has to do with power, with the family. I gave you the choice to act on your own behalf. I thought you would jump at the chance to bed your darling Thomas, considering the type of girl you are. But you didn't, so I'm taking away your choice—I'm telling you to do this. The decision has been made for you."

"You are telling me to commit adultery, and heresy. You would tell your own flesh and blood to do such a thing?"

"You are little more than flesh and blood. You are the vessel by which the Howards lay claim to the greatest power we can wield."

"If it has so little to do with me, then I wish you had chosen a different vessel, a different pawn to use in your game!"

"Don't you think I would have claimed it for myself if I could?" The duchess's voice is sharp, her gray eyes shining wet in a way I've never seen before. "Don't you think

I wanted it to be me? Or that Norfolk, or any other of the Howard clan would want to be where you are now, at the king's side?"

"Then why didn't you, if you were so crafty to get him to fall in love with me? Why didn't you do it for yourself?"

"We knew we couldn't. With this king, we know the best way to get close to him is to get one of our pretty young things in his bed. So we created you, we told him all about you, told him exactly what he wanted to hear, and he fell in love with all of our words. He took you and made you his wife, the potential mother of his sons, his heirs."

"I didn't ask for you to create me, if that's what you did. I asked for none of this, and yet I'm made to suffer for it. It isn't fair!"

"You are right, it isn't fair. No. It isn't. You always go on about what is fair and what is not—you, dressed in velvet and furs, seated beneath the cloth of state with the royal jewels around your neck, dining beside the king with all of court bent in half at your feet. You get all of this, and you are nothing. You are a child."

Her eyes widen, as if taking me all in. I wish that she wouldn't look at me that way, with that pain so vivid in her eyes. I don't know whether I want to embrace her or run and hide.

"I've dreamed for years of sitting there, as queen," she says, her voice hoarse. "It was my only dream. But I was never pretty enough to do it, to catch his eye. Now I'm barren and no good to anyone."

I look away, knocked sideways by the anguish in her voice. She puts her hand on my shoulder and pulls, making me face her.

"The king needed a vital young maiden. Now the king needs sons, more than he ever did before. Do your duty, Catherine, and give the king what he needs."

"What about the baby, if there is one?" I gasp, breathless. "What if it—it doesn't look like—"

"You have reddish hair, yourself. Not completely unlike the Tudor red." She strokes my hair with delicate fingers, her voice softened. "Remember, Catherine: the Tudors stole the throne from the Plantagenets to begin with. We must be practical and work with what we have. You have bigger things to worry about right now than the shade of downy hair on the head of a babe."

I look up at her. She smiles, faintly, her hand resting upon my shoulder.

"Once it's done, it will be done, and you will be safe."

The duchess pulls me into her arms. I whimper for a moment, but she does not reprimand me. She has given me so much I never asked for, and yet this is all that I have ever wanted from her. I wrap my trembling arms around her, knowing the moment will not last long, and likely will not happen again.

Now I know what must happen: I will do as I've been told.

I DREAM OF visiting the lion encaged in Henry's menagerie. It is twilight in the dream, and the lion's eyes sparkle like stars from the darkness of the cage. Suddenly there is no cage; the bars separating us have vanished.

Now I've got the best of him. Henry's voice echoes in my ears, but the lion and I are alone. He is gaunt, his glorious mane falling from his head in tufts. But I'm held captive by the wild gleam in his eyes. His nose twitches, the sinews of his legs taut and ready to spring. He can smell me, smell the blood and bones and meat of me. He is hungry. His golden eyes spark like flames in the darkness.

What will become of you? I ask the lion. *What will become of me?*

Between our eyes there is a kinship, an understanding. I know that he wants to devour me alive. I have felt this before: everyone's eyes upon me, my name whispered upon everyone's lips. Everyone fit to devour me, destroy me.

What will become of me? I ask again. The lion pounces.

I sit bolt upright in bed, gasping as if someone were pushing the breath from my body.

I SIT IN THE DARKNESS of a secluded chamber, shivering beneath my dark cloak. It is midnight, and Jane should be here shortly. She will bring Thomas, and then she will leave the two of us alone. It has all been arranged.

Earlier this afternoon I took a somber turn around the palace with my ladies, passing by hallways filled with whispering courtiers who turned and offered deference as I passed. I wanted them all to see me in my sober blue gown, my eyes worn and red. I wanted them to see the gentle swell of my belly in this too-small stomacher, just enough to confirm the rumors already so rampant among them.

Tonight it will happen. The decision has been made for me; it was never my decision to make to begin with. There are no such things as my own motives or desires. My womb is the future of England. My actions are the voice through which the ambition of the Howard family sings. I only hope that it works.

I sit quietly, taking even, measured breaths. I wear a silk nightgown beneath this cloak, my skin scented with rose oil. Tonight has a dual purpose in my heart, in spite of my fear. After tonight, my curiosity will be sated. I can be rid of this love-haunting, once and for all.

The door to the chamber opens and closes briskly. I can see nothing in the darkness, but I feel Jane's hands grasping my own. She is wheezing frightfully, as if she has run a great distance.

"Jane, what is it? What is wrong?"

"He spoke," she utters between gasps. "He spoke."

"What happened?"

"It's the king, Catherine. He has spoken, he has come out of his fever. They say he will live. I must put you back to bed, again."

"Is anyone awake? Do they know that he is well?"

"No, I heard of it from Thomas. Thomas was the first to hear him speak."

As Jane pulls me into the dark hallway toward my chamber, a bleak heaviness settles inside of me, weighing me down. It grows larger and darker with every step I take.

XXVII When I next see Henry it is for a private dinner in his chambers. As soon as I enter, I rush toward him, as if to leap into his embrace. But I halt just in time—such an aggressive show of affection may have a negative effect upon him. I hold back, and bow instead. He grasps my hand and pulls me up to face him, smiling sheepishly.

"I'm sorry not to have been well enough to visit you as of late," he tells me, caressing the side of my face. Though he smiles, I can sense his embarrassment in the way he blinks his eyes.

"Do not apologize, my lord." I press my lips firmly to his ringed hand, my eyes now burning with tears. "I am only glad that you are with me, now."

"Come, sit," he says, urging me into a seat before the fire. I entertain him with my usual chatter, trying to keep the conversation bright and lively.

"It will be spring soon, Henry," I say, breathless with excitement. "Perhaps we shall plan a masque later this month, to celebrate."

He smiles at this, but a bit wanly, and sips at his wine.

"Whatever pleases you, my love." He smiles, the ever-indulgent husband.

With these words, he waves his fingers slightly. A groom hurries over and begins adjusting the cushions that support the king's back in his chair. Henry looks away from me, his eyes lingering on the fire in the hearth. I sit dumbly in my pink dress the color of a rose petal. Fool I am! I thought that this would cheer him, the blushing color and low neckline reminding him of the passions we shared months ago. Instead I am a cruel reminder of the youth he once had, the vigor he tried to reclaim, and lost again. I worry that it pains him to look at me.

I bid him an affectionate good-bye. I know that he will not visit my bedchamber tonight. He is not well enough. I wonder how long—how long I will wait.

"I love you, my husband," I whisper in his ear, my arms draped around his great shoulders as he remains seated in his chair. He strokes my hair and back lovingly, but does not sweep me into his lap as he was wont to do.

"And I love you, my dear wife. I shall see you tomorrow for dinner."

I must not tarry; Henry is clearly tired and needs his rest. And there are tears burning like fire behind my eyes. I dare not think of why they are so desperate to be released.

"I look forward to it." I smile brightly and bow out of the room.

But in the hallway, in my chamber, I can find no safe place in which to allow these tears their due. I hold them inside of me, a great roiling cloud of guilt and shame and fear.

EASTER MARKS THE first banquet after Henry's recovery, and it is a particularly joyous affair. I sit beside a smiling Henry, surveying the elegance of the courtiers on their best behavior, the renewed vigor of the minstrels and tumblers who perform for our entertainment. Henry's cheeks are pink with health, his eyes sparkling. Though he emits raucous peals of laughter over the antics of his favorite fool, sitting close to him I can see the strain in his brow, see the way he gingerly adjusts his weight upon his chair.

"Is there anything I can do for you, my lord?" I ask brightly, pretending not to notice the wince that flutters across his eyes.

"No, my love, you are doing quite a bit as it is. It does me well just to see you looking so pretty in your silk and pearls."

I smile and turn away, but in the corner of my eye I see Henry's hand rise slightly, his fingers twitch. He is calling a groom over to tend to him. He is calling—no, oh no, I must not look. I hide my face behind my goblet and drink, pretending not to notice Thomas standing beside the king, not to see his dark eyes glistening in the candlelit hall.

I must live with my treachery—it burns a hole inside of me, a flame that no amount of wine can abate, though I take a few more greedy gulps before setting down the goblet. It is not only what I planned to do with Thomas, I realize now, seated upon my throne before the eyes of all the court. No, it is even more than that. It is that some part of me, in spite of my fear, had dared become resigned to the king's death.

"Sweet Catherine," Henry says, his great hand warm upon my back. I turn, a brilliant smile on my face. Thomas is still standing next to him, but I stare determinedly into Henry's eyes. "I've thanked your cousin for looking after you."

I breathe, I smile. I don't know how to respond.

"Leave it to you Howards to all look out for each other. My, what a family you all are!" He turns to Thomas and laughs at this, and Thomas laughs with him.

IN SPITE OF the warmth of his gaze, the king's infirmities overrule his passions. Will I simply be stuck here in the midst of fear and danger without a way to create an heir and fulfill my role, waiting for whatever may happen to me when this old king dies? *No, no.* I mustn't think of such things. It's an abomination to think of such things, especially after what I nearly did.

I glance at the bed, the soft covers turned down to reveal the yielding mattress beneath. But this bed seems cold, lonely. Dreams pull at me with warm, tantalizing fingers— but no, I can't. Dreams nearly caught me, recently, nearly pulled me in with the tide and into the deep. It is dangerous to dream.

But what if there is more to love, and I am missing out on it? Little did I know, on the night of my first kiss with Thomas, that our love would be interrupted—that his kiss would hang, suspended, in the air over the garden, hovering over the flowers at midnight, hovering like a ghost over my bed. This type of love can be the most lingering, the most powerful, for there is no time in which to discover a single fault or flaw. It remains forever as one kiss: one solemn, perfect promise of the world.

Perhaps this is what happened to Henry, when he first saw me. Perhaps my image hovered over the royal bed that very night; a sweet and beguiling ghost, my voice haunting his dreams.

THE RAW COLD of winter has begun to thaw into a sparkling spring, and I'm glad of it. I've taken to heading straight to the stables after Mass and riding my silver mare hard over the pastures, her swift hooves soaring until I am nearly breathless. There is a lot inside of me that needs dampening, burying, and the pounding of the horse's hooves upon the cracked earth, the cold air burning my cheeks, and the pale sky over my head seem clean, pure. I make my mind as blank as the sky. I listen to my heartbeat. I listen to my breath. I do my best to think of nothing. By the time I dismount, my legs and back are aching, but the pain itself is a welcome distraction.

I see Henry in the afternoons, and his health has gradually improved. We take walks in the garden together, for his physicians agree that the sunshine will do much to improve his health. I watch the king, and I watch those around him. All of court looks different to me now, somehow both clearer and more confusing than it appeared when this year began. Henry is besieged by those who undoubtedly would do him ill if it would benefit them to do so. During dinner I see him conferring with Edward Seymour, and the sight of it nearly knocks the wind out of me. I scan the faces before us and imagine in each of them a unique self-interest, a unique abuse or destruction of our king in the name of God or family or the true church—whatever that church may be.

And I know, now, that I am no different from any of them.

PREPARATIONS FOR A progress to the northern regions have already begun, in an effort to suppress the potential rebellion before it begins. The king will journey farther north than he ever has in the course of his reign. In spite of his fear of dirt and disease, he will smile while shaking the grimy hands of his populace, their dirty lips pressed to his jeweled fingers. He will stand in the midst of the masses, sparkling and brilliant, like a god on earth, to inspire their devotion and impress upon them the magnitude of his power.

"I've seen them packing the finest gold plate and carved goblets," Dorothy remarks as she unlaces my corset to ready me for bed. "I've heard rumors that your coronation will take place in York."

I pretend not to hear this, and look up to admire my reflection in the mirror. I'm wearing the gold circlet Henry gifted to me recently, in honor of spring and the day of my birth. I am now sixteen years old. The circlet is studded with sapphires and diamonds, and seems to spark in the light of the fire. When the king placed it upon my head, I know we were both thinking about the day when I would wear the true crown.

"We have all heard such rumors."

"There could be nothing more pleasing for the king, certainly, to crown a queen clearly pregnant with a royal heir."

I do not respond, absorbed by the look of the jewels upon my fingers, but the bite of this remark is not lost on me.

"The people are unhappy with your husband, Catherine," Lisbeth remarks. "A coronation may be just the distraction they all need."

"What do you mean?" I ask, too curious to rebuke her. Lisbeth's eyes flash up to the mirror to meet mine.

"The Countess of Salisbury was executed this morning."

"No!" Katherine gasps. "She was an old woman!"

"An old woman not even allowed the benefit of a trial, only to be dispatched by a novice executioner."

"She was executed without trial?" Dorothy asks.

"The king signed a Bill of Attainder—it renders a sentence without need of a trial. And her sentence was death."

"Oh, Lisbeth, stop—it's too gruesome."

"Then shut your ears," Lisbeth snaps. "I think our queen has the right to hear it. It's the talk of all of court—all of England. It took three swings of the ax to do her in."

"Oh! How awful, Lisbeth!" Malyn wails. "Stop, don't tell us any more."

"I thought Her Majesty might want to hear the truth. You must be disappointed, Catherine, after all you did to try to save her."

"Indeed." I swallow. Now they can all see how little power I have over the king. "It is most unfortunate." *The king's will be done.*

There is a soft knock upon the door—Jane finally returned from her conference with the duchess—and Dorothy rushes to answer it. I break away from Lisbeth and move to the opened window, breathing in the smell of early honeysuckle. But the smell only fills me with a strange, familiar dread.

The door opens, but Jane isn't standing there. It is the king. The ladies drop to the floor in obeisance.

"You are dismissed," I tell them, turning to face Henry. They depart the room in silence, their eyes cast down.

"I wanted to tell you how beautiful you looked at dinner tonight, my love," he tells me, bringing my hand to his lips. "I regret that it has been so long since I have last visited you."

"I understand, my lord." My voice sounds different, far away, but Henry doesn't seem to notice.

"The progress is not as important—nor as pleasurable—as tending to you."

He leans forward and kisses me, his lips warm upon mine. We have not been intimate since his illness, and I yield to him with the warmth he always responds to. But I have already separated from myself, from my body. My mind is elsewhere, in a different spring, transported by a similar dread in the sweet smell of honeysuckle. It was during spring, near the time of my eleventh birthday, that I learned about Cousin Anne's execution and heard tales of her bravery moments before the sword. I always take for granted that spring is a time of rebirth, but perhaps this is not the case. Perhaps all the flower petals and perfume are merely a mask for death.

Like the sparkling jewels upon my husband's fingers, the fingers that pull this gown from my shoulders and caress my naked flesh.

XXVIII

The royal progress finally departs on the last day of June. At the beginning of our journey, torrential rain burst through the thick, humid air and bogged down our elaborate caravan. I wonder if Henry, gruff and irritable, speculated as to whether the brutal execution of an elderly woman could have inspired the rage of Our Lord in the form of weeks of rain.

We ventured out once the rain cleared, but progress was slow, coaches mired in the muddy roads. Now the sun is bright and the roads are dry, and we progress at a consistent pace in a long train winding up rough roads twisting through the wild, overgrown, virulent green of the northern region.

Dozens of wagons are stuffed with provisions, followed by guards on horseback in their dark green velvet livery. I ride on a magnificent white horse not far behind Henry's entourage. I am surrounded by my ladies, Lady Rochford and Joan riding on either side. Henry rides ahead surrounded by guards, advisers, and gentlemen of the privy chamber—Thomas among them. It seems as if all of court is traveling, except for the Privy Council, as well as Archbishop Cranmer and Sir Thomas Wriothesley, left behind to tend to matters in the king's absence.

Being away from the suffocation of court feels freeing; a brisk wind rushes over the sloping hills of green, blanketed here and there with banks of heather. Here, on horseback, I can avoid the gossiping courtiers at the edges of the group, who rail against the king's decision to summarily execute all prisoners in the Tower before our departure. It has proved an unpopular move at court, and has exposed the king's fear and weakness for all to see. But I avoid this talk. The incident only serves to remind me of the limits of my influence upon the king.

The sun is warm upon my back, the smell of summer sweet with a distant threat of rain sharpening the air. It fills my lungs and releases my tension in a way unachievable while cooped up in the luxurious claustrophobia of my chambers all winter. I am also full of hope: after weeks of consistent coupling, my blood is definitely delayed. I may finally grant Henry the one gift he most desires on this progress—the one gift that he would reward with a crown. I keep my mind focused on this thought when I catch a probing gaze from one of my ladies, or when I inhale a sharp whiff of some acrid smell—dread, fear, death. It is always swirling around us; I try not to notice it.

WE'VE FINALLY ARRIVED in Lincoln, where we offer the awaiting crowds a splendid visual feast. A mass of archers with drawn bows are the first to enter the town to a great thunder of applause. The sight is intended both to impress and intimidate: hundreds of archers and the king's men riding enormous horses dressed in green Tudor livery could easily be transformed from a court into a powerful army.

Next enter the dignitaries from the area, also dressed in their most formal robes. Finally Henry and I enter, with the honored members of court behind us garbed in cloth of gold and crimson velvet. I smile at the cheers showered upon us—there is no doubt in the minds of these people who their king is, though they have never seen Henry before. He is massive and imposing upon his magnificent horse, robed in green velvet, while I wear a gown of crimson trimmed with diamonds across the bodice. Both of us sparkle brightly in the summer sun, bedecked in jewels as befits our station.

As we wind slowly down the street to the sound of deafening applause, I see that the houses are hung with banners and flags, all emblazoned with the Tudor colors and the Tudor rose. I even spy banners with my own symbol of the rose crowned; my cheeks warm at the sound of their cheers.

"Long live the king! Long live the queen!"

I turn to Henry, who manages to fix his expression in a most regal fashion: flattered, pleased, but still maintaining the dignity of a king, not easily stunned by the love poured out by his subjects. This is the respect due to a king, after all. I smile at Henry, certain that the two of us create an impressive sight. He glances at me and smiles, lifting my hand to his lips for a kiss. The cheers of the crowd grow even louder.

"God bless King Henry and Queen Catherine!"

Never have I felt more a queen than in this moment. Is this how my coronation will be? I can imagine it here, in this magical place, starting with a processional down this very street. I will be held upon a litter, wearing a silver gown, or gold, or purple—I can't decide. I will be carried through the cheering throngs to the cathedral, where the crown will finally be set upon my copper head. The thought of such triumph makes me feel tingling and warm—it could all happen here. Then I could truly claim my victory over his previous wives, for Queen Katherine should never have been Henry's bride, Queen Jane never had a coronation, and Queen Anne won her crown through dark enchantments that clouded Henry's judgment. I will be a true queen, more so than the others had been.

Henry and I are immediately taken to a tent prepared for our arrival, where we change out of our velvet into more formal attire: Henry in a cloak and doublet of cloth of gold, I in a gown of silver, sparkling like a bright star. We set off again on horseback to the cathedral. Here, in the echoing chamber, we stand before the northern people, Henry tall and glorious and golden, I dainty in my delicate silver tissue gown. The priest swings incense over our heads in a filmy cloud before we both receive the sacrament. A Catholic king and queen, for all to see.

HENRY'S NORTHERN SUBJECTS are not like those at court: they are kind and reverent and bow respectfully before me, without the hint of a smirk upon their lips. After all, I am the only Queen of England any of them have seen.

Each evening, before the banqueting begins in the great hall, the loyal citizens of Lincoln are welcomed into the royal presence with a bounty of favors. I am glad that Henry is welcoming these people into his heart again. Even the rebels whose devotion has faltered are received by their sovereign; I watch as they bend prostrate and beg the king's forgiveness, offering gold and jewels to ensure his mercy. I stand beside Henry for all of this, but step back so as not to interfere with the full glory of His Majesty. The people—both loyal and disloyal—stand before him in awe.

Since our arrival, the entertainments each night have been raucous and the food bountiful. Over two hundred deer have been enclosed in the nearby forest, their capture offering daily sport and diversion for the king and his hunting party. Now their carcasses are piled by the smoking fires, and dozens of servants prepare them for our banquet. Great nets of silver, squirming fish and boatloads of river birds are hauled in for the royal feast, including swans whose limp white necks sag over the rough wooden tables.

Though the formality of court is imposed upon the wildness of our surroundings, the lush countryside makes the festivities feel less cloistered. Tonight, we dine and dance beneath the bright stars. I wear my cloth of silver gown and a mask studded with diamonds and pearls. Lisbeth,

Katherine, Joan, and I are all giggling and breathless after a particularly vigorous dance. The ladies leap back into the dance, but I wave to a servitor who speedily brings me a goblet of wine.

Hovering near the banqueting tables, I'm startled by sudden laughter. The young lords have been drinking all night; the effect of the wine is easy to hear. In the center of their riotous merriment a white swan flaps its enormous wings, feathers fluttering over the grass. The creatures had escaped earlier from the King's cooks, only to be injured now by these drunkards. A bloody gash mars the perfect whiteness of its neck.

"Oh, poor old Margaret Pole!" one lord hollers. "No amount of gold could have saved you, could it have?" The others howl in response. The bird staggers, wings flapping awkwardly; its eyes glisten, ink black.

"It took three chops for that old woman's head to roll," one lord states.

"I heard it took four."

"I heard she made the executioner chase her around the block!" Their laughter is like the wild baying of wolves.

"My queen." Thomas suddenly emerges from the crowd before me, his dark brows furrowed. He glances swiftly at the scene taking place behind me and discreetly offers his arm. "Come away from here, my queen."

I smile, but somehow I cannot command myself to speak. Thomas delivers me to the king, with whom I survey the celebratory dance from a regal distance. I smile, but my cheeks hurt, my mouth is dry.

Margaret Pole, an innocent old woman, was executed

upon the king's—my husband's—orders. Even knowing this, I enjoyed myself, I reveled in the honor and luxury of being queen. The shame of this makes me feel suddenly ill. I sway, slightly, catch myself on the king's massive arm for balance. He turns to me and smiles, pats my hand lovingly.

He is a murderer, but I must cleave to him. It is my duty, as his queen. It is my only hope for survival.

I glance across the mass of dancers to the host of drunken lords. For a moment I imagine I see a flash of red—a red-and-black devil's mask staring back at me. But I blink and the image is gone. It must be my mind, my fear playing tricks on me.

A MAN IN an executioner's mask wields a polished ax, its sharp edge bright in the sunlight. But just before he swings, the mask is pulled aside: it's Henry, smiling, leering. *It's Henry!* His eyes are livid, the way I've seen them before. He tips back his head and laughs loudly, like the roar of a raging bear. He lifts the ax in his hands to strike—

"Catherine." A rough whisper in my ear. I wake with a start: I'm in my sleeping tent, and I can barely see in the darkness. My straw mattress shifts uncomfortably.

"Henry!" I gasp, but he covers my mouth with his. His kisses are forceful. He pulls at my nightdress with eager, insistent fingers. *The king's will be done*—no, no, I must not think of such things. My mind must be blank, must be clean. I must submit and make him happy with what I have to offer. If only I could tell him that I'm pregnant, then maybe it would calm him. But I find that fear has swallowed my voice. I close my eyes and meekly submit. I must make him happy.

"My wife, my wife," he whispers in my ear. I smell wine upon his breath. "My wife and my heir." Then he already knows about my pregnancy. He kisses me again, as though not to allow any denial. I know that he is about to claim me. But suddenly he stops, his shoulders tense. His heavy breathing snags.

"Henry?" I ask gently. He's already pulling away from me. The air in the tent is stagnant, heavy upon my flesh. "What is wrong?"

"Don't touch me!" he snaps. I draw my hand away from him quickly, as if he struck out to bite it. He turns away, his massive form casting a shadow over me in the darkness. I lie on the bed, quivering in fear. I have displeased him in some way, I have displeased him. I open my mouth to say something, but can think of nothing. I lie here still as stone and make no sound as he reaches for his robe.

Dread settles in my belly as he leaves the tent. I pull the furs close around my shoulders and try to sleep.

I OPEN MY EYES. I must have slept, but I do not feel rested. My body aches as if I've held it taut all night, like an animal ready to spring from danger. I stretch beneath the covers, my back aching with every move. Thoughts of last night come rushing back to me and the heaviness of dread settles in my belly again. I pull back the covers to rise from bed.

The ladies are still sleeping, so I'm the only one who sees it: a stain of blood upon my nightshift, upon my underclothes. My blood has returned.

I wonder if perhaps Henry is cursed, and thereby I am cursed through him.

XXIX

As we travel from Lincoln to Pontefract Castle, my horse's gait over the rough, broken roads makes my belly lurch. For the first time I'm not merely sad to tell Henry that I'm not pregnant, I am afraid. After what happened last night, I doubt that he will be eager to visit my chamber again. He has indulged me for nearly a year and I have still not given him what he so desires. What if he moves on to another? What will happen to me?

By the time we're installed in proper chambers at Pontefract, my mind is fraught with fear and possibility. After days on the road, I've had time to conjure all the terrible things that may happen if my lack of pregnancy were to be made known.

"You look pale, Catherine," Lady Rochford remarks, having shut the doors to my bedchamber. She is the only one who knows that my blood has returned. "You must rest before the banquet tonight. We will simply tell the king that you are tired, that he cannot visit you tonight. No doubt he will think it because of your pregnancy." She glances up at me furtively. "By tomorrow night you will be ready to greet him again. He will notice nothing amiss."

"The king will not visit me tomorrow night. I don't know that he will ever visit me again."

"What are you saying, Catherine?"

I look straight into her eyes.

"We must make this happen," I tell her, my voice barely audible. "We cannot count upon the king's help. We must make this happen for me, for us, on our own."

"I understand," she says, nodding slightly. "By tomorrow

night, you will be ready." Her voice is placid, calm. "I will arrange everything, Catherine. Do not worry. We will make this happen. No one else will know."

TONIGHT, THE LADIES chatter jubilantly as they dress me in my cloth-of-silver gown. Only Lady Rochford is quiet as she clasps my wild curls into a silver coronet. Our eyes meet in the mirror before us. Her eyes tell me more than she dares say in words.

"Smile, Catherine," she whispers. "You look beautiful."

I sit beside the king during the night's festivities. I smile and laugh when he smiles and laughs. I applaud the acrobats and jugglers and laugh jovially at the jokes of the fool, all the while watching the king for his reaction. Though he presses his hand against mine in the usual manner, I know that he will not visit my bedchamber tonight. I am already pregnant as far as he is concerned. I'm sure he pushes the thought of his recent failure from his mind.

The ladies ready me for bed tonight just as they do every other night, but I am wary. I keep my eyes on Lady Rochford, hoping that she has found some way to remedy my problem. Once my hair has been brushed and I lie in bed in my nightgown, I dismiss the others. They file out dutifully and head to their own beds, and my chamber door is shut behind them. Jane stands beside my bed. We stare at each other for a moment.

Wordless, she lifts my cloak from a nearby chest. I had not realized it, but I'm shivering uncontrollably, though the room is perfectly warm. She drapes the cloak over my shoulders.

"Not here, Jane," I whisper, suddenly desperate. "It can't

happen here." Not within sight of the royal jewels, upon a bed fit for a queen. No, no, it can't happen here. She merely nods in agreement and takes my hand, leading me to a door at the opposite end of my bedchamber. Before passing over the threshold, she pulls the hood of the cloak over my hair.

The hallway before us is pitch black; I lean upon Jane's arm for guidance. She shows me to a small adjacent bedchamber with clean linens upon the narrow bed. No candles are lit, and the chamber is windowless; the air is completely still. I am glad of this, though the darkness is unnerving. I begin pacing, for fear that spies may linger in the shadows.

"Calm yourself," she whispers in my ear. She pulls the cloak from my shoulders and shows me to the bed. "Only Joan Bulmer and I know where you will be."

My breath stops in my throat: *Joan knows?* Does it not follow that all of the ladies of Lambeth will know?

"We need someone, a lady-in-waiting, to guard the chamber upstairs while I guard the door to this one. Joan promised to keep it a secret. Who would you have suggested?"

I shake my head, mutely. Jane is right. Better it be Joan than any of the others.

"There is no other way to access this chamber but through the door I will guard. You will be perfectly safe."

She lifts my hand and I feel a different hand grasp it—a warm hand with long fingers. Thomas is already here, he has been waiting here in the darkness for my arrival. Jane pats my shoulder reassuringly. I hear her open and close the door behind her. The room is silent; but for his hand in mine I would think I sat here alone.

"Catherine," he whispers in my ear. He sits upon the bed beside me.

"I can't see you."

"Catherine, it's me, Thomas. Don't worry."

I lift a hand and touch his hair, his face, tenderly—the soft-ness of his lips, the crinkling skin at the corners of his eyes. It is him. I sigh with certainty, but I'm still trembling. He clasps his hands around my arms, rubbing them warm. I'm about to say something else when he moves forward and kisses me.

It is a peculiar thing to feel that you are living your dream. I had thought never to experience another kiss like this, from him, but here I am. Here we are. His lips are full and warm and tentative upon mine. There is perfection here—just like that night in the garden—sweet perfection in the gentleness of his touch that reminds me of all the hope I ever had for the two of us. It makes tears well in my eyes to think of it, my breath catching in my throat.

"Shh, shh," he whispers, calming me. He kisses me again and slips into the bed beside me. His hands are warm upon my skin, and there is something careful and reverent about his touch. He, too, is caught in the wonderment of this, of us, together again. That we are doing something that I know we have both spent countless nights merely dreaming of. He pulls the nightdress over my head, his bare chest pressed against my bare chest. He covers me, covers all of me, and I feel warm and protected. I feel loved and in love.

A WOMAN LIES upon the stone floor, draped in silk, await-ing her lover's arrival. He comes to her in darkness, hover-ing for a moment over her sleeping form. We can see clearly their two shapes in the torchlight: the languid, stretching body of the woman, and the body of the man standing over her, with broad white wings upon his back.

We are in the hall of Pontefract Castle, watching a tableau unfold before us: the myth of Cupid and Psyche. Psyche is visited nightly by a lover she is forbidden to see in the light of day. The hall is silent as we watch the two of them, watching him as he watches her, gazing lovingly at her face, her body. A soft gasp and sigh pours from the crowd as the winged Cupid moves forward, waking his love with a kiss.

When the curtain is drawn over the scene, the silent hall erupts in thunderous applause. I glance over carefully, very carefully, in the dimness—just a flash of eyes to see that Thomas is watching me.

I try not to think about him but, like Psyche, I can't help myself: I think about him during Mass, during royal ceremonies and banquets. I think about him as local dignitaries are presented to me, bowing over my hand in veneration. I can feel his eyes upon me, can feel my skin warm and tingling where he last touched me, can feel his lips upon my lips. I have never felt anything so intoxicating, so overwhelming. We've had three nights together—three stolen nights, dreamlike, unreal. But they have awoken something within me that is all too real, something that lay dormant for years, awaiting his touch.

I look at Henry and fear what I have done. But I had no other choice to save myself, to give Henry what he thinks I already have. This is the only thing I know will please him, the one thing that is required. I imagine how happy he will be at my first announcement of pregnancy, and I feel full of joy and relief for both of us. I will have no choice but to push all thoughts of Thomas aside then so as not to tarnish this gift I am giving to Henry—the gift of a healthy son. I have done all of this for him.

But that does not stop me from craving Thomas, now. My mind is wary, but my body follows its own responses. Kisses repeat themselves in my head through the day. I am sitting here in this hall, applauding the performers and smiling at all assembled, but only half of me is here. The other part of me is already gone, already reveling in what the night may bring. When I look at Henry I smile, and merely pretend that it is all a dream. I've long lived a double life with my dreams, so I am accustomed to this feeling. I am like Psyche, indulging in a night of love that will flee as soon as the sun rises.

IT IS MID-SEPTEMBER and we've left Pontefract for York. My blood has arrived, again. Late, but here it is. I have no alternative, or else the date of birth would be suspect: I must seduce the king, in spite of our last disastrous attempt at coupling. I must be sweet and seductive. I must not think about Thomas.

Upon our arrival in York, I sit beside Henry all during the evening festivities, not even getting up to dance.

"I suppose I'm too tired," I tell him, my voice low. "I feel already eager for bed." My words are innocent but my eyes are seductive, and Henry does not miss their meaning. I am relieved that I can still have this effect upon him, though the effort to charm him—to be laughing and giddy and seem free of any worry or care—does tire me. I make an effort to think about Henry in the blandest, most basic sense: he is my husband, and I must do my duty by him. I drink an extra glass of wine before following him to his bedchamber.

MY NIGHTS WITH the king have passed easily, and he seemed pleased with my affections. I am hopeful that my blood will cease, but other thoughts invade the simplicity of these prayers: Thomas's long fingers upon my pale skin, Thomas's full lips pressed to mine. Thomas's dark eyes glistening in the light of a single candle, staring at my nakedness. I cannot look at myself—my own hands, lips, breasts—without imagining him kissing, caressing me. If only I had something to hold close to me so that I might always remember what it was like to be held in his arms. Some token of our love so that I might be reminded of it every day of my life.

In the middle of the night, I rise from bed and write a brief note by candlelight.

> *Master Culpeper,*
> *I never longed for anything so much as to see you.*
> *It maketh my heart to die when I do think that I*
> *cannot always be in your company. Please write*
> *to me in secret, for I long to relive the tender words*
> *you have bestowed upon me in private. Come to me*
> *when Lady Rochford is here, for then I shall be best*
> *at leisure to be at your commandment . . . And thus*
> *I take my leave of you, trusting to see you shortly*
> *again. And I would you were with me now, that you*
> *might see what pain I take in writing to you, my*
> *little sweet fool.*
> > *Yours as long as life endures,*
> > *Catherine*

I hope he will return a love letter to me, via Jane, before I arrange our next meeting. Then I can replace all of those old letters I so foolishly put to the flames. And I will be able to read his words of love over and over again, and hear his voice even when he cannot lie beside me, whispering in the dark.

XXX It's been two days and I've not received a visit from the king. And I've not received a letter from Thomas, though he did give me a message in person:

"Tonight?" he whispered to me yesterday, in the midst of a graceful pavane. His expression remained measured, cautious.

I only smiled in return, a picture of innocence, garlanded in pink roses in celebration of summer.

"Please—make it be soon. I beg you." He smiled, but his eyes were burning. "Please."

I had hoped for a letter, but the sight of Thomas's ardent gaze is dangerously exciting. The king is distracted with the renovations to St. Mary's and preparations to meet his nephew James; I know not when next he will visit me. By then I could have missed my chance to feel Thomas's weight pressed upon me in bed. Other young women get to feel this. Why should I deny myself, if my love is here and waiting for me? How can I deny my passion? Perhaps I should be stronger, but I'm not. Besides, I have to be certain of a pregnancy.

"I should like to meet with Thomas again," I inform Lady Rochford quietly, when we are alone in my bedchamber. She glances at me, her eyebrows raised.

"You'd best be cautious, Your Majesty."

"You're lecturing about caution? Now?"

"This is not a time to indulge your crude fantasies," she informs me. "This is a means to a particular end."

"Yes, and don't you agree that we should be well assured of that end? This is my chance, these next few nights. The king is otherwise occupied. Still, I ought to use the time to my best advantage."

"You are certainly the duchess's granddaughter." She sighs. I'm not sure how I feel about this comparison, but Jane nods her head in resignation. "I will arrange it."

"Do not act so pious with me now," I scold her. "This was not my idea at first, you will remember. Besides, you've been at court longer than I have." I eye her carefully as I say this. "I've heard tell of the corruption you've witnessed. This is nothing so depraved as all that. It's a means to a particular end, as you said."

She is quiet for a moment, and doesn't return my gaze.

"Are you talking about Anne?" she asks.

"Yes. Am I allowed to talk about her?"

Anne indulged in the most sordid, immoral, lustful impulses with a lowly court musician, as well as her own brother—Jane's husband—in addition to the enchantments she cast upon the king, to fool him into marrying her. All I want is a baby, just like the king. And I am in love with Thomas, truly in love. What I am doing, though certainly a sin, cannot be quite so horrible as the acts Queen Anne committed for pure pleasure.

"You should not, but I suppose you are allowed."

"She deserved what happened to her, didn't she?" Jane would know this better than anyone.

"You must understand this, Catherine. The Howards only support those who will benefit the family."

"I know that."

"No, I do not think you do. If Anne was accused of being unable to bear a son, a continuation of the king's curse, then they would abandon her. If she was to be found a witch, then the Boleyns and the Howards would be the first to light the pyre at her feet so that they would come out of the flames on the other side: clean and pure and loyal to their king, unblemished by their daughter's sins. And they did—just look where you are now."

Jane is looking at me strangely, her eyes lit uncannily by the light of the fire. Her words make my heart beat loudly in my ears.

"If Anne had been exiled, she would have existed as a reminder of the unclean thing that was once crowned Queen of England. It was best for the family not only to remove Anne from the throne, but to dispose of her completely."

"I know. That was what the king wanted."

"True, he did—even before Anne knew it, I think. But what happened to her, in the end, was for the best for all involved. They snuffed out her very existence, as if she had never happened."

"I am doing what the duchess told me to do, what you told me to do," I remind her. "All I want is to be pregnant."

"And you will be pregnant, and soon. I am sure of it." She reaches out and rests her hand upon mine. "I am only telling you what I know. You are the king's wife. Your life is in his hands."

"And in my family's hands."

She considers this, her eyes lost for a moment in the flames. "Yes," she says. "Yes, I suppose you are right."

IN YORK, THOMAS utilizes a secluded back stairway to gain entrance to my bedchamber at the top of the stairs: a tower room with tall, cloudy windows draped in dusty velvet. The room is dark when he appears in the doorway, closing the door quietly behind him.

"Joan will guard the stairway," Lady Rochford tells me. My gaze is locked with Thomas's. He smiles, and moves a step closer to the bed. "But it is too dangerous for me to leave this room unguarded. Are you listening, Catherine?"

"Can you stand guard within the main chamber?"

"Will it not seem suspicious that I am not in here, in bed? I must stay here, for your safety." With these words she sits upon a chair, close to the door. "I'm sure that the duchess would agree."

Lady Rochford's presence is not enough to dissuade me from spending a night in Thomas's arms. The room is shadowy already, but I put a damper on the flames in the hearth.

"I never thought you to be so concerned with privacy, Catherine," she remarks, "with what I've heard about your trysts at Lambeth."

I ignore this comment and walk over to Thomas.

"Your guard is at her station, I see?" he says with a grin, sitting upon the great carved bed. I blow out a few of the candles lit beside the bed, but he takes my hand in his and pulls me toward him.

"Yes, she has insisted on staying."

"Do not think about it." His voice is deep, rich. "We are alone here. Tonight is about you and me." He pulls me closer, to sit on the bed beside him.

"Did you receive my letter?"

"Yes, I did," he tells me, brushing his lips against my neck.

"You did not write me back," I whisper in his ear. "I was hoping that you would write so that I may replace all of your old letters that I lost so long ago."

"I will give you something better than a letter." He smiles, and moves in for a kiss.

But I want a letter, I think in the midst of the kiss. How do I explain it to him? Why do I want one so desperately? I follow the trail of this desire all the way down to the pit of my heart, my being: because a letter will be something that I can keep, and touch, and reread. It will remain real once all of this dream is over, and we are back at court and must resume our real lives.

"Catherine? What's wrong? You're shivering."

"Nothing," I tell him, and pull him close to me. "Nothing, my little sweet fool." I hold him so tightly that my arms begin to ache.

The world consists of only this chamber, this bed, and the two of us upon it. As he pulls me free of my corset, I can only wonder if he, too, realizes that this will end soon, when the progress is over and we return to London. I try to banish the thought from my mind, focusing instead on the feeling of his skin against my skin.

Lying naked together in the dark, Thomas whispers to me: "I love you, Catherine."

My eyes snap open. Jane snores softly in a corner of the room.

"Marry me, Catherine," he whispers. "Marry me."

"I am married." My voice is barely a whisper. "You know that I am married. You cannot ask me that."

"But I love you," he tells me. "You were meant to be with me."

"*He* says I was meant for him, too. And he is king, there is no refusing."

"So you will refuse your own heart, instead?"

"You know that it is not my decision to make, and it never was. Neither of us can make our own decisions—we were fools to think otherwise."

I cut my eyes at his, angry at the thoughts he is dredging up within me. I do not want to think of the king now, nor of our sad predicament.

"Did you not know what you were doing, putting me in the king's path all the time? Lady Rochford said you helped them arrange all of this. Is that true?"

His gaze breaks away from mine, fractured.

"You cannot accuse me of refusing my heart now, when you had a hand in it all along."

"No, no, please don't. I'm sorry. You're right—neither of us has ever been offered a question without first being given the response. I did what I was told, just as you did."

"We are obedient children."

"Indeed, we are," he says, moving his hand up my thigh. I elbow him softly, a bit annoyed. I prefer not to think of this love affair as yet another of the duchess's schemes.

"Listen to me, Catherine. Please, just listen to me. There will be a time when you will be given the opportunity to decide for yourself. There might not be long to wait."

I roll over and face him. The chamber is dark; all of the

candles have burned out. Only a pale slice of moonlight permeates the room. His dark eyes glitter in the silvery light.

"Promise me that you will choose me then, when it is for you to choose."

When the king is dead. That is when I will be able to choose. Somehow the danger of the words he dares not say makes clear to me the graveness of our current actions. The hard glitter in his eyes frightens me. I touch his face, I kiss him, but I dare not answer him.

"What you are saying is treason."

"We already share treason, Catherine. We harbor it in our hearts each day. We enjoy it upon this bed at night."

I close my eyes in shame but he presses his lips to mine, passionately.

"Will you marry me?"

"You know that I will," I tell him.

At the sound of these words coming out of my mouth, I suddenly feel that I am falling. I wrap my arms around Thomas but the sensation only persists: we are both falling, spiraling through the great black void.

XXXI

By the torchlight in the banquet hall, I am wary of Thomas's presence. Tonight I sit beside the king and abstain from dancing. I am glad to be here, surrounded by people, with so many things to look at and distract me from my own thoughts. I pretend to be entertained by the antics of fools and minstrels. One fool reads a long, bawdy rhyme that makes the whole hall echo with laughter. The king laughs heartily and pats my hand.

In my chamber, Malyn brushes my hair. Joan approaches, dropping a hasty bow.

"My queen, you have a visitor."

Her voice sounds odd, stilted. I look up; her face is blanched. Her eyes dart furtively, as if acknowledging the other ladies in the room.

"Of course," I tell her, and manage a small smile to hide my wariness. "We will meet in the main chamber. Ladies, you are dismissed. Joan will stay with me."

Emerging into the main chamber with Joan, I find myself face-to-face with Francis Dereham. He smiles at my approach, then sweeps an elaborate, mocking bow.

I knew it was him—that red-and-black mask! I curse myself for not doing anything, but what could I have done? I did not want to admit it. I wanted to imagine it was a bad dream. It is a bad dream.

"I'm sure you are surprised to see me." His voice is loud, brazen. I can tell that he is drunk. "Perhaps you assumed I was murdered by pirates, or lost at sea?"

"I am pleased to see you, of course."

"Of course you are." His voice is thick with mockery. "I thought this the perfect time to present myself to my queen, seeing as you've now appointed all of our old friends to positions in your household." He stares at me, smiling. "Now we can all be together again."

"Indeed. I expected that you would visit me, soon."

"You have always been very adept at guessing the intentions of men, Your Majesty. I suppose that's how you've managed such impressive conquests."

I hold out my hand, beseeching calm. He looks at me, his blue eyes full of spite.

"You know there was nothing that I could do, Francis."

"There was nothing you wanted to do." He laughs bitterly. "You rejected me long before the king was involved. Don't deny that—at least, don't deny that to me. If you could have your way, I'm sure you would put both me and King Henry aside for your chance at Culpeper." I flinch at his words and he steps closer, reaching out quickly and grasping one of my full velvet sleeves. "Or is it someone new these days, my queen?"

I strike out at his hand, snapping my gown from his grasp. He only smiles.

"Regardless of what you may have wanted, remember this, Queen Catherine: you are still my wife, and all of this royal marriage is a sham."

"You must not say such things, for your own good as well as mine."

"It only matters to me that *you* know it. That you are still my wife. We are precontracted to one another, rendering whatever union you have made with that beast of a man null and void. It is a tack Henry has taken before in matters of divorce."

"Henry does not intend to divorce his wife," I state carefully. I rest my hands protectively over my belly; the gesture is not lost on Francis. Though I can't yet be certain, there is a possibility. "I must warn you, Francis, of your treason."

"Then I shall likewise warn you of your own. After all, the king thought he married a virgin when he married you."

I stare at him for a moment, mute with terror. This proud boy from Lambeth, who once pledged his heart to me, now stares at me and bares his vicious teeth.

"The question now is, what are you going to do for me?" He laughs, and his laugh frightens me, for he sounds a little mad. "What will you do for your husband?"

"All I can do is to offer you a position here. You will have the opportunity to work your way up at court. I am sure that you can do this, with my favor. It will be a very profitable life for you—more profitable than having married me."

He opens his mouth as if to scoff at this, but I lift a hand to silence him.

"I have brought you in now, Francis, and I am showing you a queen's favor and generosity, which may prove very agreeable to you. But in this new agreement you must make a vow, for your sake and for mine: take heed what words you speak. I know better the dangers of court than you do. You do not know the peril you put us both in just by speaking to me in this way, just by being here."

With these words I turn away from him.

"You are dismissed," I say, and Joan escorts him into the hall.

I walk to my chamber and dismiss my ladies. As they retreat, I pull Lady Rochford aside.

"Jane, I shall have no visitors tonight." I would not put it past Francis to arrive again, unannounced, at midnight. "You must guard this door." Jane nods assent. I shut the door behind me and stand before the fire breathing slowly, my heart pounding.

I do not know what else I could have done. I think of the duchess, how she told me to pull the ladies of Lambeth close to me when they requested positions in my household. Now I will have to do the same with Francis, and hope that I can reward him into submission and loyalty. Though I suppose I showed little to him, in the years since our tearful good-bye. That seems an entirely different life, lived by a different girl.

A creak, a scratch makes me jump. With wide eyes I see the hidden door in the back of my chamber open. Thomas enters.

"What are you doing here?"

"Please, Catherine, do not be angry with me." He approaches me timidly, taking my hand in his. "It pains me not to see you. I was worried about you."

"As well you should be. We should all be worried about me."

"Catherine, what is wrong? You know that I will protect you."

"Francis Dereham is here," I whisper. But how will I explain? "He was—"

"I know," he says, and pulls me into his embrace. "I know. The duchess told me, long ago. She feared that he might come back, sniffing around for money and favor. I will protect you, Catherine. You can trust me."

I had wanted to be strong, but instead I fold easily into his embrace.

"You cannot stay here tonight," I tell him, but he is already kissing my neck. "You should not stay here. If Francis were to see you—"

"I don't care about Francis and neither should you. All I want is to be with you. I can't bear not to be with you."

It is like a sickness, this desire that I hold within me, that he ignites so easily in spite of my better judgment. It's as if

I'm dying, and Thomas is the only thing keeping me alive. Or perhaps it is his love that is killing me, causing me all of this pain and anguish and joy. I cannot separate my joy from my heartache: the two live side by side.

I STRETCH MY bare limbs against his, then fold myself again in Thomas's arms.

"This can't go on," I whisper. "You know that, don't you?"

"Then you will give yourself to me, then take your love away just as easily?"

"None of this is easy, Thomas."

"I know, I know," he murmurs, running his fingers along my arm. "But I fear for you. I fear for both of us, and for all of England."

"Why?" I lift my head from his chest, leaning on one elbow. "I may be already with child—with Henry's child. And all will be well."

"That may not be enough," he says darkly. He looks at me steadily, slipping his arm around my bare back and pulling me close, his face inches away from mine. "Catherine, there are those who say the king is no longer fit to rule."

"What are you saying?" My limbs freeze in his embrace.

"Do not act surprised, Catherine. I'm sure you've thought it, too. I have served the king longer than you, though in a different capacity, I'll admit, but we can't deny the evidence of his madness. You've heard what he did to the monasteries, to Becket's tomb. Even old Margaret Pole was not safe from the king's brutality."

"I don't want to talk about this." These words are treason, danger, death. I roll away from Thomas, pulling the sheets up to my chin. He rolls with me and wraps his arms around me, my back pressed against his chest. He lays his face upon my hair and whispers directly into my ear.

"We need to talk about this, for your own safety. The king has become—dangerous. More so as the years progress. He's too easily swayed to violence, too easily swayed by his madness. You can't tell me that you haven't seen it."

I think of the roar that I've heard emanate from Henry's throat. I think of the times he has pushed me aside. I realize that I've stopped breathing; my breath is stuck in my chest.

"The people have begun to tire of him. Not just here, but in London, too. The funds from those monasteries he destroyed went directly into the king's coffers, you know, to pay for his banquets and robes and jewels. It was less about religious reform than it was about his indulging his greed."

"Or my greed, you mean?" I feel suddenly sick, trapped in Thomas's arms.

"No, this is about the king. He is old, Catherine," Thomas continues, his whisper sharp in my ear, inescapable. "He will die soon. Wouldn't it be better for him, for all of us, if he were to die before there can be any further abuse of his power?"

I cannot ask what he is suggesting, for I already know. A cloud passes over my vision, turning the moonlit shadows a sickly, underwater blue.

"There could be a way to do it, discreetly. He is already old and ill, no matter how he attempts to conceal it. All would owe their allegiance to you, his pregnant widow."

"What good would that do us?" I hiss, frightened by his words. "What good would that do anyone?"

"You are right: Prince Edward would be crowned king, and no doubt a Seymour named lord protector. But there have long been doubts about Edward's health." He rests his hand gently upon my belly. "I think it quite likely that your baby will find his way to the throne."

"And what if I don't have a boy? What if he never places the crown upon my head? He may be a madman, but he is all that protects me."

"I will protect you."

"You cannot. That's not enough." I wrestle free from his embrace. "You've let this—what we've done here—affect your loyalty, your judgment." When I turn to look at him, his face is stunned and pale, his eyes like pools of ink.

"How can I not let your love affect me? How can you turn away from me, now?" His voice is sharp, cutting through the shadows. He sighs, reaching out for me again. "You can't deny that you've thought of this, Catherine. We've all thought it. He is a danger to himself and others."

"You must promise me, Thomas, that you will not do anything. Please promise me that you will not do anything against the king. I am worried for your safety."

"I promise I will do anything to protect you."

I pull him close to me and kiss him, but the kiss is already tainted. I thought in Thomas's arms I would be safe. But his words are even more reckless than our actions.

This ends now, but I don't have the heart to tell him.

I'M AT A GRAND MASQUE at Hampton Court, and the whole hall is bright with decorations of red and gold, and the room is lit with torches. I hear screaming in the distance:

it's Queen Jane, screaming through her labor pains. The music gets louder to drown out the screaming. The dancing is mad and unstoppable, my legs impelled through the vigorous steps. The room is spinning. A cold hand grasps mine—I look up and see Anne Boleyn. She grips both of my hands; her skin is like ice. She laughs at me and in laughing she tilts her head back. A gaping red wound stretches across her pale neck.

I wake from this dream, sweating, my heart pounding. I've had this dream before. I lean over the side of the bed and heave into my chamber pot. Jane hears me and rushes to my side, pressing her cool hands to my hot forehead. The room is still spinning. I can still hear the echoes of the mad music playing in my head.

I FEAR BOTH days and nights. Jane reports that Thomas has not taken kindly to my refusal to continue our meetings.

"Perhaps a letter would soothe him, or a token of your affection?"

"No," I tell her, unwilling to elaborate and condemn Thomas in the process. "Not with Francis around. It is not safe, no matter what he says."

Indeed, Francis creates his own problem. He is constantly stalking around me, watching my every move, every dart of my eyes. He behaves overly familiar with me in front of the other courtiers. I try to brush it off as the flattery of a young man to his queen, but he has not the poetic grace of my other paramours at court. There is something base about his display of affection, as if I am not a queen who deserves the loftiness of poetry but a common harlot well pleased with a smirk and a bawdy remark. I see disapproval in the eyes of the other members of my household, male and female alike.

"I notice that you have posted a new secretary," the king mentioned to me only days after Francis's arrival. "Who is the young man?"

"Francis Dereham, my lord. A former pensioner of my uncle's." I know better than to describe him as a friend.

Luckily for me, Henry has greater problems to deal with than the appearance of a young man receiving a favored position in his wife's household. King James of Scotland did not arrive for the appointed meeting with his uncle. Henry is furious, but has done well to hide his wrath from the people of York. Preparations have begun to move us to Hull by the beginning of October, where Henry will inspect the fortifications: a monarch must always be prepared for battle.

Meanwhile, in my heart and during the nightly celebrations, I've been waging a quiet battle of my own.

"I must see you," Thomas whispered to me last night, in the midst of a dance. I could barely hear him through the shrieking of the bagpipes.

"Too dangerous," I murmured quietly, smiling all the while. I could feel his eyes burning upon me, but could not return his gaze.

It is all too dangerous. My hand in his as we continued the dance, my skin thrilling to his touch. My body knows nothing of its own danger; it knows only the pleasure he has taught it.

I must listen to my mind, now, before it is too late.

XXXII

It is mid-October and our procession moves slowly from Hull back to Hampton Court. After months on progress, our caravan appears a bit more ragged than it did at the beginning of the summer. And I might be the most ragged of all: my blood returned just yesterday, and I am humbled by the memory of my sin. My rash acts of desperation have not provided the succor I require, yet still the fact of my sin remains. I've tasted what may have been love, but it has not cured me of my troubles, and in fact may have created more. Now I find myself on the other side of sin, alone. I will suffer my penitence willingly, for this is God's lesson for me. A dream cannot be realized through lustful indiscretion. I pray for absolution; until then, I am not worthy of God's blessing.

In spite of this, we return home in the glory of a successful progress. The northern people approved of their new queen, and Henry seems all the more enamored of me after seeing me play my role before the public. Henry is happy with me, and I must be satisfied with that. I am grateful to be leaving *all* the wild dangers of the northern countryside safely behind me.

Measured hoofbeats gain upon me, sidling up to my silver mare.

"You are not unwell, my queen?" I recognize the voice instantly, in spite of its rigid formality.

"I will be glad to be off this horse," I say wearily. I glance surreptitiously at Thomas's profile. He stares straight ahead. We have done well to avoid each other these last few days of the progress. I can only hope that he understood the necessity.

"I trust that you are relieved the progress has ended," he says quietly.

"Yes, and no," I reply. "I shall always remember it. But such things cannot last forever. Court awaits us. Life awaits us." Reality, and all its complications, cannot be escaped. Thomas seems subdued, compared to our last meeting; perhaps reality has returned to him, as well.

"I must agree," he says, "It is unfortunate. I rather like the countryside."

"As do I."

"Perhaps you will return there, someday. Perhaps—" He stops himself, midstream. "Forgive me. I do not mean to be presumptuous. Please forgive me."

"There is no need to ask for forgiveness."

"I only hope that you are well, that you will feel better once we arrive at court."

"I trust that I will. Thank you."

He tugs the reins of his horse, moving up through the throng toward the king's retinue, where he belongs.

Please, Thomas, forgive me. Please understand: it is not my choice. He has been at court long enough to appreciate this. It was dangerous for us to think that he could protect me. Only the king can protect me, as frightening as that prospect may seem. I must be a wife to King Henry, and to no one else. It is hard enough to live this way, splitting my heart in two. But I cannot doubt my decision now. I must leave all of this behind me. I must leave my own heart behind me.

This road is rough, and I am weary. There is so little that I understand about this life—I wonder if I am the only one who feels so lost. We are all merely wandering down a road, in single file. We are not sure where this path will lead us.

We do not know when we are walking headfirst into darkness. We are not sure when, or if, the sun will shine again.

UPON RETURNING TO HAMPTON, we were greeted with sad news: Henry's sister Margaret died in early October while we were on progress, and Prince Edward has fallen ill in our absence.

Soon after our arrival, I accompanied Henry on a visit to his son. I could not help but think of Thomas's dark words when I saw the boy, and the thoughts made my throat constrict. The four-year-old prince has a sallow complexion. He is certainly well fed, but lacks the athletic prowess and energy his father displayed even at such a young age. Perhaps the nature of a lone prince's life is too cloistered for his own good. We walked outside with little Edward; his nursemaids draped a heavy cloak over him in spite of the fine weather.

Over the few days since our return we've received word that the prince's health is much improved, and a breath of relief is sighed throughout court. Sighed by all, perhaps, save Henry.

"We are disappearing, we Tudors," he laments, looking up at me with woeful eyes. We are having a quiet dinner in his chamber, and I am glad of the privacy. I stand from my chair and walk around the food-laden table to him. I sit upon his lap and wrap my arms around his neck. He does not resist, only rests his head upon my shoulder. Now that I've been given a taste of his vile moods, I'm amazed by how tender he can still be with me. And I'm glad to be able to comfort him in a way that a wife should.

"That is not true," I tell him, lightly stroking his hair, "You still have your children. You still have Prince Edward."

"And I have you," he whispers in my ear. "Thanks be to God that I have you."

I AM GLAD TO BE BACK at court, back to the ordinary rudiments of daily life. The weather is fine and the king is in good spirits. I have been attending Mass more frequently, offering my mute confession up to God. My heart is raw, wounded—better to pay it no mind at all. In time it will become a phantom pain, one I am accustomed to ignoring. There are many in this world who must survive without their heart.

Henry is finding joy in me just as he did when we were first married. Today, the first of November, he has planned a special thanksgiving service in the Chapel Royal. I attend Mass with him every morning since we returned from the progress. Standing beside him in the church reminds me of that magical moment of taking the sacrament at the chapel in Lincoln. We kneel before the altar to offer our thanks.

"I thank the Lord for the good life I have led and trust to lead with my queen. I thank the Lord for granting me a wife so entirely conformed to my inclinations as her I now have," Henry murmurs, his voice low and humble. He asks the bishop present to make prayer and give like thanks with him. My cheeks turn warm; the king is happy, and feels blessed to have me.

As we leave the chapel, Archbishop Cranmer shuffles forward and hands a sealed letter to Henry.

"What is this?"

"A short letter," Cranmer says, bowing hastily, "for you to read later, Your Grace. In private."

As Henry puts the letter in the pocket of his doublet, Cranmer's eyes flutter briefly over mine. He turns and hastily leaves the chapel.

THE NEW GOWN I've had made is truly special, just as I dreamed it would be: dark purple velvet with gold lace panels in the skirt and tissue of gold set into the sleeves. The neckline is embellished with a series of amethysts, matching the smaller series of stones on the trim of my purple velvet hood.

The main chamber is full of ladies already sipping from goblets of wine as they help to ready me for tonight's banquet—a celebration of the successful northern progress which was at first postponed in light of the prince's ill health. All the members of my household line up accordingly to prepare for our ascent to the main hall.

"Where is Francis?" Joan asks, peering through the crowds of people.

"I don't know, I haven't seen him." I turn back to the mirror for one last inspection of my gown and hair in the glass.

"Perhaps he's gone hawking?" Dorothy suggests.

"He should know enough to return in time for supper," Lady Rochford snaps.

"I say good riddance," I remark quietly. In spite of the favors and gifts I've bestowed upon Francis in order to ensure his good behavior, I still shiver to see him—a ghost virulent with wicked secrets—walking among the dazzling array of courtiers that is a part of my new life. I suppose it will merely take time for me to become accustomed to his presence, just as it did when the ladies of Lambeth became a part of my household.

"Beautiful, Catherine!" Henry exclaims, taking my hand in his. He laughs as I spin before him. "You were born to wear royal purple!"

Henry pulls me onto the dance floor, before all assembled. I feel that bliss of triumph as he spins me to the song of the lute and drum and wooden pipe. I hear the crowd gasp in admiration as my velvet gown spreads out around me in waves of violet, the gold lace sparkling in the candlelight. Perhaps I can be happy as Henry's queen, perhaps I can put all the past behind me.

Henry pulls me close when our dance is complete and whispers in my ear.

"You look beautiful, my love, my queen."

I hop up and kiss him on the cheek, spontaneously; the audience breaks into laughter and applause.

JOAN, LISBETH, AND Dorothy huddle around me in the warm dimness of my chamber, pulling the rings from my fingers and brushing my hair smooth. Katherine is busy putting my velvet gown away in an oak chest; in the mirror I can see her admiring it, caressing the folds of the fabric.

A knock at the door makes the ladies fly to attention, ready for their obeisance to the king. But a page appears instead. I pull closed my fur-trimmed robe to receive his message.

"I'm afraid the king will be unable to visit you this

evening." The page bows formally before me. "He is busy tending to official matters."

With another bow, the page departs, his shoes clicking harshly upon the flagstones.

"Surely you will see him at dinner, tomorrow," Lady Rochford says, consolingly, no doubt noting the furrow of my brow.

"The king did not seem unwell at supper this evening," I remark thoughtfully.

"No, on the contrary, he seemed quite well. Quite happy."

"He has not complained to me of pains in his leg as of late. Have you heard of any such pains?"

"No, but I could ask his grooms about his condition. I could ask—"

"No, don't bother," I say quickly, pulling myself into bed. I don't want to hear the name she is about to say. "You are right. I'm sure I will see him tomorrow."

I sink beneath the covers as Jane blows out the candles, and the ladies retire for the night. I'm left here, blinking in the firelight, not ready for sleep. My mind wanders to forbidden, secret places: the hidden chamber at Pontefract. His warm fingertips trailing down my back. His low voice. His eyes and teeth gleaming in the darkness. His kiss. My chest clenches, alive and pulsing, in pain. I open my eyes, blinking, as if trying to pull myself from the waters of the deep, pull myself up from drowning.

Please, God, forgive me for my sins . . . I think that perhaps, like Henry, I am a complicated creature, with a prayer upon my lips, and my heart full of sin. *Please, God, please, Henry, forgive me for my sins* . . .

I T I S E A R L Y and the windows of the main chamber are open, letting the fresh breeze waft through the room, shifting the tapestries upon the walls. I am waiting for the king to arrive, to escort me to Mass in the Chapel Royal. While I am waiting, the girls see fit to entertain me. Katherine stands in the middle of the room, a smile upon her face.

"No no no, Malyn—it goes like this. Watch me." She flicks her wrist toward me and I begin to play a lively tune upon my lute. Katherine dances, lifting the skirt of her full gown in her fingertips so that we may better see the swift movement of her feet. The girls cheer in response.

"All right, now we all must try it."

"We need another minstrel to play for us."

"I'm sure you know the song by heart. We'll simply sing the notes aloud. Come." I join the circle and flash my eyes at the other ladies. Dorothy and Joan are already giggling; Lisbeth shushes them, but this only makes them giggle more. As soon as I sing the first note, the rest jump into the dance in a rush of footsteps and overlapping voices. We turn in a circle, gliding and hopping around the room. I sing the song faster, and the ladies do their best to keep up until Katherine steps on Joan's train, and both come tumbling into each other, laughing in a heap upon the floor. We all applaud anyway, our cheeks pink from laughter.

When I turn, I'm startled to see two of the king's guards in the doorway of my chamber. I greet them warily.

"I was expecting the king," I say, trying to conceal my concern. "I trust there is nothing wrong with my lord?"

"We are here by order of King Henry," one guard explains. "You are to remain here, and await the king's pleasure."

"Remain here?" I ask, nearly laughing, "Whatever do you mean? I've been waiting for him to arrive. We were just practicing our dancing while we waited."

"This is no more the time for dancing," a guard informs me as he strides into the room. I shiver at the sound of this. I watch as he opens a box of jewels from my dressing table. He inspects the contents briefly, then snaps the lid shut.

"Will I meet the king for dinner?"

"No. You will keep to your apartments. Your meals will be brought to you, here."

"What is happening?" I demand, panic making my voice rise. Something must be terribly wrong.

"You are to keep to your chambers." His words are slow and deliberate. "We are here on the king's orders."

When the other guard moves into the chamber, I see my chance and take it. I dash out the door, down the hallway. Unless he is ill, Henry will be on his way to Mass. I streak down the gallery, my slippered feet pounding like a heartbeat upon the stone floor. I have to see Henry. I have to see if he is well, if he knows what's happening. Did something happen to him? What could have happened?

"Henry!"

Suddenly I realize that I'm screaming. The courtiers in the hallway turn to look at me in shock and fear. Not even the queen uses the king's name in public, but I can't help myself. I run down the hallway, cutting through straggling onlookers.

"Henry! Henry!"

The guards are close behind me. I hear them calling my

name. I am his rose without a thorn, I want to tell them— why wouldn't he want to see me? What is wrong with him? Why will they not let me see him? Is he sick? Is he dead? I can't stop these thoughts from entering my brain, along with others, even more frightening: Is he angry with me? Have I done something to offend the king? The hallway echoes with my voice.

"Henry! Henry! Henry!"

I see him entering the chapel, and the sight of him sends a shock through my bones. A moment later, the door of the chapel is slammed shut. The guards catch me roughly by the arms and pull me back.

"Henry! Henry!" I cry, but it's as if no one hears me, as if I no longer make a sound. They pull me back to my chamber. When they close the door behind me, I hear a key turn in the lock, a bolt dropping into its catch. The ladies stand in a shocked circle, staring at me.

"You look like a ghost, Catherine," Joan says, grasping my hands in hers and pulling me close to the fire. "What did you see? Tell me, what did you see?"

I feel as if I have seen a ghost. I saw Henry, but not the Henry that I have known. This Henry was so old, decrepit, his face gray, his back hunched in weariness and defeat. This Henry would not look upon the face of his wife, would not respond to her calls. He created me, transformed me into what he desired. I am nothing without his desire. What will I be without him? I fear that I may vanish from the earth, no longer fit to exist.

I do not know what has happened, but from what I just saw of Henry I can imagine what is true: he has discovered a thorn on his rose. I have shattered the heart of the King of England. God knows what will become of me, now.

XXXIII

Breakfast was brought to my room, but I have no interest in eating. I alternate between pacing the main chamber and sitting listless before the fire.

Since my imprisonment, the days have passed in strangely mundane fashion. I am kept to my suite of rooms here at Hampton, but I have not been robbed of my privy keys. I have relative freedom, walking through the connecting chambers where my ladies continue to play cards, work on their embroidery, sit chattering before the fire. It appears so ordinary, this sequestered life, and there are moments when I could fool myself into believing that nothing is amiss. But then the panic returns—black clouds rolling in, obscuring my vision—and I am caught midstep, speechless, motionless with fear.

Apparently, little is known beyond these walls. I interrogate my ladies upon their return from dinner, but they assure me they've heard nothing whispered in the great hall. They have also not seen the king, but that is not out of the ordinary, either. If he is angry with me, which he must be, his response thus far has been lenient. I am still wearing the royal jewels. I am still his queen. But beyond these facts lies the hovering darkness of the unknown: like a lion waiting to pounce upon his prey.

It is just before supper, when I would be going to sit with Henry for a meal in his chambers. I look up to the door, expecting to see him there. Instead, Archbishop Cranmer and my uncle Norfolk stand before me. The duchess has warned me that Cranmer harbors heretical beliefs and will not support a Catholic queen. I am relieved that Norfolk is here as well.

"Am I to see the king?" I ask. "I need to see him."

"No," Cranmer answers. He lifts a hand to dismiss all of my ladies. I watch, helpless, as they file into adjacent chambers and shut the doors quietly behind them. Now I am alone. I look directly at my uncle for my appeal.

"Please, please let me see him."

My legs tremble beneath me. Cranmer leads me to a chair, I sit upon it heavily.

"We must ask you some questions, Your Grace, about matters that have recently come to light," Norfolk begins. He glances at Cranmer, whose eyes don't leave my face.

"What was the nature of your relationship with Henry Manox, while you were living with the duchess at her Horsham residence?"

My eyes race from one dour face to the other. If they are asking me, that means they already know.

"How do you—why? Why do you ask?"

"We have an account from Mary Hall. The evidence she has offered requires that these questions be asked, my queen," Norfolk answers; his words are deferential but his tone is stiff.

"Mary Hall? I know no Mary Hall."

"The account was delivered to me by her brother, John Lassells," Cranmer obligingly supplies. "I must ask again, what was the nature of your relationship with Henry Manox?"

Mary Lassells—the duchess's chamberwoman who years ago had scolded Manox for his foolish dalliance with me. *But what else do they know? What else?*

"He was my music tutor."

"Did you have carnal relations with Henry Manox?"

"No."

"How well did you know him, in other physical ways?"

I look at Norfolk for guidance, but his sharp eyes pierce through me. He had not been interested in my past when the king was first showing me favor. I look down and notice that I'm kneading the skirt of my gown, leaving dark blotches of sweat upon the blue satin. My face burns hot with shame.

"He was my music tutor . . . and we kissed." They must already know this. But how much more do they know?

"You kissed him. And did he touch you? And did he know you carnally?"

"No, he did not. He did not."

"Francis Dereham," Norfolk says, his voice icy cold. "What was your relationship to Francis Dereham? Did you have carnal relations with him?"

"That's all gone," I blurt out, looking down at my hands. "I burned it. I burned it all just like you told me to." But I'm crying now, and I don't know if they can hear me. I'm sweating through the satin, but also shivering violently. *You told them I was just like Jane, you formulated the lie!* I want to scream this but the sight of Norfolk's cold eyes frightens me. His mouth is turned down in disgust.

"Were you naked when you lay with Dereham in bed? Was he without both doublet and hose?"

"I—I don't know. No."

"Did he know you carnally? Were there others in the room who saw you?"

My eyes wander the room frantically, alighting upon the tea set, the carafe of wine, the deck of cards, the embroidery sample abandoned midstitch by one of my ladies. It is all so ordinary, so miraculously unchanged.

"I burned all of that life—I burned it." Now my shivering has become shuddering. Tears stream down my cheeks. "I burned it just like she told me to."

"Burned what?" Cranmer asks, "As who told you to?"

"Ask the duchess! She will tell you there was nothing to it, nothing that couldn't be burned and forgotten. She knows all!"

"We have already spoken to the duchess," Norfolk remarks calmly. "She has assured us she knew nothing of the immoral life you led before your betrothal to the king."

Burn your life, Catherine. The duchess's words echo through me. Perhaps now she's taken her own advice, seeing as I have already been strapped to the pyre. Just as Jane warned me—she warned me! This is how the Howards work: better to be the one to light the flame than to end up burning yourself.

I feel like I am burning, right now. I can feel the flames upon my flesh. I can't stop myself from screaming.

"Catherine—Catherine!"

Their voices are very far away. My head tips to one side. It just keeps tipping. I'm falling, falling a very long way down.

———

"IT WAS NOTHING out of the ordinary," I mutter, worrying my handkerchief in my damp hands. My eyes sting, the skin around them tight with dried tears. It is late, and I've not eaten all day. A tray of food lies untouched upon a nearby table, but the sight of it makes my stomach turn. The ladies sit around me by the light of the fire.

"Of course it wasn't, dear," Joan consoles me. "We all know that."

"We all did such things, especially at Lambeth." I flash my eyes at all of them; they know they are guilty of similar acts. No one in this room is wholly innocent. But I suppose their indiscretions mean little, while the concealment of mine was an act of treason.

"Many young girls do. And you told me yourself that Francis promised to marry you."

"But I could not marry him," I tell them. "The king chose me. He proposed marriage. There was nothing I could do. You cannot turn down the hand of the king."

"I'm sure they will understand that, dear. Francis will tell them. They cannot trouble you now for what was done before your marriage to the king."

"And what you did with Francis was not out of bounds, considering your precontract."

Precontract. That word meant divorce for Anne of Cleves, and she had not consummated her betrothal. What will my family do with me if the king divorces me?

"Francis will tell them?" I look up again. This time the ladies avert their eyes from mine.

"We thought he was out hawking," Lisbeth murmurs. "No one has seen him."

"We believe that he's been taken in for questioning," Joan tells me, but there is more to this than they dare to say aloud.

"Then he's been taken to the Tower," I breathe. But this cannot be real. Nothing as horrifying as this can be real. In fact, this whole room seems unnatural: the glowing fire, the quiet circle of ladies. Where is Lady Rochford? I need to talk to her about this. I turn and see Jane sitting in the shadows. She's usually in the center of the circle, right by my side. It's odd to see her lurking in a corner—wrong, wrong. All of this is wrong.

"Lady Rochford?" I ask. "Jane?" But her bent form offers no response. She clutches at her dark skirt, wringing the fabric. Something about her pale hands in the shadows seems familiar, frightening. I can't understand why.

"Don't worry about her," Joan tells me. "You had best get some rest."

The other ladies do their best to coddle me, to calm me; they comb my hair and ready me for bed. I am so exhausted from worrying and crying that I actually fall asleep.

I RUN DOWN THE GALLERY, calling the king's name. My feet ache with every step and my throat is raw, but that does not stop me. I see the face of the king—old and ruined—and the door of the chapel slams shut before my face by unseen hands, as if God Himself is locking me out. As the guards pull me away I'm screaming, straining against their arms. But the dream continues: another run down the gallery, screaming, the faces of staring courtiers blurring by me as I run. The look on the king's face and the slam of the chapel door shudders through my bones.

I WAKE SUDDENLY, my whole body tense, my legs cramped. Joan sleeps in the bed beside me. For a moment I cannot tell what is real and what a dream.

I look around—I'm in my bedchamber. Things slowly start to look familiar. And I realize that my head is different than it was before, split into separate chambers: in one there is sleep and dreaming, a place of oblivion haunted by ghosts (Henry's face: old, ruined). In another chamber is a great, towering fear imposing itself upon me—I scurry away from this chamber as soon as I sense its foreboding presence.

But the third chamber—I will dwell here for a while: it is clear, though small and cramped. There is something I must do, something urgent that must not wait another moment. A message must be sent—one too sensitive for ink and parchment.

Stepping from my bedchamber, I make my way toward the fire, which barely flickers in the hearth. Quietly, I approach Lady Rochford, who is seated in a chair by the fire.

"Jane," I whisper, but there is no response. I touch her shoulder, but she gasps and flinches from my touch. I'm taken aback at the sight of her face: she is ghostly pale, mumbling a fervent stream of words beneath her breath.

"Jane?" I ask, but she does not answer. She is staring at me with wide eyes, but I don't think she can see me. I don't know what she sees.

"Catherine." Joan is beside me, pulling me away from the muttering Jane. She pulls me back into the bedchamber.

"You must find Thomas," I whisper. "He must leave court, immediately." I must trust Joan, I have no other choice. I think to ask her about Jane, but I dare not mention it.

"Of course. I will tell him, directly. I assure you." Joan helps me back into bed.

This is my only hope, now, that this will end here. That nothing more will be discovered. What I did is done, and I've prayed to God for forgiveness, and I've put it all behind me. Now I can only hope that I will receive forgiveness, and protection. I will gladly bear my sorrow and terror, at least knowing that Thomas is safe.

I settle back into bed, blinking. When I close my eyes, I see hawks circling overhead, shrieking. Their black wings spread against the blue sky.

XXXIV

Cranmer arrives midday, this time alone. He spins out the same questions, persisting in order to uncover even the most intimate details of my relationship with Francis. Though I've attempted all day to prepare myself for further interrogation, I can feel the great black maw of fear opening up beneath me, threatening to swallow me whole. I'm worried that the words aren't coming out of my mouth in the right sequence, or that I'm not even speaking English anymore. I don't know how much they know, and I fear saying too much and incriminating myself further.

"Dereham has been heard to say that if the king were dead, then he may claim you as his wife," Cranmer informs me. "He says that you were betrothed to him before your marriage to the king. This prior betrothal would render you an unsuitable bride for the king. You married King Henry under false pretenses, already the promised wife of another."

"There was no proper marriage contract," I insist. "I never intended to marry Francis Dereham."

"And yet you allowed carnal relations with him, even without benefit of a precontract?"

"No, I mean, I—" Am I damning myself further? Which is worse? Which makes me more unfit to have married the king? "He called me his wife, but we were not married. It was his own pride, his own boastfulness to claim me as his own. I've only once been properly married. Only once!"

I slide off my chair and fall to my knees on the ground, my head lowered. "Please, I beg you, please let me see the king. I must explain all of this to him."

"You will not see the king, Catherine, but I am here to offer you the possibility of His Majesty's mercy. Your only hope is to make a full confession of your faults."

"Is this the king's decision?" I ask, thinking suddenly of the king's illness earlier this year, and how I was barred from his chambers. "The king does not want to see me?"

Cranmer shifts slightly in his chair.

"Please, please allow me to see my husband. He chose me as his queen; I should at least be granted the opportunity to explain my actions directly to him."

"No, the king has made his requirements plain." There is something sharp, jagged, lying beneath the archbishop's calming tones. "You must confess all if you hope to receive the king's mercy."

"You are asking me to admit to a precontract that did not

exist. I will not do it." My ladies are right: they cannot condemn me for actions that took place before my marriage, before I ever met Henry, before I ever came to court.

"Did your carnal relationship with Dereham continue after your marriage to the king?"

"No."

"You appointed your former lover to a position in your household, is that correct?"

"Yes, he came to me, he wanted a position. I didn't think . . . I didn't . . . nothing happened between us."

"My queen." Cranmer's voice is softly menacing. "Dereham has already condemned himself by speaking of the king's death. It is already over for him. Now you must think of yourself. A complete written confession is your only hope for mercy."

Dereham has condemned himself. Speaking of the king's death. I try to make my mind blank, to disconnect myself from these thoughts.

He leads me to a writing desk, produces a piece of parchment, and urges me gently into the chair. All of my life there has been someone to tell me what to do, what to say, how to act, what to wear. My family has already deserted me, disowned me in disgust with my behavior. Now here I sit across from my Lutheran enemy, urged to write a confession of my sins against my husband, the king. Do I have the option to refuse?

"Catherine, these are grave offenses against His Majesty," Cranmer murmurs. "But the king is willing to be merciful if you are completely honest."

Completely honest. How vexing I find those words.

As I submit to his insistence to write my confession, I feel that I am barely here anymore, barely living in this skin and bones that are my body on this earth. I float up above the proceedings, disconnected, watching it unfold like a play, or a farce.

> *I deeply regret that I have injured the heart of my dear sweet prince whose kindness and favor mean everything to me in my life. I will confess to concealing former faults in the light of my love for you, my dear king. I confess to you now in the hopes that you will look with sorrow and mercy upon the weakness of my female mind and female flesh, so desirous to be taken into Your Grace's favor . . .*

I write the truth about Manox in as brief and succinct prose as I can manage: we kissed and I was a foolish child who should have known better. In regard to the matter of Francis—no doubt he has told them, I can tell by their questioning that they already know the truth. Torture aided his confession, most likely, in addition to the bitterness he felt toward me for rejecting his love.

Still, I must choose my words carefully. I admit that I allowed him to court me in secret when I was but a child unschooled in the ways of proper love and honor. I confess the details of our relationship: the tokens of affection we exchanged, and the habit we began of calling each other husband and wife—terms of endearment, merely. But in spite of the various times he took liberties with my person upon my bed in the maidens' chamber of Lambeth, I never made any formal promise to marry him.

"How could I have?" I turn to Cranmer, who peers over my shoulder at the paper before me. "I am only a girl. A girl does not choose whom she will marry."

I end with a solemn request for compassion for a girl who was pulled too strongly by her emotions and granted little guidance in such affairs. Henry already finds the female flesh weak, so I think this will be the most effective way to explain myself. Indeed, I can think of no other explanation at my disposal. A king's lust and obsessions are called love and become law, but these same impulses in a queen are treason.

I think Henry and I are more alike than we will ever know.

"Come now, Catherine." Cranmer's voice is soothing, cajoling. "What new fantasy has come into your head? If there is more, you must tell it. You can confide it in me." I lift my hands and feel the tears pouring down my face. I am gasping—the sound of my sobs frightening to hear.

"The king's mercy makes my offenses appear even more heinous than they did before," I cry, my voice wavering with sobs. "The more I consider the greatness of his mercy, the more I do sorrow that I should have so injured the heart of His Majesty. Please tell him that. Tell him that he is my husband—my only husband—and that I will die claiming him so!"

Let him give the king my confession, and tell him of my bitter repentance. I am not Francis Dereham's wife, I am Henry's wife. His beloved wife, for whose love he was thanking God mere days ago. He will need to see me, and he will forgive me. I will not allow Cranmer and Norfolk and all his council—men with their own intentions—to convince me otherwise. Henry's great old heart has been through too much heartache to permit any more. He will welcome me back into his arms, into his heart, and we will be all the sweeter with each other when he does. I can see it all when I close my eyes: Henry and I, together, our tearstained cheeks pressed side by side.

When I look up and blink my eyes, my vision is fogged. Cranmer is leaving, and the ladies rush into the room to my aid. But I will be fine—I have confessed, and now await the king's mercy. And he will be merciful, for Henry loves me. I am not like cousin Anne, whom he wanted to be rid of. I am Catherine. We danced just a few nights ago, before all of court, and he told me I looked beautiful. He told me that he loved me. I clamp my hand over my mouth, to keep the words inside. Henry loves me. He will save me from all of this.

XXXV

I've been imprisoned in my chambers for mere days, but it feels like years. I often walk from room to room, restless. It is a double imprisonment, spent visiting and revisiting old thoughts and fears as I walk, unseeing, from one room to the next, then back again to where I began. I'm waiting for Cranmer and Norfolk to arrive again, but I know that I will not say anything more to them. I will speak only to my husband, my king.

Joan sets a tray of food upon the table before me; her

hands are trembling, and the tray clatters upon the polished table. I look up and see that her face is white as snow.

"Joan?"

"I've just overheard, Your Grace." She kneels before me, gathering my hands in hers. "The king has left Hampton, with only a few attendants."

"The king has left?"

"Yes. They say he has gone to Oatlands Palace." Her eyes flutter away from mine, nervously.

"The king has left me here, alone?"

"Was I right to tell you?"

"Of course. Perhaps he is going to read my confession, in private," I remark lightly. "Oatlands Palace in Surrey—that is where we were married."

"I know, Your Majesty." She bends forward and presses my hand to her lips. "You will tell me if you need anything?"

"Of course I will, Joan."

I need to see my husband. I need to calm his fears. I need for his love to save me.

THE TRAYS OF FOOD ARRIVE, and hours later they are taken away in the same state. This is one of the few ways in which I can see that time is still passing, that it does not stand completely still. I watch the sun rise in the window, and then I watch it set, and I sit and hum softly to myself in the blackness. The blackness is particularly dangerous, full of evil, whispering things.

Cranmer and Norfolk came to visit, but I told them nothing. How am I to gauge what to tell them so as not to reveal more than what they already know? Jane went into my privy chamber upon their arrival and she has not been out since.

"What are you doing?" I ask Lisbeth and Dorothy, when I see them removing the knife from my dinner platter and wrapping it in a napkin. They look at each other.

"Tell me—what are you doing? You can eat the dinner yourselves, you know that I will not. But you must answer my question."

"Norfolk told us to, my queen." Dorothy dips a quick bow as she says this, but I see that she cannot look me in the eye. "He was afraid you may attempt to harm your-self."

"Indeed, Norfolk is very concerned about my well-being."

"*We* are concerned, Your Grace." Lisbeth reaches her hand out to my arm, but I shrug her away. I return to the window again, because that is where time moves. That is the only place where time still moves.

THE SUN HAS SET, and my chambers were raided: Joan, Dorothy, Lisbeth, Katherine, Malyn—all of them have been taken in for questioning, to glean what they know about my dalliance with Francis.

In the silence of their departure, weariness threatens to overtake me, pull me under. But when I close my eyes, the screaming gets closer, louder, until it fills my head: *Manox and Dereham, locked within the Tower, stretched upon the rack. What will they do to them? What will they confess? Will Thomas be safe? What about my ladies?*

But I already know: my ladies will not need torture. The words will spew out of their mouths without a second thought. They will betray my confidence to save themselves, I am certain. Had they not been thinking solely of their own gain when they requested posts in my chambers? There was nothing I could have done to stop them. Nothing I could have done. Instead it appears that I was reliving my days at Lambeth here at court, with all of my ladies around me and my paramour given a position in my household. I cannot deny the wickedness of this vision. Is this what Henry thinks of me, now? Is this how far I have fallen in his eyes?

The images shift, change: now I see Henry. I'm lying beside him upon his great royal bed, with the sheer golden curtains. Henry is sleeping. I can't think of Thomas now, or else the king will know: he will see my dreams, he will know all. I hover over the king's sleeping face in the darkness. His eyes fly open suddenly, and he wakes with a horrifying roar, his eyes livid with fire.

The thought of a girl already spoiled by another man disgusts him.

I've made a fool of the king on his marriage bed! I hadn't meant to but I did. He grasps my neck, ready to choke me to death.

A strangled cry in the darkness startles me. I am awake now, completely awake, sitting upon a window seat and fully dressed. I peer into the darkness and fumble forward on trembling legs. A hand grabs my arm. I gasp in fear, but I can't release myself from the icy grip.

"Be careful! Be careful where you step."

"Jane? Jane, what is wrong?"

"Be careful where you step, the hole has opened up." She points a white hand into the shadows before us. "The pit of darkness."

"Jane, you must talk to me." I put my hand upon her arm, cautiously. "We must decide what we will tell them—and not tell them. They are going to question you, soon enough."

"It does not matter what we tell them, fool!" she snaps.

"Watch your words, Jane."

"Watch my words? I'm watching them. I can see them pouring out of my mouth." She pants, frantically.

"Then stop pouring them. Watch what you say—say nothing. Answer none of their questions."

"It is too late, Catherine, for you and for me." She steps close to me, a slice of cold moonlight from the window lights upon her face. Her eyes are wide, unblinking. "It has been a long time coming for me. Guilt or innocence does not matter. I know more about court than you do, my queen. I've seen far more than you've seen."

"What have you seen?"

"Or haven't seen, more like." She laughs at this, a thin, wheezing laugh that sends a chill through my bones. "I haven't seen many things I've said I've seen. You must understand this about court, Catherine: if they want to do away with you, they will find some way to do it. They will find any way to do it, it does not matter if it's true or not." A slight smile sharpens the corners of her mouth. "Just like we did to your cousin Queen Anne."

"What do you mean, *what we did*, Jane? What did you do?"

"I did what they wanted me to do. I played an important service to the king. He was tired of her—he was sick at the sight of her. But how to be rid of her, really rid of her noxious presence? They said she was a witch, and in some ways it was true, mark me!"

She shakes my arm viciously at this, pushing her face close to mine.

"But there had to be more than that, there had to be much more. So I told them about her couplings with courtiers, a lowly court musician—even her own brother."

"Your husband."

"Yes! My husband, my darling husband, already sick at the sight of me, from the moment we were wed."

I see fire in her eyes, now, a dark flame smoldering there. Her look burns me.

"So I said that I saw them together, in her high royal bed. A travesty against God. You can see many things, if you want to see them, if it is convenient to see them."

"Then it was all a lie?"

"They wanted to be rid of her, and so did I. And her rotten brother along with her! So I helped them. I helped them using Anne's own words against her—and then I added my own, for good measure." She laughs again: a startling, guttural sound.

"Who are they, Jane? The king wanted to be rid of Anne, but who else?"

"The king; the king and more than the king. All the rest of them—the Boleyns, the Howards."

She laughs at the shock upon my face, her mouth wide open.

"There was no enchantment, no witchcraft, Catherine. Anne was just a girl—a girl they propped up on the throne, just as they did with you. But she was common, brutal, challenging. The king tired of her. And when the king tired of her, her family had little use for her anymore."

I remember now, suddenly: that night in the midst of Anne's trial. The cloaked figure at the duchess's chamber door. The dark cloak and white hands—a woman's hands. And then Jane testified, and soon after Anne's fate was sealed.

"You met with the duchess, before Anne's trial," I tell her.

"Of course I did," she says. "The duchess is rather brilliant at lying—but I'm sure you know that now. I met with all manner of Boleyns and Howards. We had to get our stories straight. We had to get our lies lined up, in order. The king wanted to be rid of her, Catherine, and we were helping him. There was no saving her, so we decided we might as well help him get rid of her as quickly as possible, and save ourselves."

She laughs, but the laughter falters, as if stuck in her throat. She swallows. "And now my time has come."

"What are you saying? Jane!" Her gaze wanders from me, suddenly, as if gazing at some other horror standing in the room beside me. Jane's own ghosts have found her, here. I shake her rudely to wake her from her reverie.

"And now our time has come. They will not need to lie, Catherine. We did this to ourselves."

"You told me that I would be safe—that you would keep my secret. I was in danger, Jane. You told me it was the only thing that I could do."

"You could have been safe, you could have been. But now they've found a means to be rid of you—Cranmer, the Privy

Council, the rest of them, they've all wanted to be rid of you, before you bear a child. Not the king, this time, but the power that surrounds him. They've found a means to be rid of you, and it will be enough. More than enough. But they didn't have to make up anything, did they, Catherine? They only needed to find out the truth."

She stares at me, her dark eyes wide and unblinking; but her gaze seems distant, as though she is staring straight through me.

"Be careful where you step, Catherine."

She points toward the floor in the center of the dark room.

"The blackness is there: madness, death. It's opened up. Be careful not to step into it. If it swallows you, there is no coming back again."

She releases my arm and sinks back into the shadows, muttering to herself. I stand here numbly, dumbly. I think that my whole world has changed: the witch wasn't a witch, after all. *Anne was just a girl*—a girl not unlike me.

But the king wanted to be rid of her. The king doesn't want to be rid of me, I am sure of it. Just this month, this very month, he gave thanks for me, his loving wife. The others may want to be rid of me, but not Henry, my Henry. He is a king—his power must be greater than any they can muster, in the end.

TIME HAS PASSED, and my ladies have still not returned from questioning. Several meek, lowly maidens tend to my needs as I wait for them to return. But when the guards arrive, they arrive alone.

"Jane Boleyn, Lady Rochford," they announce as they enter my chamber. We all know what they mean by this.

"She is not well," I say, my voice rough and croaking from my throat. But they pay this no mind. They follow a maid to the privy chamber, where Jane has been staying. The moment the door opens, I hear her scream. The guards lift her in their arms, unperturbed by her wild cries. When she sees me, she begins to scream louder, as if she has seen the devil, himself.

Anything she tells them will be no more than the ravings of a madwoman—how can they glean any truth from that? Or perhaps the truth is not necessary. They will hear what they want to hear.

And what about that truth? Was I really acting out of Henry's desperation to secure an heir, or my passionate desire to spend a night with Thomas? I relive every scene from the summer progress, unwillingly, until they become jumbled in my memory—nights with the king and nights with Thomas overlapping in a frightening series of images, too fast for me to fully understand. Was I simply desperate to be with him, and used this as my excuse?

It was all for the baby, I remind myself. *It was all to save my life.* Now, imprisoned in my chambers at Hampton Court, I wonder if this was enough of a pretext for treason.

XXXVI

Cranmer and Norfolk arrive, and call all of the remainder of my household into the main chamber.

"Am I to see the king?" I rush up to Norfolk and ask quietly. He pretends not to have heard me.

"You will be departing today for Syon House, for the remainder of your confinement. You will be permitted to take three ladies with you. You will be under house arrest, but served as queen."

"With only three ladies to attend to me?"

"Three should be enough."

I watch, dumbfounded, as he chooses my maids for me: three bland girls whose names I don't remember from the group of inexperienced ladies who found their way into my household.

"What gowns am I permitted to take?" They glare at me: a foolish, prattling girl to be concerned about such insignificant matters as my wardrobe in the midst of my imprisonment. But there is nothing I can do to stop myself. I watch as the ladies gather my belongings: six gowns, six hoods, all of them in somber colors and simple design, unadorned with any cloth of gold or jewels or elaborate embroidery. All of my jewelry will be left behind here, at Hampton.

I stand with the ladies, inspecting the clothing I'm allowed to take with me. If I don't inspect this hood closely enough, then I will fall into the great abyss of fear that has opened up before me—just what Jane told me about. I can see it today, even in bright daylight: a black hole in the middle of the stone floor. I carefully step around it whenever necessary, even lifting my gown over the spot so as not to dip it into the blackness. The guards see me do this, but say nothing.

We are taken by barge to Syon House. It was Syon Abbey for years, until Henry reclaimed it during the dissolution and converted it into a residence. I'm given a suite of rooms with a private bedchamber. These rooms lack the rich tapestries, the luxuriant abundance of velvet pillows of my previous residences. It seems that everything in life has been robbed of its sparkle: my own gown is bland, as bland as the three ladies who stand before me in dark, plain gowns, their faces pale and blank as stone.

"This is a suitable place for a nunnery," I remark upon entering my chamber, "and now I shall dress as a nun, as well. I shall dress as you do."

The ladies lower their heads, and I laugh at them.

"Perhaps God will come to me, here." I feel unable to stop laughing. "No, no, that won't happen. God left here a long time ago. King Henry evicted Him."

Suddenly I hear the door behind us being shut, and locked. This is not a nunnery, or a queen's chamber: this is a prison. I must not forget that.

When I turn, I see a pale form staring back at me. I gasp at the sight of the ghost—her face so pale, her eyes so dark. It is Anne Boleyn, staring at me, mocking me in my despair.

I was no witch! the ghost shrieks. She lifts her arm and points at me, in accusation. *I was no witch! I was only a girl!*

"I am only a girl! This can't happen to me!"

"What's wrong, Your Grace? What's the matter?"

"Don't you see her? Don't you see?" I point toward the ghost, still standing in her accusatory pose. My lady looks at the ghost, blankly, then returns her gaze to me.

"It is a mirror, my queen."

I turn to glare at her; she winces at my expression, but does not falter from my gaze. I step forward, and the revenant steps closer. I reach out and my fingers make contact with a sheet of cold glass.

Now I can see: it is my own reflection staring back at me.

MARY, MATHILDE, AND ELSIE are a more subdued trio of ladies than I have ever had in my company. Even their names are plain, and part of me would like to tell them so. But even when I am cross they seem untroubled by my behavior. They are quiet, sedate, but also diligent. This room does still seem a queen's chamber, if only for their fastidiousness in dressing me, arranging my hair, bringing my meals, and offering whatever meager comforts they can manage. Truly, it is not so mean an existence as I had expected; I am still being treated with some mercy, perhaps there is hope yet for more.

"You know I won't eat that," I inform Mathilde as she places a breakfast tray upon the table.

"Whatever you wish, my queen. But, for your sake, I humbly beg you to eat. You must be hungry, and it is important for you to keep your strength."

"I see no reason for strength, if I am stuck here all day. I don't know what is happening in the world beyond these walls."

"We want you to be prepared for whatever happens, my queen."

The other ladies look up from their embroidery, their gazes locked on my face.

"We all must be prepared for whatever may happen." Mathilde reaches forward and places her hand lightly upon my arm.

"What do you know?" My voice is sharp with sudden anger, my eyes burning. "Tell me right now—I order you. Tell me what you know."

"I know nothing, my queen, save what you have already been told. Your ladies, along with Henry Manox and Francis Dereham, have been taken to the Tower for questioning."

"For *torture* and questioning," I tell her, just to see her eyelids quiver with fear.

"I have not heard it said aloud, but it is most likely true. Yes." She gazes down at my hand as she says this. "Beyond that, I know nothing more. We none of us know more, but we would tell you if we did."

"I don't know what I'm doing here," I whisper. The sound of my own voice frightens me. "I don't know what I'm waiting for."

"We are here," she tells me. Her voice is calm. "We will wait with you. We will wait for whatever is to come."

The hole in the floor is there. I look away from it. I look back to Mathilde's face.

"You are tired, you must get some sleep." She sits on a cushion beside me and reaches up to stroke my hair. I am tired, it's true, but I've been too afraid to sleep, too afraid of dreaming. But the ladies are all seated around me, and a fire is lit. I place my head upon a pillow, just to rest.

THESE GIRLS ARE not the usual type one finds at court. Perhaps I would have been better met with them as companions than the ladies of Lambeth, in my youth. I dream of this often, in fact: the dream of an alternate life, an alternate Catherine. This Catherine never caught the king's eye, but instead married Thomas Culpeper and became the mother of his children. I imagine our wedding in lavish detail: the gown, the church, all of my family present, proud of me. It is all so precious, so beautiful, until the moment the king appears to grant his blessing to us both and I awake, screaming and shaking uncontrollably.

"Breathe, my queen, breathe. Breathe." Always when I wake, one of the ladies is here, beside me. At first they were interchangeable, but now I notice slight differences: Mathilde is the oldest, her eyes lined with age. Mary is the prettiest, with soft hands and a soothing voice. Elsie is the youngest, and talks just above a whisper. She must not be any more than thirteen years old. I should tell her to be wary of King Henry, who likes a fresh young girl, but I think her plain face will keep her safe from all of the trouble I have endured.

"They will not let me see my husband," I tell Mary. The room is dark. I don't know when it became nighttime—have I been swallowed by the darkness? But then how would Mary be with me, if I've already been consumed? I blink; Elsie is stretching forward from her chair and lighting a candle. The shadows stretch up and light her gaunt, tired face.

"Have they told you why?" Mary asks.

"No, they have not told me why. I need to see him, I need to explain."

"You have offered him your confession, Catherine." Mathilde rests her cool hands against my hot forehead. "All we can do now is pray for mercy."

Mary and Elsie take my hands, and we are linked together

in a circle. They are quiet, their eyes closed, praying. I have confessed, I have—but not everything. I can't even bear the thought of confessing it all to these ladies, for fear of what they may think of me. I clench my lips tightly shut, for fear the damning truth will spring free of its own accord. Will God deem me worthy of mercy? I close my eyes, in spite of my fear. I pray, silently, for mercy, a stream of words I dare not say aloud.

FOOTSTEPS. I OPEN MY EYES again, sit up from bed. The ladies are sleeping. I enter the main chamber to find Thomas Wriothesley—another heretical council member, according to Norfolk. But what is he now, ally or enemy? I should assume enmity in everyone, my own uncle Norfolk included.

"Will I be permitted to see the king?" I ask, before he can say a word. "I would like to see him and speak to him in person. It is my only request."

Wriothesley only nods at this solemnly, and gestures to a chair in the middle of the room—the interrogation chair. But I have no interest in sitting there.

"Am I to see the king, my husband?"

"Not yet," he says, studying my face. "I have more questions that must be answered."

What could he possibly want now? I've already offered my confession. I've already written—

"What was the nature of your relationship with Thomas Culpeper?"

I blink at him, as if I don't understand the question. *Did he really say that? Am I dreaming?* The room is full of blue shadows; it is either dawn or twilight. This could be a dream, I could be—

"Catherine," he says sternly. He is calling my name, as if calling me back from a far-off place. "You must answer me. You must know the answer. What was the nature of your relationship with Thomas Culpeper?"

"He is my cousin," I tell him.

"Yes, and perhaps much more than that, according to your ladies. Only your full confession will grant you any mercy from the king. You must tell all."

But how would mercy be possible, once I've told all? Does he realize what he is asking me to admit? What do they already know? I can't tell the truth! There is no mercy for treason. *The king's will be done!*

"Culpeper has been taken in for questioning," he continues efficiently. The words echo deafeningly in my head: Thomas has been taken in for questioning. Thomas is in the Tower. *The Tower!*

"Did you have a precontract to Culpeper, before your marriage to the king?"

"No, I didn't."

"Did you allow him carnal knowledge of your person before or after you consummated your marriage to the king?"

This is my only hope, to protect him, to protect us both. He is my love, my one true love, and he will never fail me.

"No," I tell him.

"This was found on Culpeper's person and identified as a gift from you." He brandishes the ring before my face—the token I had bestowed on Thomas, in secret. But what does that mean? That means nothing, on its own.

"Did you love Thomas Culpeper?"

"No," I tell him. "I did not love him. Nothing transpired between us."

"Do you admit to having met with Culpeper, in private?"

"No."

"Lady Rochford tells a different story, Catherine."

Of course, Jane told them. Then it is too late, isn't it, to deny it in its entirety?

"She urged me to meet with him. She arranged the meetings. But it was entirely innocent. The ring was merely a gift, a trifle."

The ring glitters on Wriothesley's fat finger. It winks at me like a cruel, bloodred eye. The blackness is here—close, so close to me.

"Did you ever tell Thomas Culpeper that you loved him?"

"No." But my voice is growing smaller. I am separating from myself, like the cream curdling away from the milk. I am floating up from my head, floating up above this room, above it all. I think I am safer, here. I don't know when I will ever come down, and live in my body, again.

"No," is all I manage to repeat. "No, no, no, no."

Thomas is in the Tower, but he will protect me. If there is anyone sworn to protect me, it is him. I would stake my life upon this. It is quite possible that I already have.

XXXVII

This world is a dangerous place and I float above it, safe from its insistent grasp. I float and I am safe. The ladies try to call me back to eat, to talk to them, to lie down and sleep. But I know it is better this way. I stay away from the black hole in the floor, though it gets bigger by the day. I watch as the others sidestep it, or nearly fall in. But they won't fall in. That hole was meant for me. It is my madness, it is my fear.

But I am not a part of this world. I am not living in flesh, anymore, as I've lived my life until now. I sit upon this window seat with a fur pulled over me, but I can't feel the warmth of the fur, or the cool of the stone wall pressed against my cheek. I can't smell the food, or hear the fire crackle. Sometimes I start shivering, but soon enough the quakes pass through me and I move on, through the storm. Elsie's voice calls to me, from very far away, but I don't answer her. I don't have a voice left to answer. When I look again, I see little Elsie, her mousy-brown head bent over her embroidery sample, and she is crying. I don't know why she's crying. I look at it like a painting: *Girl in Tears*. I turn away. I float.

"Do you have anything else to confess, Catherine? You must confess it now." Voices are dim, are far away. I look at my uncle, but he is only a shadow. I am only a shadow. I can't answer him.

I dream of Thomas. I feel as if he is near me, now, and I hope that he can feel me near him, no matter where he is. No matter what they are doing to him. It has to be all right, it has to. Hope is not yet dead, though there are those bent upon destroying it. He is my love, and he will not fail me.

The sky beyond the window is dark, and I see my own face reflected dimly in the warped glass. *Who is that girl?* I wonder, staring at the contour of my cheek, the shape of my full lips. I barely recognize myself, or perhaps I never really looked at myself this hard, this carefully. I half expect the image of my face to dissolve before my eyes.

There is a flicker of movement in the window. I see a stark face reflected beside my own, staring at me. White face, black eyes, black hair. I turn my head, and she's still here.

It is Anne Boleyn.

"I was a girl, just like you," she tells me, "can you imagine such a thing?"

She sits up on the window seat, across from me. She rolls her shoulders back and stretches her long, slender torso. She is sharp and elegant and womanly and proud, just as I saw her that day, on her coronation. But as she stretches I can see the red streak across her white neck—I look away, but she only laughs.

"No, I wasn't just like you. We are quite different. I was crowned queen and I produced an heir. But here you are, so soon, so soon. Here you are, waiting and waiting and waiting."

I feel dizzy looking at her; I can't breathe. She makes my vision blur: her skin so pale, her hair so dark, the wound upon her neck dripping red.

"What will you do now, Catherine?" She cocks one slim eyebrow as she asks me this. "How far will you go to save yourself?"

Henry loves me, Henry will save me. Thomas will protect me. Love will save me in the end. Anne laughs suddenly, as if reading my thoughts. Nothing is safe from her. She stares at me, her eyes gleaming, feral.

"Love will not save you, Catherine. Especially not love from Henry, for he loves nothing so much as himself. You should know that by now." She turns her head to the side again, craning her elegant neck, brandishing the wound before me. "You are not so special, so singular, to have been granted the king's love."

"But he chose me, he married me." I whisper.

"He chose you for lust, not love. He glorifies his lust into love—he would glorify the spot where he shits if he could." She bristles, eyes gleaming. "His tiny man-member wagged, and he followed wherever it led him, destroying all that stood in his path. His family, his country, his church—his lust was paramount to all. Do you think he will hesitate to destroy you?"

I am his wife, I think, but dare not say aloud.

"This is the predicament of a woman's power." She tilts her chin down, lifting her eyes to mine—her eyes glisten like onyx. "We are blamed for a man's lust. You can see this now, can't you?"

I nod my head slightly. She smiles, her mouth a gleaming red crescent.

"We inspire lust in men; it is our power. But does it really make us powerful, or vulnerable? We are desired, and then we are debased. First we are goddesses, then mere mortal women, then harlots. It was this way with me, and now with you, too." She narrows her eyes at me, inspecting me carefully. "I am sure you had no idea of the danger of the power you possessed."

He loved me. He thanked God for me. I grit my teeth angrily. *He does not want to be rid of me, the way he wanted to be rid of you.*

"That can hardly matter now, Catherine." Anne responds to my thoughts. As she stares at me, I can see a realization dawn in her eyes; she smiles with malicious amusement. "You still think he will save you, don't you? How can you possibly think such a thing?"

"What do I do?" I ask her. My voice is a shameful croak.

"There is nothing left for you, Catherine." Her eyes are black, depthless. I can feel myself falling into them, like the hole of madness pulsing in the middle of the floor. "You've learned nothing from me. I cannot help you, now."

"THIS IS YOUR final chance to confess, Catherine," Norfolk tells me. He is leaning over me. He looks very, very tall. I shift my head away from the window. My hair is matted in a tangle against my cheek.

"I have nothing to confess," I tell him; my voice is quiet, hoarse. They will not fool me into betraying my love.

"Then it is too late for you."

I flash my eyes at his. *Too late for me? Too late for what?* In response to my brittle gaze, Cranmer pulls a roll of parchment from his pocket.

"*'I intended to do ill with the queen, and the queen likewise intended to do ill with me,'*" he reads.

"Who would say—"

"Your beloved Thomas Culpeper," Cranmer informs me, "your *'little sweet fool.'*"

My breath catches in my throat, my heart tumbles over itself.

"Jane, she arranged it," I mutter, inconsequentially. "It was her idea."

"She disagrees with that, as well. She assures us that the meetings were entirely your idea, and that she tried to dissuade you from such danger, but that you would not listen to her."

I open my mouth to speak, but Cranmer cuts my words short.

"Before you try blaming your lover, Catherine, I think it best that you know he has already placed the blame on you." Cranmer lowers himself to my level. His face is very close to mine; I can feel his warm, stale breath as he speaks. He turns back to his paper and reads: "*'The queen demanded to meet with me, every night. The queen was languishing and dying of love for me.'*"

"But nothing happened—we met together, but nothing happened."

"But the intent was there, do you admit it?"

"I—I don't—"

"Your ladies have corroborated this story with their testimony." Norfolk moves on smoothly. "They all saw the way you looked at Culpeper, they saw that clearly you were in love with him. You made little effort to hide it."

"And look where it has led you." Cranmer leans closer to my face. "Were you in love with him, Catherine? Now is your final chance to confess." But I can already see the truth of it: nothing I say will make any difference, now.

"I thought I was," I tell them, "I thought he loved me. But I was wrong."

"I am afraid that what you may feel now matters little." Norfolk sighs, he pulls a ragged piece of paper from his doublet pocket and holds it before my face. *Master Culpeper...*

I never longed for anything so much as to see you . . . Yours as long as life endures, Catherine.

"Let's be clear on this point, little niece." Norfolk's voice is harsh and sneering. "When you signed this letter, you signed your own death warrant into law. There is no mercy for you, now."

The screaming begins. It's a horrible, animal sound pouring out of me, and I can't stop it. Nothing can stop it. Norfolk and Cranmer stand back, disgust and horror in their eyes. I am on this earth again, I feel stuck to this earth, unable to rend myself from it. My skin burns at the contact with reality. I look down and realize I'm raking my ragged fingernails over my arms, tearing my flesh.

Cranmer and Norfolk recede into the shadows. The ladies rush in to comfort me. But there is no mercy, no comfort for me, now.

"Confess to God," Mathilde urges me. "Forget about Cranmer. Forget about any of them. Confess your sins to God, and be forgiven."

"There is no forgiveness for me."

The black hole in the floor pulses, spreads. I watch it, and all I can do is scream.

"There is always forgiveness, Catherine," Mathilde tells me. "But only if you are willing—"

"What about Thomas?" I ask them. "What will happen to him? I will lose him now, I will surely lose him—" I begin screaming again, tears streaming down my face. Mathilde looks at me with pursed lips, then slaps me suddenly across the face. I'm so shocked that I stop crying. The room is silent.

"Catherine, I'm sorry—but don't you see what he's done to you? He could have saved you, but he didn't. He could have sacrificed himself for your sake, but he didn't. His words have condemned you both."

"Then he did not love me?" My voice is high and whining, like a child's. I cannot look into her eyes for shame. She reaches out and lifts my chin so that I must face her; her eyes are not stern, they are soft, wet.

"It doesn't mean that he did not love you, or that he does not love you, now," she says softly. "He was tortured, Catherine. He was afraid. Perhaps he thought you had betrayed him. I wish it had not been so. But I promised to tell you the truth."

"I didn't betray him. He betrayed me."

"I know. This is not a poem, or a song, or a dream about romance—this is life and death. Perhaps he loved you very much, and then pain and fear swallowed him whole. But I want you to stop thinking about him for a moment, and think instead of yourself."

She takes my hand in hers. The others are seated on the floor beside us. They shuffle closer; Mary takes my other hand, and Elsie's completes the link.

"Pray for forgiveness for yourself, and for all of them. We all must pray."

"God will think me weak and a fool."

"God will think that you are His child," she says soothingly, "and that you were led down the wrong path. Tell Him that. Pray."

I close my eyes and do as she says. Thomas betrayed me, but my love for him still burns inside my heart. I can only hope that Henry feels the same way about me. The remembrance of our love and happiness could still save me, Henry could still save me. I close my eyes and pray for this: for Henry's love and mercy.

THE FIRE IS WARM, I can feel its heat radiating out to me. I'm wrapped up in a blanket on this window seat, my head propped up by a satin cushion. I don't spend much time in this room anymore, floating in and out. Floating around. This life is where nightmares live—I avoid it as much as I can.

I look out the window. The glass is foggy and misshapen, but I can see that the sun has set outside. It is twilight, the sky a rich blue. I hear footsteps, hoofbeats, the call of a hawk. I look down to the path below my window: Thomas Culpeper is standing there. I press my palm flat against the dim glass.

He smiles at me. His eyes are black against his pale face— I have not forgotten how dark his eyes are, nor the way they crinkle in the corners. I have not forgotten, Thomas. *I have not forgotten you.* He lifts his hand and waves at me, smiling, then turns to leave. I pound my hand against the glass to get his attention.

My pounding ceases suddenly when Mary grabs my wrist. I struggle for a moment, scowling, but say nothing.

"Who are you waving to, my lady?"

"Thomas," I tell her. "He's come to see me."

I turn to look back out to the dim street but she pulls me away, shaking me slightly.

"He is dead, Catherine," she whispers. "It is over, he is dead."

"No, I just saw him." I push her arms away and turn again to the window. But Thomas is gone. Her words made him leave—her dark, evil words. Why would she say such things? Why?

"Perhaps he came to say good-bye," she says, resting her hand upon my shoulder, but I shrug her off.

"Why? Am I going somewhere?" I ask.

"No." Mary tucks me back into my place on the window seat. I lean my head back and think of Thomas: his long-fingered hands, his sinewy arms and bare chest, his spine like a row of sharp stones beneath my fingertips.

WHEN I LOOK again at the dark window, I see her beside me. I knew she would be back.

"Your lovers are dead, Catherine," Anne tells me. Her long slender fingers are stark white against her black gown. "And they've left you here, waiting, waiting. It is a sad story."

"You don't seem sad," I croak.

"No. Because everyone will remember me. But how will history remember you, Catherine, have you thought of that?"

I turn back to the window, hoping to see Thomas on the street below. But the sky is too dark. All I can see is my own face reflected there, and Anne Boleyn's reflected beside it. Her eyes are endlessly black, cavernous, like the sky. I could get lost in them.

"You didn't even manage to add your own blood to the line of succession," Anne reminds me, the words rolling seductively off her tongue. "That was my triumph—my daughter still lives, waiting for the day when she may take the crown in my stead."

"Perhaps it's for the best."

"You do not really think that, do you?" Anne's laughter is sharp, like broken glass. "You cannot possibly be satisfied with mediocrity. Can you?"

But I was never ambitious the way Anne was, harboring ambition that stretches beyond the grave. I would have liked to have had a baby, to watch him grow. But while the crown may secure riches, it does not secure happiness. Henry is living proof of that.

"There is only one way that you will be remembered, if at all." She moves closer, whispering in my ear. "As the second, and less remarkable, of Henry's executed queens."

"Maybe I don't want to be remembered," I tell her, though she laughs at the mere idea of it. "Maybe I wish I never was queen."

"And you aren't anymore." Anne shivers in delight. "Those girls already told you. You are no longer queen. You are merely Catherine Howard."

Merely Catherine Howard. I close my eyes, willing Anne to leave me. It is true: a proclamation was released by the Privy Council that I had forfeited my honor, and in so doing would no longer be named queen, but merely Catherine Howard. Now, to be Catherine Howard is no inconsequential thing, nor is it a promising thing. It is to be in the very heart of danger, hovering over the mouth of hell.

XXXVIII

"Your family will most likely be released, soon. Perhaps in the new year," Mary tells me by way of consolation. We are seated together before the fire. The days have grown colder, bitter. I did not want to move, but the ladies pulled me bodily from my window seat and settled me here, upon a cushioned chair close to the flames. I had wanted to sit by the window, in the hopes of seeing Thomas again, but I dare not tell them this. I know they will not understand.

"Who?" I ask, as though just waking up from a long nap. "Where are they?"

"The Tower," Elsie tells me, but chokes on the word as soon as she says it.

"Nearly all of the Howards at court have been incarcerated," Mary continues. "The Tower is so crowded that even the royal chambers have been opened for use."

"And how are they charged?"

"With misrepresentation to the king."

Yes, yes, they told me about this. They are all guilty for having represented me as a virgin: the duchess, my siblings, various cousins, aunts and uncles—everyone who found places of honor at court upon my marriage to the king. Now they all seek to assure the Privy Council that they knew nothing of my wild misdeeds, either before or during my marriage. My eyes flash from one to another of the ladies. I wonder what they know of my "evil demeanor."

"What about Norfolk?" I ask.

"He wrote a beseeching letter to the king, stating his innocence in the matter."

I laugh at this, and I can see that the sound of it startles them.

"And the king has granted him mercy?"

Mary darts her eyes from mine, but Mathilde nods, warily.

"And what of the duchess?"

"The duchess was caught destroying the contents of Dereham's coffer, thinking it might contain evidence," Mathilde informs me, squinting at the head of a needle and a bit of thread. "She was also imprisoned, but I heard that she told them where eight hundred pounds could be found, hidden in various places at Lambeth. I think that will help her case."

At the thought of the duchess's hiding places, a harsh laugh bursts from my lips. Elsie jumps at the sound of it and stares at me with wide eyes. But I can't stop laughing—a gasping, hysterical laughter. The ladies are pale and frightened, but I don't know how to stop.

"Oh, come now, laugh with me, won't you? We must find something to laugh about."

The ladies try to laugh, but they are unsuccessful. I drown them all out with the sound of my howls. Anne Boleyn stands across the room, watching me; her image ripples as tears spring to my eyes. I don't know if the others can see her, standing there. She smiles, knowingly. Her smile is for me alone.

"You must wait for Parliament to reconvene before you learn your fate," Norfolk informs me. "They will meet after Advent, in the new year."

The sight of Norfolk in my chamber startles me as I awake. It has been so long since I have had any news at all. I blink in the bright light and stand before him.

"I must confess to the king. Will I see him soon? Before the trial?"

"The king has left this matter to his advisers. You will wait for their action."

"I see I have no choice. I have always done whatever I was bid—whatever you told me to do." My eyes flash at his briefly. "And this is where it led me."

"Your own sin has led you here, Catherine. You should know that by now."

"Then you have truly abandoned me, your own flesh and blood?"

"I do what is best for the Howards—would you rather the whole lot of us fell along with you? I've worked too hard for too long for that to happen. You're not the first niece of mine this court has seen fit to sacrifice. There are always other opportunities."

"You will do what is best for yourself. That is all you do."

"You may think what you wish of me, Catherine. But for your sake you should heed the sin and treason in your own heart."

"And what about your sin? You pushed me into this! You who knew my faults, and now you abandon me. I must make my peace with Henry."

"You must make your peace with God, Catherine. The king is done with this matter."

"The king is done with me?" I stare at him, and his expression does not waver. "What does that mean?"

"When Parliament reconvenes, your Bill of Attainder will be drafted."

A Bill of Attainder. Just like the bill they wrote up for old Margaret Pole, the Countess of Salisbury. An uncontested death warrant.

"There will be no trial, Catherine."

"No trial? No chance to defend myself before Parliament, before the king? This is how you will do away with me?"

"You were already given your chance to confess. Your confession has been judged by Parliament, as has the evidence against you."

"Confessions exacted through torture."

"You cannot attempt to convince me that you committed no sin against the king, that you did nothing wrong."

"Then it is already decided: I will be condemned, and you will do it for him." My eyes water; the colors in the chamber seem suddenly too bright. "This was your intention from the beginning, wasn't it? As soon as Cranmer told the king about my past? You would keep me from the king, and take care of the matter yourselves."

"The king requires our protection from such matters, to shield him from further humiliation."

"Why? Are you afraid he will be too merciful? Are you ready to kill me with your own hands, to protect your ambition?"

"It is the king, the monarchy, that I am sworn to protect. And you sought to corrupt it, tainting the royal blood, the royal succession. There is nothing to be done now to protect you."

"But it was all that I could do. I had no other choice—"

"Your regrets no longer matter. In fact, they never did. That should be clear to you, by now."

Then it is true: I am beyond the realm of mercy. A king must be strong and destroy his enemies, even if one of them used to be his love. Being king has become bigger than Henry, bigger than being a man.

Norfolk turns to leave and I slump to the floor. What

Jane told me is true, though I never imagined I would have to face it: when the Howards have no more use for you, they will not hesitate to aid in your descent if it means saving their own skins. From the moment John Lassells arrived with his information about my past, there were those—perhaps Cranmer, perhaps others—who were eager to use it to get rid of me. Norfolk will go along with it to separate himself from me, release himself from blame. They need to be completely rid of me in order for Henry to move on—just as they did with Cousin Anne. No matter who you are in life, no matter who stood by you, when you face death you face it alone.

"Catherine!" The ladies descend upon me, lifting me from the floor.

"It's over," I tell them. "They've left me here. All of them."

"We are here for you, Catherine," Mathilde tells me. "You are not alone."

But I am alone. The room is dark. The great black hole has opened in the floor; the darkness seeps closer to me, creeping toward my toes. It is just me and Anne Boleyn, staring at each other over the great, black void.

"Catherine, you must confess." Mary grasps me by the upper arms, shakes me gently. "Unburden your soul."

"It won't do any good. It's too late, it's too—"

"But it will do some good, for you."

"But I can't, I can't." The words stick in my throat and the black hole at my feet grows larger, spreading closer to me. I feel cold. I'm shivering uncontrollably.

"This is guilt you are feeling, Catherine, and fear. But you have nothing to fear. We are with you."

"Tell us what happened, Catherine." This is Elsie's little voice, beside me. "Tell us about Thomas. Release it, and it will release you."

But how can I tell them? How can I confess all?

"Thomas told me that he loved me but he didn't. The king told me that he loved me but he didn't. He loves nothing. He is cruel and he ruined me, and I hate him for it. And now he's left me here—they've both left me here."

"And what about you? What did you do?"

"I told the king I loved him, just like they told me to." My voice is thin, strained. "I did everything they told me to. I acted. I lied. I didn't have any choice."

"And what else did you do?" Elsie asks.

"Catherine, you can tell us. You need not fear judgment from us."

"I was in love with Thomas. I met with him. I committed treason. I broke the king's heart."

All the words come out in a rush. I look down at my lap the whole time, at my hands clasped with theirs. I shut my eyes and the words keep coming, like a wave released inside of me. My eyes burn, my cheeks are wet with tears. Shadows move in the room, moving over us. When I open my eyes, I fear to see Anne Boleyn's smiling face, but she is gone. The fire is flickering; Mary gets up and stirs it back to life. Flames leap, lighting the room in gold. The black void in the floor is gone. It is just a room again.

"How do you feel now?" Mathilde asks. It seems a year has passed since she last asked me that, or perhaps no time at all. I feel angry, I think to tell her. I feel sad. I don't know what I feel. I feel tired—so tired. Every bone in my body aches. My eyelids droop. My throat is dry and sore.

"You need your rest, Catherine." She strokes my hair as she would a kitten, soothingly. I listen to the crackle of the fire, the sound of Mathilde's regular breathing, the feel of Elsie's cool hand on my own.

THE DAYS AND WEEKS pass in a strange blur. We are waiting—the waiting, I hope, is the worst part of all of this. Tonight it is the death of the old year, the birth of the new. The ladies soothe my spirits by reading psalms and poetry aloud.

"I wonder how they are celebrating this night at court." I can imagine court in only the most vague, distant way.

"Things are different now at court, so I hear," Mary remarks carefully. "It's been a restrained season, void of celebration. And a new law has been recently passed, restricting the king's choice of brides."

"What was that?" Mary's eyes flicker to me, then to Mathilde, who doesn't look up from her embroidery as she answers in her clear, stern voice.

"An unchaste woman who marries the king under false pretenses of purity shall be guilty of high treason."

"Then I've made my small mark upon history, after all," I muse, distantly. "I've changed the way the game is played."

"What game?" Elsie asks.

"The merry game of dangling a host of pretty girls before the king's face to see which one he snatches up."

"Oh," Elsie says, her eyes wide.

"Court is not so full of blushing maiden faces as it would like to pretend." I look at Elsie: she is sweet, unspoiled. I wish that she would leave court, never go back there again. "I wager there is not a single fresh young damsel who has a family member willing to risk treason to vouch for her purity."

Perhaps this will be better for everyone—no other young girl will be used as a pawn, as I was. And perhaps it will be better for Henry. In the case of each of his wives, it is possible that Henry was the only one to feel love. None of them, save perhaps his first bride, felt any true love for him. Yet, like a trusting child, he never suspected that our affections were anything but genuine.

I've read the indictment released about my own crimes, that through deceit I criminally fooled the king into loving me—just what the Howards asked of me. That which catapulted me to the throne now condemns me in the eyes of Parliament. Perhaps Henry and I were both blinded by his love for me. I drowned in all of those words of love and forgot that beneath the rich crimson velvet, the glittering eyes, the bejeweled fingers and joyous laugh lay the reaper, in the flesh. I never thought he would abandon me, I never thought I would be forced to accept my death at Henry's hand.

But it was not him, not really. I took the path that led me here. The blood upon my hands is my own. If Henry wanted me dead, or wanted to save me, I will simply never know. In the face of his shame, he can't show any softness, any compassion. My crimes have been too serious, and the price of kingship too harsh.

I turn away from the fire, away from these thoughts, my head resting on a pillow propped upon Mary's lap. Elsie lifts a book and resumes her poetry reading.

"That's Thomas Wyatt you're reading," I tell Elsie.

"You are correct, my queen."

I wonder what it would be like to have the mind of a poet, if maybe poetry could take all of my sad choices and make them into something beautiful, something worthwhile that people could understand.

I think back to my first kiss with Thomas, the kiss that felt like poetry upon my lips. If only I had known then that we would never be permitted such a pure moment together again, I would have made him tarry longer, I would have held him longer, and kissed him many times. Or maybe it would have been better, safer, not to have kissed him at all. As it is, that single kiss burned into me like a scar. It began as a strength, then became a weakness, then a tool of our destruction.

But I can't think of Thomas anymore; the pain it gives me is too great, too confused a thing for a heart to bear. His love and his betrayal sit together, like twin stones buried inside of me. And he is gone. I will never see him again, never be able to understand what happened, in the end. This realization comes to me again and again.

I close my eyes and think of Wyatt. Perhaps I will pray to him, to a poet. No doubt God is weary of my prayers. This is my prayer, tonight: give words to one who could never speak for herself, who could never find just the right words to explain.

XXXIX

It is February, cold and snowy. Cranmer arrives with other members of the Privy Council, and this time they are not here for confession. They've come for me. The moment we've been waiting for is here, but why do I still feel so shocked by it?

"Parliament has reconvened," Norfolk informs me.

I know that, now just get on with it. I grip my skirt with both hands.

"The Bill of Attainder requiring your death has been signed into law," Cranmer states woodenly. "We are here to convey you to the Tower of London, where you and Lady Rochford will await the scheduling of your executions. One wish you requested has been granted: the executions will be carried out in private, on the Tower Green."

Just like my cousin Anne Boleyn. The witch, the whore. I wonder what names they are calling me, at court.

"Who signed it?" I ask suddenly. "Did King Henry's hand sign my death into law?"

Cranmer's eyes dart away from my face. I stare at him, unwavering.

"Of course the bill was signed by the king."

But I know this isn't true. They've done it for him, they've taken care of all of this nasty business for him, so that the king will be protected—or so they could be sure to be rid of me, worried perhaps that his resolve might have swayed, in the end. While the king can bend the law to his will, he cannot buckle beneath it.

We exit Syon House in the midst of a crowd of officers and council members, buffering me on all sides. The ladies grip my hands tightly. The sun is setting, and the wind is cold against my cheek. I start to shiver beneath my cloak.

As soon as I see the barges, draped in black, waiting at the water gate, I am struck with sudden clarity of my situation, like a mighty blow to the head. I think to sit on the ground for a moment, perhaps attach myself somehow to the soil near Syon House. But the guards will not permit it. As soon as my steps falter, I am lifted from the ground and forcibly placed upon the barge.

"Be careful!" the ladies cry. "Be careful with her!"

I am too frightened to struggle. The barge shudders beneath my feet. I am glad for the black drapings, preventing inquisitive eyes from peering in to see the shamed queen being led to her doom. The barge slips over the dark Thames, like a river in the underworld in an ancient myth.

The Thames is a messenger of fortune, be it good or ill. It has always delivered me to my destiny: to Westminster, to take up my first position at court, then back to Lambeth to await my betrothal to the king. This morning is cold, misty, gray. Still, memory flickers before my eyes: I remember the moonlight on the water, the silver light sparkling on the sapphire around my neck. I remember the fear in my heart, though it was a different breed of fear than what resides there, now. That voyage ended in the king's bed. This will end with my head upon the block. All paths lead to death, inevitably.

The land beyond the black water is veiled in gray mist like a bridal veil, or a shroud. The Thames barely ripples beneath the boat, as if it can't be bothered to notice our passage here. The river will forget me, as will everything else. I feel as if I barely exist anymore, out in the middle of this dark water with the gray fog obscuring the world I once knew. It is both a frightening and comforting feeling, to no longer exist: if I am not here, then no one can hurt me or anyone I love, for perhaps they don't exist, either.

I peer from behind the curtains. The sun has already set; the sky is too dark for me to see the heads of Thomas and Francis impaled upon London Bridge, weathering whatever gusts of rain and snow may fall upon them. Now the gate of the Tower emerges from the strange dimness: a dark, opened mouth, ready to swallow me whole. *Traitor's Gate.* Perhaps the sprawling Tower itself rose out of this black river one day, grew and spread like a massive tree, straight from the waters of hell.

The barge stops at the water gate. I step from it onto dry land, a flight of stairs. The guards urge me up each step: I will not stumble, or have a chance to escape. I am rushed into the Tower and up the stairs to my apartments. The stairs are narrow, winding; I paw along the cold stone wall, faltering on the uneven steps, feeling dizzy in my ascent. All the while I hear voices echoing down the hallways: *Catherine!* The residual echoes of torture have sunk into these walls. *Catherine! Catherine! Catherine!* I've heard those cries before, in my darkest dreams—Thomas and Francis calling to me.

But they are dead, I have to remind myself. Thomas wails in the distance, his voice piercing my heart like a sword.

The ladies pull me into my chamber and shut the door behind me. This chamber is not the prison cell I had imagined, but it feels icy in spite of the fire raging in the hearth. I step into the room and hear muttering. Jane is seated in a corner. As I approach her, she wails, cringing away from me. Her eyes are wide and unblinking, and foam collects in the corner of her mouth. I know the look in her eyes.

"You stepped into it, didn't you?" I ask her. "You stepped into the blackness?"

But it's too late to pull her out, now. Mary puts her arm around my shoulders and pulls me away.

"Catherine is here—Catherine is here! The king's beloved is here!" Jane laughs suddenly, her eyes are wide and glassy, unfocused. "I heard that the king called for a sword, to slay you himself! He would slay his own heart if need be. He would cut out his own heart if it beat in a way that did not please him."

"That is what is required of a king," I murmur.

"Then you forgive him, Catherine? You forgive the man that used you so rudely and now throws you to the dogs?"

I am too tired to answer her, too tired to consider my own emotions.

"Well, I don't forgive *you!*" she screams viciously. I jump back in fear, and the other ladies crowd around me, pulling me back.

"It is your fault that I'm here. You were never good at writing letters, Catherine. You were never very good. That's why I was there. The duchess put me beside you, to watch you. From the very beginning. I was to watch your every move. Just as I did with your cousin Anne!"

"You did a fine job of watching me, didn't you?"

"I saw everything you did—you know what I saw." She laughs at this again, tilting her head back with the force of her laughter. "I was to watch you—not to end up here!"

The ladies pull me away, pull me into my bedchamber. I can hear Jane beyond the door, weeping and muttering to herself in her own darkness.

I lean against a wall as the ladies scurry around the room, stoking the flames in the hearth and turning down the bed-clothes. They act as if I am a guest of honor, not a girl condemned. I press my hands to the rough stone wall and close my eyes.

My fingers find scratches, etchings of the names of those who came and went before me. I trace them with my fingertip: *Bishop Fisher, Thomas More, Anne Boleyn, Margaret Pole.*

IT IS DIFFICULT to convince yourself, when you are healthy and lovely and young, that soon you will die. I avoid looking at myself in the mirror, but I inspect my hands, my arms, my belly. I'm still a marvel of youth and health. Where is death? Death is not here.

"We shall wait now for Cranmer to set the date," I tell the ladies. "I'm not sure how long we will have to wait."

Mathilde rises from her chair and stands beside me. She takes my hands in hers. "I think you will not have long to wait, Catherine. And there is something that you must understand." She pauses for a moment, and looks directly into my eyes. "There will be no reprieve for you."

"What?" My throat is cracked, dry. "What are you saying?"

"We've had hope, between us, but that hope is gone. I want you to prepare yourself for what is to come."

I feel my mouth twist in anger—how dare she look inside me and see my one last hope, and destroy it? But I don't know what to say. I squeeze her hands in mine.

"I'm sorry," she says, her eyes soft as a doe's. "You wanted me to tell you the truth. It is the least that I can do."

"Will you pray for me? In spite of what I've done, in spite of the fact that I may deserve—"

"Of course we will pray for you." Mary and Elsie join us, their hands on my arms. "We will pray for you, Your Grace, and we will weep."

"And what happens then? When it is over?"

"When it is all over," Mathilde says carefully, "and your soul has departed this earth, we will be as kind to you in death as we have been now. We will bury you ourselves, with a prayer."

There is nothing I can say. I fold myself into their arms.

FROM THE WINDOW of my chambers I have a perfect view of the scaffold being built, not twenty yards beyond where I stand. I can hear the banging of hammer against wood all day. The workers continue late into the night, anxious to finish their construction. I watch them now, their forms move like shadows against the deep twilight. Beyond the scaffold another twenty yards is the chapel of St. Peter ad Vincula—St. Peter in chains.

"You will be laid to rest next to your infamous cousin Queen Anne Boleyn," a voice says from the darkness behind me. "Overshadowed, both in life and in death."

Anne smiles, her teeth gleaming white, reflected beside me in the dark window. The ladies have fallen asleep before the fire. The familiar madness has returned: the black hole is in the ground, waiting for me. I've been sidestepping it since I arrived here, with their help. But now, with Anne smiling at me, I can feel it again—a deep void, a spiraling fear opening inside of me.

"What will you do, Catherine? What will you say?" she asks, sidling up to me. "I gave a fine speech before the swordsman did his job. No one present will forget my grace, my poise, in the last moments of my life."

"Yes, I heard about that. You were an actress up to the very end." I turn and meet Anne's gaze, not daring to turn away from the sharp wildness blazing from her eyes. "Maybe I am done with acting, with playing a role. Maybe now I can be myself again, the girl I used to be."

"What good is that?" she asks me, her maniacal laughter bubbling up in her throat, threatening to break free. "What good will that do? No one will remember it, Catherine. No one will be impressed with that."

"You made a very impressive speech, it's true. But it didn't change anything for you, did it? You were still executed. You're still dead."

Anne opens her mouth for a bitter retort, but her voice doesn't register in my ears. The image of her dissipates like so much smoke before my eyes. It's not really Anne, after all, just my image of her—her perfection, her triumph, her condemnation. She has haunted me from the moment I first laid eyes upon her, a glittering image gliding upon the Thames. Now she is gone; I've no need for her judgment anymore.

I look across to the chapel, alone. Saint Peter did not fear death, and God sent an angel to release him from his chains. I don't expect an angel to save me, but the least I can do is to prepare myself. I draw a great breath, slowly; my chest expands. I must have peace, now. It is all there is left to me—but that does not mean it is nothing. It is a far greater thing than I ever realized.

Turning away from the window, I gaze around the room. Mary and Mathilde are asleep before the fire. Elsie is asleep upon the bed, curled in exactly the position I found her when I awoke beside her, her arm slung over me. I sit at the small desk in this room and scrawl upon a piece of parchment a list of notes: what gowns and trinkets left to me will be granted to these three ladies, upon my death.

It is very well to flatter and cater to a woman who is royalty, it is quite another to stand beside the condemned. For this small thing, I am so grateful. My heart grows in my chest at the thought of it, until I fear it might burst. There is danger there—I press my cold hands to my still-dry eyes. Once I fall apart, there will be no putting me back together again.

I wonder how history will remember me. Will the details be obscured, exaggerated by time, or will all be washed away, forgotten as the years pass? My portrait was never painted, and only one small coin bears my royal symbol, to remind everyone that I was once queen. That I existed at all.

I only wish I had more time, but I know this wish is not unique to me. I would have liked to have been a mother. Infants appreciate the world around them in ways that are easily forgotten—its brightness and its newness is their birthright. I think of the things that I loved as a child: the tall grass where I would curl up and sleep, the rough cracked bark of the trees I would climb, the trailing branches of the willow tree, the sun on my neck, the wind in my hair.

All of my life I felt as if I belonged to someone else: my father's pretty daughter, my grandmother's charge, Anne Boleyn's cousin, betrothed to Francis, beloved of Thomas, then wife to King Henry. I think back now to when I was truly myself, and I can see it in my mind: I'm a child, lying in the grass and singing, the face of a kitten moving close and sniffing the tip of my nose. I had nothing then, or I thought I had nothing, but really I had everything: I had myself. That was truly me, on my own and complete. It makes me smile, just to think of it.

CRANMER ARRIVES TO inform me that my execution has been scheduled for tomorrow morning.

"You must prepare your soul for death," he says.

"How does one do such a thing?" But he has no guidance to give me. He stands before me, his palms open in a sign of offering. I ponder this, at a loss for words. I stare out the window, thinking.

I hear it, suddenly: a roar, from somewhere else in the Tower. It's coming from the menagerie—that beautiful, majestic lion that the king had encaged until he became a sad, withered creature. He roars again, and I can feel it as if the sound is moving through my own body, a powerful feeling that makes my breath shudder in my chest. Perhaps the old beast is not so broken, after all. Perhaps there are still some things left to us, even in imprisonment: our courage, our dignity.

I turn to Cranmer and blink, slowly.

"Bring the block to my room," I tell him.

I SIT BEFORE THE MIRROR and glance at myself, warily. The room is dark, only a few candles are lit. My hair is matted and my eyes shadowed, my skin is pale; the other half of my face is submerged in darkness. I barely recognize myself.

We all harbor the potential for evil within us. The royal court that I dreamed of for so long nurtures this evil. All of the dashing, handsome courtiers and beautiful ladies are consumed by darkness, consumed by themselves, harboring treason and betrayal in their hearts—betrayal even of those they love, for the sake of power. And I am one of them. I am no better than any of the most greedy, the most vile.

But at least I did not betray my love, my true love. No, he did that for me. Thomas betrayed me. But that can't matter anymore—it is too painful to matter. It is over and done.

The life I have left to me now, brief though it is, is mine alone. I need counsel from no one on my decisions. What will I do now, on my own, with my life and with my death? I will stand and face it all, for that is all there is left for me to do. I have my dignity, something I've thought little of before this moment.

I request a basin of cold water with which to wash my

face. I have not washed properly in weeks, not wanting the bracing cold of water to wake me, to wash the sleep from my eyes, but I know it's time. My gaze is cold and clear. I do not cry, knowing that to do so would be to split myself in two in fear and sorrow. The one thing I can do is remain whole. A strange calm washes over me. I am entering a new stage of my life: like Lambeth, like court, like the king's bed. And like all the others, this next step requires me to leave the past behind. I am still an actress, given a script I have no choice but to play out tomorrow upon the great, grim stage of the Tower Green. Death is a foreign role, and therefore frightening to me. That is why it is frightening to us all.

I settle my neck upon the block simply to know how it is done, to know that I can do it without crumbling. With practice, I can do it like a queen. This is how it is done, easily, and then it will be over. All of this fear will be over. I don't know where I am going after this—to heaven or hell—but no one can know that for certain. All I can do now is pray, and hope that it will do me some good. I settle my neck upon the block, again, again. All I can do is practice until I know that I will be able to do it right.

XL February 13 is a cold day, the earth crisp and white with snow. I wear a white gown, a simple silver circlet for the day of my death. It is pure, virginal. My hair is tied up, away from my neck.

The sun is bright and dazzling reflected off the white snow. It's been so long since I've seen the sun. It makes my eyes hurt to look at it as I step out onto the Tower Green.

Lady Rochford walks behind me; I can hear her sniveling, but I block the sound from my ears. Ravens caw like squalling children, circling overhead. My ladies cluster around me like a shield from the press of the assembled crowd. As I make my way to the scaffold I keep my eyes averted from the block, the hooded executioner, the people squinting at me in the sun. My body feels both heavy and light all at once; my feet are heavy, shuffling along the path.

We pause before the scaffold. The ladies' faces are smeared with tears. I had thought to thank them here, but I cannot force the words from my throat. I touch their faces with my cold fingertips. The wind catches the hems of our dresses and lifts them like clouds, swirling and billowing around us. They look like three angels, standing around me. And they are here to watch my ascent.

My feet are so heavy I can hardly lift them. The ladies hook their arms beneath mine and help me up the stairs of the scaffold. There is straw spread on the ground before us, around the block; it has a dull, ordinary gleam in the pale light. The murmuring of the crowd increases: the faces spread out in an ocean before me, undulating waves. When I turn to face them, I see that their faces are sad, dismayed, not angry. I feel the tears well in my eyes. *Be brave.* I have decided to be brave. My breath forms a cloud before my face in the cold air—I can see life puffing out of me. I had never thought to look at it, before.

I place a coin in the hand of the executioner, just as I rehearsed last night. I grant him my forgiveness for what he is about to do. His gloved hand feels rough against my hand of ice.

"She's just a child," I hear someone cry. "So young, too young."

"God save you, child," another voice from the crowd cries. "God save you."

I can sense their horror, gazing up at me upon the scaffold, my white gown billowing in the wind.

"Pray for me," I ask them. My voice is weak, I don't know if they can hear me. "Please, pray for me."

I lift my hand to shield my eyes from the brightness of the sun, but someone moves forward and covers my eyes with a cloth, ties it behind my head. My legs fold neatly under me. I don't need to cry. I am braver than I thought was.

"God, my soul is Yours. Please forgive me." *Please.*

As I lean forward to press my neck to the block, I hear the beating of drums.

AND AFTER A MOMENT OF PAIN there is falling, but I hold my faith close to me, I let myself fall. After a moment of falling it's all over, and I feel I'm being lifted. The brightness is gone. When I open my eyes there is light, but it does not make my eyes squint, it does not cause me pain.

When I open my eyes, I know where I am. It is not London, nor court, nor the Tower. The grass is green, the sun is warm, and I hear singing: a young voice, light and sweet. The voice is pouring out of my own throat—it is pouring out of me.

I know I am finally home.

Description of the Contrarious Passions in a Lover

I find no peace, and all my war is done;
I fear and hope, I burn, and freeze like ice;
I fly aloft, yet can I not arise;
And nought I have, and all the world I seize on,
That locks nor loseth, holdeth me in prison,
And holds me not, yet can I scape no wise:
Nor lets me live, nor die, at my devise,
And yet of death it giveth me occasion.
Without eye I see; without tongue I plain:
I wish to perish, yet I ask for health;
I love another, and thus I hate myself;
I feed me in sorrow, and laugh in all my pain.
　　Lo, thus displeaseth me both death and life,
　　And my delight is causer of this strife.

—*Sir Thomas Wyatt*

AUTHOR'S NOTE ❧ It has been recorded that the king's advisers, seeking to spare the king from the humiliating details of Catherine's betrayal, took it upon themselves to arrange her condemnation in his absence. The Privy Council went so far as to sign her death warrant, with the king's approval. Whether they did this to spare the king's feelings, or out of their own concern that the king might falter in condemning Catherine Howard to death, is unknown. It is true that at the time the accusations were revealed, Henry was happy with his wife and did not want to be rid of her. His initial reaction to the allegations against her was one of doubt and suspicion, for he believed in his wife's honesty and purity—this is interesting to note, considering the king's proclivity toward paranoia and distrust of those around him.

In regard to Catherine's crimes against the king, the confessions in this novel are all based on historical accounts. Thomas Culpeper confessed to the "intent to do ill" with the queen, but he did not confess to having had a sexual relationship with her before or during her marriage to the king. According to the laws of treason at the time, the intent to commit treason alone was enough to condemn them both to death. The idea that they did have an adulterous affair for the sake of pregnancy is merely conjecture, for the sake of fiction.

As for Catherine's part in this treason, a letter was discovered among Thomas Culpeper's belongings, addressed to *Master Culpeper* and signed *yours as long as life endures, Katheryn*, on which the letter in this account is loosely based. Assuming it is genuine, this letter was certainly enough evidence of Catherine's affection for Thomas Culpeper, and surely helped secure her condemnation.

Years later, when King Henry's daughter Mary Tudor ascended to the throne, she revoked from the records all laws that had been signed by the king's advisers in his stead. This included the Bill of Attainder for Catherine Howard's execution.

Little good it did Catherine then, more than ten years after her death.

ACKNOWLEDGMENTS ঌ Thank you to Thomas Libby, for being both a supportive husband and an enthusiastic research assistant. Thank you to my mother, Bernice; my grandma Sunny; my sisters, Marcie, Valerie, and Susan; and the best in-laws anyone could wish for, Florence and Eugene Libby.

Thank you to my agent, Esmond Harmsworth, for his patience and dedication, and to my editor, Julie Strauss-Gabel, for taking on this project with complete enthusiasm and invaluable insight.

An extraordinary thank-you to Hazel and Roy Brock for being the most wonderful hostesses in all of England: welcoming us to their home, schlepping us around in their tiny red car, enjoying a surprise snow day, filling us with wonderful food, and gracing us with their delightful company.

I have a few thank-yous whose names, unfortunately, have been lost—scrawled on the backs of admission tickets and lost receipts. Still, I would like to thank the Yeoman Warder at the Tower of London who permitted us on to the altar in the Chapel of St. Peter ad Vincula to see the rarely visited grave of Catherine Howard. Also, millions of thanks to the thoughtful and generous tour guide who let two Americans join his already-overbooked evening tour of "Haunted Hampton Court."

And I would like to thank Catherine Howard. I did not see your ghost haunting that legendary gallery at Hampton Court. I had hoped you might convey to me some message from beyond the grave, some truth about your life you would want expressed within the pages of this book, or at least a blessing for me to tell your story in what manner I saw fit. But I think it's for the best that I didn't meet your ghostly presence. I did leave a stone upon the marble crest marking your burial site in the chapel, to signify that you did receive a visitor, for a change, on the 465th anniversary of your execution.

Catherine, may you rest in peace.